ZERO-G

ALSO BY ALTON GANSKY

ALTON GANSKY

BESTSELLING
SUSPENSE
AUTHOR

ZERO-G

ZONDERVAN®

ZONDERVAN.com/
AUTHORTRACKER
follow your favorite authors

ZONDERVAN®

Zero – G
Copyright © 2007 by Alton Gansky

Requests for information should be addressed to:
Zondervan, *Grand Rapids, Michigan* 49530

Library of Congress Cataloging-in-Publication Data

Gansky, Alton.
     Zero-G / Alton Gansky.
        p. cm.
     ISBN-10: 0-310-27211-4
     ISBN-13: 978-0-310-27211-3
     1. Astronauts – Fiction. I. Title.
  PS3557.A5195Z35 2007
  813'.54 – dc22
                                    2007016781

Interior design by Michelle Espinoza

Printed in the United States of America

---

07 08 09 10 11 12 • 23 22 21 20 19 18 17 16 15 14 13 12 11 10 9 8 7 6 5 4 3 2 1

TO JIM AND BONNIE HARRIS
GOOD FRIENDS

*When once you have tasted flight, you will forever walk
the earth with your eyes turned skyward, for there you
have been, and there you will always long to return.*

Leonardo da Vinci, 1452–1519

• • •

*Without thinking, as we paused at one of the three-
dimensional exhibits, I asked Dad the question I
always asked: "What's it like, out in space?" Mother
shot me a frightened glance. It was too late. Dad stood
there for a full half minute trying to find an answer,
then he shrugged. "It's the best thing in a lifetime of
best things."*

The Rocket Man by Ray Bradbury

• • •

*Where can I go from your Spirit?
Where can I flee from your presence?
If I go up to the heavens, you are there;
if I make my bed in the depths, you are there.*

Psalm 139:7–8

ZERO-G

ONE

"Daddy. A story. Please. Then I'll go right to sleep."

"I suppose you want a space story. Maybe something with space pirates."

His five-year-old son lay on the bed in his room, sheets and a cobalt blue comforter with cartoon images of Saturn, Earth, and distant stars pulled under his chin, all held in place by small hands. Benjamin Tucker could see only his son's head and the dancing eyes that always warmed him.

"No, Daddy. This time I want a castle story."

"What? A castle story? No spaceships? No ray guns?"

"No. A castle. And a knight. Swords are okay."

"Is it okay if the swords shoot death rays?"

"No, Daddy. Don't be silly. Swords don't shoot death rays."

Tuck sat on the edge of the bed and tousled little Gary's hair. "Okay. If you insist."

"I 'sist."

Tuck's greatest fear was forgetting moments like these. A father and his little boy ...

But ... something didn't fit. Gary wasn't five anymore; he was eleven. Had a birthday just last month.

The warmth he felt a moment before chilled. The room began to recede.

• • •

"Waaaaait a minute, wait just one minute. What happened here?"

Tuck sat at the dining room table, a thick manual open in front of him. Outside, a Carolina wren chanted its two-syllable prayer in the front yard's mulberry tree. A humid breeze pressed through the screened windows.

"Mom helped me do it. She said it was okay."

Tuck gazed at his eleven-year-old daughter, her brown hair now bleach-bottle blonde. "Are you wearing makeup?"

Penny lowered her head. "A little. Mom helped me with that too."

He planned to let his little girl, whom he wanted to remain little forever, squirm in his silence. Five seconds later, he caved. "You look gorgeous, young lady."

"Thank you, Daddy." She ran to him and climbed on his lap. Everything was right with the world.

He wrapped his arms around her and pulled her tight to his chest. He could feel her thin arms and narrow shoulders. "But no wearing makeup outside. Not yet, anyway."

"But, Daddy ..."

"No, you don't. You're not going to 'but Daddy' me into changing my mind. You go out like that and boys will be following you home like lost puppies. I'm not ready for that. Neither are you."

"I'm not a little girl, Daddy." Despite her protest, she kept her arms around him.

"Of course you are. And when you grow up and get really old, say thirty-six or so, and you're all wrinkled like a prune, and everyone in the world calls you 'ma'am' and 'old lady Penny,' you'll still be my little girl."

Penny giggled.

"Now and forever, my little girl."

Penny dissolved into nothing.

• • •

"Do you Benjamin Tucker take Myra to be your lawfully wedded wife, and do you promise to love her above all others and cherish her more than life itself, to honor—"

"I do."

The preacher blinked hard. "Um, I wasn't finished."

"I heard it in rehearsal. I did then and I do now."

The congregation laughed. The woman, who stood near him, the woman whose hand he held, smiled and mouthed the word, "Behave."

"Okay then," the minister said and turned to Tuck's bride-to-be.

"Myra, do you take this man—"

"I do."

It took a solid two minutes for the congregation to settle.

The preacher leaned close to the couple but spoke loud enough for all to hear. "Can I at least do the ring ceremony?"

Tuck felt a smile creep across his face. They allowed the minister to finish the ritual without interruption. He could still remember how the ring became stuck at his second knuckle and Myra pushed so hard to get it in place that the knuckle popped.

He wiggled that finger, then the whole hand. He could not feel the ring. He could sense his hand and arm floating shoulder-high, but no ring. Of course he felt no ring. He left it with Myra for safekeeping. He never wore it on a mission—

Tuck's eyes snapped open. An instant later, he wished they had stayed shut.

He forced his mind to clear, demanding it to come to attention. First, his eyes gazed through the window: black, then the eye-piercing glare of the sun, then a sliver of blue horizon, then stars, then black and sun again ...

Spinning.

"Not good." His words sounded strange to him.

"Atlantis, *Houston, do you read?*"

"Houst ..." He coughed. "Houston, *Atlantis.*"

"*Commander Tucker. Man, it is good to ... your voice. Can you give us a sit-rep?*"

"Stand ... stand by, Houston."

An arm floated in front of Tuck's face.

A viscous fog clouded his mind. Tuck prided himself on his mental acuity and on his ability to assess any situation in seconds, but those skills had gone missing. It seemed formaldehyde was pickling his brain.

"*Your transmission is breaking up ... spinning ... LOS.*"

A second or two stumbled by before Tuck made sense of the fragmented sentence. Loss of signal. They were spinning, taking the antenna in and out of alignment. How could that be?

"Does it matter?"

"*Say again, Atlantis.*"

"Stand by one, Houston." Looking out the window made Tuck sick. He forced his eyes to glance around the flight deck. He sat in the commander's chair of the orbiter *Atlantis.* The black on the other side of the window was space—cold, vacuous space—two hundred miles above the surface of Earth.

Memories began to form, images appeared and played on his mind, but his thinking still crawled like a baby.

"*You still with us, Tuck?*"

His eyes closed. Sleep dogged him, and he wanted nothing more than to surrender to it.

"Talk to ... Tuck."

"Raygun?" The word dripped from Tuck's lips.

"... haven't been called that ... Navy ..."

An image of a man too good-looking for his own good crowded out some of the confusion. Rick Van Duren, former hot-shot Navy pilot turned astronaut. Enough of Tuck's mind remained for him to remember that Rick sat in the CAPCOM chair.

"Ricky? The Rick-man. The Rickster." Tuck chuckled.

"I need you ... to think. Pull it to ... else I'll come up there and slap you around. Do ... me?"

Where had Rick's humor gone? He always joked around. Always. Except on mission. Again, Tuck's eyes opened. The flight deck was still there and he was still strapped in the commander's seat. A body floated forward and over the instrument panel. Tuck pushed it back without a thought. He could process only one thing at a time, and that thought had to do with the spinning orbiter.

He studied the instrument panel in front of him. The eight-ball, which indicated flight attitude, spun wildly. Tuck took hold of the flight controller between his legs and gave it a gentle nudge to the right. *Atlantis*'s spin changed. He did it again. Then forward, then left, then right.

"Atlantis, *Houston, we ... RCS activation ... you?"*

Tuck didn't respond. Working the Reaction Control System required every brain cell still working. He made adjustments on instinct honed from decades of flying military and civilian aircraft. With each touch of the rotational hand controller—the "stick"—several of the forty-four small rocket motors on the tail and nose of the craft responded with short bursts. It took longer than he thought it should, but the wild spinning ceased.

Still, something about the orbiter's position seemed wrong. He couldn't see Earth. Shouldn't he be able to see Earth?

"Houston. Attitude is stabilized."

"Outstanding, Tuck. Can you tell us what happened?"

"I can't see the Earth. The Earth is gone."

"We're still here, buddy. Atlantis is just upside down to its normal flight position. That can be fixed."

"I don't know what happened." Tuck rubbed his neck. The sleepiness hadn't given up. "I ..." He looked around the flight deck. Someone, a woman, sat slumped in the pilot's seat. The body of a man in a blue jumpsuit hung in the air, pressed against one of the side instrument panels.

"Everyone is out. I don't know why."

"How are you feeling?"

"Sleepy. So sleepy. Sick."

"SAS?"

SAS. Space Adaptation Syndrome. "Yeah, motion sick."

"We show good ECLS, do you concur?"

He looked at the gauges for the Environmental Control and Life Support System. "ECLSS seems nominal."

"Surgeon has some questions for you. Do you think you can answer them?"

"I don't know. Light-headed." Tuck chuckled. "Of course, I am in microgravity. We're all light-headed." He laughed. "Get it, Rick? Microgravity? Light-headed?"

"I get it, Tuck. Surgeon wants to ask those questions now. We'd like to keep the loop open with your permission."

The more Tuck talked, the more alert he became, but it was minimal success, baby steps when he needed to be making Goliath-like strides. "Sure. Why not?"

"Atlantis, *Surgeon.*"

"Go ahead, Bob."

"The loop is still open, Tuck. Do you understand?"

"Yes." The giddiness loosened its grip. Tuck rubbed his temples, but his head still felt packed with cotton. He had a thought. He placed his index finger inside his mouth and his thumb to his cheek then pinched hard. The pain helped. His mind cleared for a moment, but the nausea and faint feeling remained. The urge to sleep washed back in like a wave. Tuck forced it back with another masochistic pinch. "Oww."

"Say again?"

"Nothing. Just a little self-treatment. I understand the loop is open. I have no secrets from the guys and gals in flight control." The flight surgeon had done the ethical thing in informing him about the open loop. Only the surgeon could have a private talk with any of the astronauts—doctor/patient privilege extended even into orbital space.

"Do you recall passing out, Commander?"

"No. I can't remember. My head hurts something fierce."

"The others on the flight deck are out too?"

Tuck looked around again. Moving his head sent bolts of pain down his neck. "Best I can tell. I'll go check."

"No. Not yet."

"My crew. My responsibility."

"How's your vision?"

"My vision? Okay. I'm seeing fine. Nothing's out of focus."

"Both eyes?"

Tuck closed his left eye then a moment later did the same with his right. "Roger that. Both eyes nominal." He moved his head from side to side, working the muscles in his neck. The motion made his head pound. "Someone is playing the drums in my skull, and whoever it is likes it loud." He groaned.

"You still with me, Commander?"

"I was thinking about going out for some fresh air."

"We'd like you to stay put for a moment and see if your head clears and memory returns."

"Negative, Houston. Checking on the crew." Tuck popped the latch on the harness that held him in his seat and pushed against the cushion. A second later, he was afloat in microgravity.

The flight deck had seats for four of the crew; mid-deck held three other seats. The other two seats on the flight deck—the mission specialists' seats—were empty. His mind struggled to make sense of this. He had been in the commander's seat, the left seat, when he came to. The mission pilot, Jessica Ault, was strapped in place. If he and the pilot were in flight position, then why weren't the others?

Tuck struggled again to clear his mind. He would check on Jess in a moment; his first concern was the free-floating crewman. Tuck braced a knee against the port seat and reached for the body. He didn't need to see the face to know he had taken hold of Mission Specialist Jared Finn, a civilian with the Canadian Space Agency. Tuck's heart stumbled to a stop when he pulled Finn to him—the pale face and open, fixed eyes told Tuck what he didn't want to know.

Although the effort made Tuck's head throb, he pulled Finn to the chair, then pushed him into its seat.

A dark part of Tuck's brain processed the actions: Finn's body moved easily and bent in all the right places. He could see no sign of rigor mortis. Did it take longer for rigor to begin in space? He had no idea.

Breathing came in gulps as Tuck struggled to snap the harness around the dead astronaut. Once done, Tuck did what he knew to be a useless act. He felt for a carotid pulse and found none. As he moved his hand, he felt some plastic under his fingers. He knew an SAS patch when he felt one. He should. Like all the others aboard, he wore one behind his left ear.

Feeling the patch forced a memory to the top of his mind. This was the first time the entire crew wore the medicated transdermal device. Space Adaptation Syndrome had always been a problem for astronauts. Upwards of 70 percent of astronauts experienced SAS to some degree. Headaches, vertigo, and worse, nausea and vomiting, could come over the most experienced crewmen, including those who never felt motion sickness even when flying fighter jets.

No one had been able to come up with a definitive reason for the syndrome, although doctors had put forth several ideas. Almost everyone agreed, however, that it had to do with the effects of microgravity on the brain and the inability to sense "down." The problem was serious enough that spacewalks—also known as extra-vehicular activities or EVAs—never occurred until after the first seventy-two hours of a mission had passed. By then, most had adjusted to their environment.

To combat SAS, flight doctors had tried several med-ications including scopolamine, but the drugs could act like a sedative or blur vision, neither welcome on space flight. The patch was the latest and most promising. It released a combination of meds over time, was easy to apply, and could be manufactured to suit the needs of each astronaut based on age, weight, gender, and susceptibility to the disorder.

Tuck didn't like them because they were worthless to him. He was a definite "lead head," a term other astronauts used to describe those who were oblivious to the effects of space travel. Since Tuck appeared immune to SAS, he had requested the smallest dose possible and only wore one as part of the experiment.

Tuck had never felt SAS until he awoke a few minutes ago. In a gesture of instinctive frustration, he ripped the patch off his neck.

Tuck shook his head. "Stop woolgathering." He forced his mind to focus on Finn. He felt as if he were swimming in syrup. Nothing moved at the right speed.

"Houston, *Atlantis*."

"*Go*, Atlantis." The voice was CAPCOM again.

"We ... um ... recommend alternate frequency." Encryption was the word he really wanted, but that alone might alert any eavesdropping country or amateur radio operator to the problem. Of course, he had said enough to raise the hackles of anyone with just a little knowledge of the mission.

"*Understood*, Atlantis."

Tuck spun and pulled himself to the front console. A quick adjustment and the encryption communication went active.

"Houston, how do you read?"

"*We hear you just fine, Tuck. Media is off loop. I took them off-line when contact broke.*"

"Tell DH he may want to lock the doors."

There was a pause. The phrase sounded innocuous enough, but everyone associated with the Space Shuttle knew the reference. On February 1, 2003, *Columbia* burned up on reentry. The first sign of trouble came when Flight Director Leroy Cain said, "Lock the doors," meaning that no data was to leave the mission control room. He locked down communications with the outside. Tuck wanted Dieter Huntz, the flight controller, to do the same. The suggestion carried a lot of painful weight.

A moment later, Rick Van Duren's voice crept into Tuck's ear. *"Already done, Tuck. Talk to us."*

"Finn is dead. He was floating around the flight deck. I have him in the PS seat now."

"Tuck, this is Surgeon again. Are you certain he is dead?"

"I know dead when I see it, Doc." Tuck moved to the pilot's seat on his right. "I'm checking on Jess now." He put a hand under her chin and lifted. Her face was pale but not cyanotic. He felt for a pulse. Nothing. He started to pull away, then tried again. It was there. Weak and thready, but it was there. "I have a pulse, but she is still unconscious."

Tuck let Jess's head down, easing her chin to her chest. He pulled his hand away and grazed the dermal patch she wore. He stopped. "Wait one, Houston."

He pulled closer and stared at the flesh-colored patch. A red line circled it and the skin beneath was swollen.

Moving to his right, Tuck performed the same finger-to-carotid-artery test on Russ Deaver. Russ was the senior payload specialist. Russ had a pulse, stronger than Jess's but not what it should be. Tuck didn't have to look long to see the red ring around the dermal patch.

"Houston, there's something going on with the SAS patch." He described the skin anomaly.

There was a pause. *"Remove patch, Commander. Right away."*

"Roger that. What about the others?"

"Yes, and bag and stow the patches."

Tuck stripped the patches from the necks of Jess and Russ, retrieved one of the many plastic bags used for sealing food and bits of trash, and placed them inside a stowage compartment.

Next, heart stuttering, Tuck pushed himself to the mission station on the starboard side of the flight deck. Mission Specialist Jodie Law's arms floated before her, her long brown hair forming a halo. No matter how hard Tuck tried, he could find no pulse.

Tears trickled from his eyes, broke free of their meager grasp on his face, and floated in air as tiny spheres. Jodie was the youngest of the crew—just thirty-two. In Houston, her five-year-old daughter waited for her mommy. Same brown hair. Same blue eyes. Same infectious smile.

Tuck began to weep.

"Atlantis, *Houston.*"

Tuck pulled himself into a ball. The motion moved him slowly forward and up toward the upper windows. Normally, Earth would fill the panes, but *Atlantis*'s unusual position and attitude only allowed a view of deep space, a blackness too profound to comprehend.

"Atlantis, *Houston. Talk to me, Tuck.*"

Tuck didn't want to talk; didn't want to listen; didn't want to feel or think or be aware of anything outside the emotional vault he was building.

"Commander Tucker, respond."

The spinning thoughts in Tuck's mind slammed together and crumbled. Vinny. Vincent Pistacchia Jr. Where was Vinny?

Adrenaline poured into his veins and Tuck snapped his head around so fast it caused his body to spin. He steadied himself.

"Moving to middeck, Houston. Stand by." Tuck didn't wait for a response. The long headset line that allowed him to move around the flight deck when in orbit was too short to reach the deck below. It took only a second for Tuck to disconnect it and start for the interdeck access hatch behind and to the port side of the commander's seat. Tuck pulled himself down the ladder headfirst like a man swimming to the bottom of a pool.

The middeck was the middle of *Atlantis*'s three decks. One deck below that was the lower deck, a place for ductwork, wires, and the like. His concern was with flesh and blood, not insulation and instrumentation.

The compartment stood empty. The sight of the abandoned space made his already tripping heart stutter. He took several deep breaths to calm himself. Each action made the pain in his head rage. Against his will, his eyes crashed shut, lids tightening until tears squeezed out.

A few moments later, the agony diminished and he felt his jaw relax. "Pull yourself together, Tuck." Sleepy. The profound weariness returned. This time he tortured the other cheek.

Sleep.

That was it.

He pushed across the open compartment making sure he didn't smash a shin on the latched table at the forward end of the small space. On the opposite side, the starboard side, were the sleep stations: three horizontal beds stacked so closely they made submarine bunks seem spacious. A vertical sleep space, essentially a sleeping bag tethered in place, was just aft of the bunks—it was empty.

Tuck launched himself to the sleeping area harder than necessary and it took some effort to keep from smashing his head into the metal structure. He pulled the first privacy screen to the side. Empty. He moved to the middle bunk. Also empty, as was the bottom.

"Think, Tuck. Think."

The head? On the orbiter the bathroom bore the more noble moniker "Waste Management Compartment." Astronauts had more colorful names for the small space where men and women did the business necessary of all biological entities.

"Be there, Vinny. Be taking a bio-break." Tuck shoved off the bunk rack and moved like a missile to the WMC at the left rear of the middeck. He jerked the privacy curtain aside.

No Vinny.

Next to the privacy curtain stood the personal hygiene station, a place where crew could shave, clean up, and do other routine personal chores. A mirror hung on the surface. Tuck let his eyes drift to his reflection. He saw his sandy brown hair, strong jaw, trim face, and near empty hazel eyes.

Uncertain what to do, Tuck let himself drift above the middeck until he felt something hard against his back. He had drifted to the airlock hatch.

Something flickered in his mind. A brief image.

Then it came through the haze like a speeding freight train.

"No. Oh, no. Dear God, no, no, no."

Tuck pushed forward and up the interdeck access, rapping his knee as he did so. The pain didn't matter.

He didn't want to do what he did next, didn't want to see what he knew he would.

His next act required more courage than anything he had done before, including sitting atop tons of rocket fuel. He forced himself to look out the aft viewing windows, the ones that looked over the orbiter's cargo bay. The cargo doors were open as they always were once the Shuttle reached orbit. What ripped his breath away was the site of the RMS sticking into the darkness like one leg of a praying mantis. The Remote Manipulator System had been in use when whatever happened, happened. At the end of the fifty-foot, thousand-pound arm stood a human figure clad in a space suit.

"Vinny." The name trickled from Tuck's lips.

Puzzle pieces of memory rained in Tuck's consciousness. Vinny was doing an extravehicular procedure. How long had he been out there?

Tuck keyed his mike. "Vinny. Do you read me, Vinny."

No response.

"Houston. I can't raise Vinny. He's EVA."

No response.

Tuck touched his mike, then realized the problem. He reeled in the loose end and plugged it into a com port. "Vinny, this is Tuck. Do you read?"

Nothing.

"Houston, I can't raise Vinny. He's EVA."

"Tuck, we know about Vinny."

A second passed before Tuck made the connection. Houston monitored vital signs of any astronaut who worked outside the safe confines of the orbiter. Vinny would have been wired up before donning his EVA suit. Once Tuck had stabilized the spinning Shuttle, communications were reestablished and FCC would be able to read Vinny's vitals.

"Why didn't you tell me, Rick? Why?"

"Tuck, your emotional state is fragile. We don't know why, but you're the only conscious crewman. We need you to be at your best and you're not. Telling you too soon could have made matters worse."

"How can it get worse?" His eyes ran to the video monitors that showed Vinny's lifeless body perched on the end of the RMS.

"How much do you remember, Tuck?"

"Not much, Rick. Not much. My brain is still clouded."

"In addition to delivering supplies to the Internation Space Station, part of your mission was a simple repair on a DOD satellite. Of course, the Department of Defense wants that part secret. Sometime during that mission, Atlantis began to spin. With the vehicle moving like it was, we lost signal from the Ku-antenna. What data we had indicated that RMS had been activated. We had no consistent contact with you for three hours."

"Three hours?"

"We couldn't maintain enough of a signal to override from down here."

"This can't be happening."

"It is, Tuck, and we aren't out of the woods yet. There are some things we want you to do."

"I know what I need to do. I'm going out to get Vinny."

"No, sir. No, sir, you are not. You're in no condition to do that. You're the only one conscious, and you can't get into an EVA suit without help."

"I have to try, Rick. I can't leave him out there."

"Listen to me, Tuck. You know you can't do that. Vinny is dead. I know that's a hard and cold thing to say, but you have to face that. Now we have a list of things for you to do."

"NASA always has lists." The pain in his head flared. He groaned and waited for it to pass.

"You got that right, buddy."

Rick had a lighter tone in his voice and Tuck recognized it for what it was—an attempt to lift his spirits and give him confidence. It failed.

"I'm going to walk you through this one step at a time, pal. Just stay with me."

Tuck pulled himself to the aft windows and stared at his friend Vinny. For a moment, he thought he saw the dead man wave.

TWO

Rick Van Duren leaned back in his chair. If any of the other members of the flight control team at FCC in Houston were to look at him they would see a man unperturbed by the disaster taking place two hundred miles overhead. The only sign of nerves came from his rhythmic stroking of the mike boom that hovered above his jawline.

"How's he doing, Rick?" The voice came over the headset and without the customary, "CAPCOM, Flight." Rick knew who was speaking. He also knew the question was nothing more than small talk leading to something more pressing.

"So far so good, Flight, all things considered. He has the Ku-antenna realigned for the present attitude. The giddiness seems to have gone, as has the melancholy. He's coming across more emotionally stable. I think removing the patch helped."

"That's my take."

Rick waited for Flight Director Dieter Huntz to get to what was really on his mind.

"You know him better than anyone, Rick. Can he fly *Atlantis*?"

Rick didn't respond at first. He and Tuck went back to their days at Annapolis and had served on the same aircraft carrier.

Dieter activated his mike again. "Give it to me straight, Rick. I don't want any of that astronaut machismo."

Rick sighed. "No, Flight, he can't. In any other circumstance, I would put my life and that of my family in his hands, but at the moment, I wouldn't let him steer a riding lawn mower."

"Flight, this is Surgeon. I concur. Commander Tuck's response time is at least 25 percent slower than normal."

"Now that the patch is off, Surgeon, can we expect him to revive?"

"Flight, we don't even know for certain that the patch is the problem. It appears related, but I have no way of telling. I need to do a tox screen and I can't do that down here. We won't know anything until we get results from the test group."

Rick thought of the three volunteer astronauts who donned the same patches. Some of the other flight surgeons were monitoring their health in hopes of determining the source of the problem. Rick would have volunteered himself, but he didn't want to leave his post.

"Our options are narrowing, gentlemen." Dieter's voice sounded distant to Rick even though only a handful of steps separated them. "Ideally we'd have them dock with the space station, off-load the crew, and use what medical equipment we have there, but Tuck isn't in any kind of condition to make that happen. If he ..."

Rick finished Dieter's sentence in his mind. *If he messes up, Tuck kills not just himself and the rest of the surviving crew but three men on the ISS.* The thought had been haunting Rick's mind.

"The longer they stay up there, the greater chance Jess and Russ will die too." Bob Celtik groaned into his mike. "Removing the patches was the right thing to do, but we don't know if we removed them too late."

"Russ and Jess need medical treatment beyond what they can get on the space station," Rick said. "Flight, I suggest we go autoland."

"The autoland system wasn't designed to bring the Shuttle back with crew on board. It was meant to allow us to land the vehicle after the crew was safe on the ISS."

Rick knew this information well. He had been one of the astronaut advisors on the project. Since *Columbia*'s tragic burnup over Texas in 2003, engineers developed new safety protocols in the event of damage to the Shuttle during launch. One of the first things a crew did once in orbit was to use the RMS arm to examine the heat tiles and wings. If the craft had sustained life-threatening damage, then the crew would dock with the International Space Station, disembark, and let FCC land it empty of the crew. The ISS, depending on the number of astronauts on the station and on the orbiter, could sustain them for eighty to one hundred ten days. NASA would send another Shuttle to bring them home.

A complete autolanding had never been done. Much of a Shuttle's return was automated, handled by a computer, but certain functions like deploying air sensors that aided the computer in its flight, lowering the landing gear, and deploying the drag chute required a human on board. Recent modifications allowed NASA to handle even those tasks.

Another problem plagued the idea of autolanding with a crew on board: tests had shown that the computers tended to bring the craft in too fast, and too fast meant possible tire failure. It would be a disaster to lose an empty Shuttle that way; it was beyond tragic to lose a crew.

"Flight, I don't think we're playing this hand; it's playing us. No matter what decision we make it will be second-guessed."

"*We* don't make this decision, Rick, *I* do."

"Negative, Flight. Whatever decision you make, you make in consultation with all of us. No one is going to leave you twisting in the wind."

"I guess this is where I make the 'failure is not an option' speech."

Rick turned his chair and looked across the space that separated them. "You know Gene Krantz never said that." They were words he should have offered with a smile, but he couldn't manage it. Krantz was a NASA icon, the mold from which every other flight director shaped himself. Krantz and his team were at the helm to bring the injured *Apollo 13* flight home.

"No, but he lived it." Dieter pursed his lips.

A motion at the back of the room caught Rick's attention. Security escorted a woman and two children into the room. With them were a couple of suits Rick recognized as NASA execs.

His gut twisted.

. . .

The pain in Tuck's head diminished to a mere crushing sensation. He had never experienced a migraine, but his wife had. Next time he would be more sympathetic.

If there is a next time.

"Atlantis, *Houston. Got time for a phone call, buddy?"*

A phone call? "I'm not interested in buying any more magazines, Rick."

"You want to take this, Tuck. And no worries. I'll pick up the long-distance charges."

"You're a pal, pal." The banter made Tuck feel better, if only for a moment. It meant that his mind was responding faster.

"Hey, baby." The voice oozed through the earpiece. Not even distance and the cold of space could change a voice he knew so well. Tears burned his eyes.

He cleared his throat. "Hey you." He heard his voice break. "It's great to hear your voice." The image of Myra flashed on his brain: dark brown hair, short on the sides, full on the top; eyes that were accustomed to expressing joy and not anger; a wit as sharp as he had ever encountered.

"They ... um ... they tell me that you're having a little trouble up there."

"I've had better trips." He shuddered. "I miss you more than I can say."

There was fear in her voice. *"I miss you too. I ... I want you to come home safe."*

Tuck started to speak but failed. It took several moments and every ounce of concentration he could muster to speak the words. "Do you still have those pork chops in the freezer?"

There was a pause before Myra responded. *"Yes."*

"I'm talking about the thick-cut ones."

"Those are the ones."

He heard her confusion. "Good. I'll be back soon and I'm thinking of having some friends over for a barbeque. Will you make potato salad?"

"Of course."

"Good. On second thought, let's make it just a family affair. Do you understand what I'm saying, Myra?"

"Yes. I know you'll make it home."

"That I will, kiddo. I've got the best team in the world on the job."

"I know, baby. I know." The effort to put on a brave front collapsed like a wall and Tuck heard every brick land. His heart ached and he lowered his head into his hands. Even two hundred miles above the Earth, traveling faster than a bullet with half his crew dead, he had to be brave for his family.

"The kids are here, baby. They want to talk to you."

What steel remained in Tuck's spine melted.

The next voice over the line was higher than Myra's. *"Daddy?"*

"Hey, gorgeous. How's my pretty Penny? Did Mom take you shopping for school?"

She was crying. *"Yes. Daddy ... Daddy ..."*

"I'm coming home, sweetheart. Got that? I'll be there to torment any boys you bring to the house."

Penny's laugh came wrapped in a sob. *"In that case, I'm going to the mall and round up some."*

"That's it. You're grounded for the next twenty-two years."

"*I . . . love you, Daddy.*"

Tuck fought back the sobs. His daughter's voice, the tone, the timbre, brought more pain than the fear of death. "Remember all those stars we see at night? My love . . . is bigger."

The connection fell silent for a moment, then Myra came across the link. "*Gary is having a little trouble right now. He wants to talk but he doesn't think he can.*"

"Tell him I understand; I'm having a little trouble myself."

"*This is kinda tough on the kids.*"

"I know. I wish it weren't so."

"*Tuck, there's so much to say, I don't know where to begin.*"

"Just tell me you love me. That will say everything I need to hear."

"*I love you more than I can say.*"

"And I love you with every breath. You take care of the kids. Make sure Gary keeps up his math and . . ." Tuck broke. Words were now useless, but the connection between them was greater than anything science and engineering could manufacture.

"*We're praying, Tuck. We're praying every minute.*"

"Me too, kid. Me too. Does Dad know?"

"*I don't think so.*"

"Good. Don't tell him yet. There's nothing he can do but worry and he doesn't need that."

"*I'll wait, but he'll be here soon. He'll find out.*"

"I understand. Do what you think is right. I'm not at my best right now."

"*They said you're feeling and acting better.*"

"My head's clearing. I'm not as foggy. Myra, listen, I'm assuming they've told you about Jodie and Jared and Vinny. They have family. You're good with people in tough situations. They're going to need some strength. Do you know what I mean? Someone with spiritual roots."

"I know what you mean. I'll do what I can."

A moment of relief ran through Tuck. Helping others would help her. "Okay, baby. Give yourself a hug for me. I've got to get back to work and see if I can't come home and annoy you some more."

"You can annoy me anytime."

"I'm coming home, Myra, but if this goes south any more ... You're the best thing that ever happened to me."

Sobs covered the first words but Tuck made out, *"... me too."*

Tuck straightened and filled his lungs. A moment later, he packed away his runaway emotions in the stowage of his mind. "Houston, *Atlantis*."

"Go ahead, Atlantis." It was Rick.

"What's next, CAPCOM?"

THREE

Tuck pushed back from Russ and studied his work. Under Bob's direction, Tuck had moved to middeck and retrieved a medical kit. With *Atlantis* stabilized, the autopilot engaged, and the downlink antenna realigned, Bob could get better information, more than Tuck could tell him. First he'd examined Jess. Now it was Russ's turn.

Guided by the flight surgeon, Tuck took Russ's blood pressure and listened to his lungs. He could tell by the way Bob spoke that he and the others considered him "skill impaired." They were probably right. It took him twice as long as necessary to do the simple task of exposing Russ's chest and attaching the leads. The onboard video cameras provided Mission Control with a real-time view of all that Tuck was doing. He felt less alone.

"Houston, ECG is in place. Ready to downlink."

"It's coming through fine, Tuck."

"Same as Jess, Houston?"

"Stand by one, Atlantis."

A minute passed like an eon. He had placed the same kind of electrodes on Jess's chest. Any reluctance he felt exposing her skin evaporated in the earnest desire to see her live. While social courtesies existed on a space mission, one could not be an astronaut and be overly modest. During liftoff or EVAs, Tuck had to wear things in places he couldn't discuss in polite company.

"Atlantis, Houston, this is Surgeon. I'm getting the same readings. Heart rate high, and blood pressure dropping. The heart is trying to keep up with the BP drop."

"What causes that, Doc?"

"A whole fistful of things. Medications for heart disease, antidepressants, narcotic analgesics, anti-anxiety meds, dehydration, anaphylaxis."

"None of those sound likely, Bob."

"We're back to the patches again. I can't think of anything else."

"Someone is going to have to make a decision." Tuck held none of his exasperation back.

"Tuck, Rick here. We are making decisions, scores of them, including the big one. We're bringing you home. We

can't risk you trying to dock with ISS. I think you know why."

"You think I'll park this thing in their living room."

"*I wouldn't have been so graphic. We're going to go with full autoland and need you to start preparing for de-orbit.*"

"What about Vinny?" Tuck gazed out the aft windows. Vinny remained like a white-cloaked statue on the end of the manipulator arm. Vinny deserved better.

"*That's first on our list. We've been doing sims down here and think we have an idea.*"

"The simulators show I can get him back inside?"

"*Negative, Commander.*"

"I'm not cutting him adrift, Rick."

"*No one is asking you to, but ... You're not going to like this either.*"

"You want me to retract and place the arm with Vinny still attached. My brain is fuzzy, Rick, but it isn't gone."

"*I'm afraid that's all we can do.*"

"You're not being creative enough, Houston. Let me get close to the ISS and then a couple of the boys can EVA to Vinny, unhook him, and come through the air lock."

"*Great idea, Tuck, but we don't have time. Surgeon thinks we may lose Jess and Russ if they don't get help soon.*"

"Vinny wouldn't do this to one of us." Anger shoved sorrow aside.

"*Yes, he would, Commander, and you know it. If he were alive, then we'd move the Moon itself to get him home. You know that. I know that. But that isn't the situation.*"

"Then what is the situation, Rick?"

"Don't make me say it."

"Spell it out."

The pause seemed interminable. "We don't risk the lives of the living for the dead. We're bringing Vinny home, but we can't do anything for him now. The longer we wait, the greater the risk that the rest of your crew will die."

Tuck rubbed his forehead, and for a moment he wished he could trade places with Vinny. He looked around the flight deck. Many had touted the *Atlantis* and her sister craft as the most complex machines ever constructed. Now it was the tomb for three dead, two dying, and one lone, afflicted man trying to make sense of it all.

"Understood, Houston. Talk me through it."

"You worked the RMS on your first mission. We want you to retract and park the manipulator arm in the pay-load bay."

"Then what?"

"Close the bay."

"What about Vinny. I mean, what about his body?"

"We'll recover him once you're home."

Tuck couldn't believe what he heard. "You want me to leave his body in the payload bay, still strapped to the manipulator arm?"

"There's no other way, Tuck. This is the absolute best we can do. As soon as that's done, we want you to start prep for de-orbit."

No words came to Tuck. The image of Vinny in his space suit, feet still strapped to the end of the fifty-foot arm of the manipulator, threw him into an emotional vacuum. He started to protest but refrained. With no solution to offer, he would just be wasting time.

For a few moments, he toyed with the idea of using the RMS to bring Vinny close, then suiting up and going out to get him, but the idea, brave and noble as it was, melted under the heat of logic. He might be able to get into a space suit by himself, but he doubted it. Just trying would eat up time that Jess and Russ didn't have. In his last dress rehearsal with a space suit, it had taken close to two hours to don the three-hundred-pound suit, and that was with help. Slipping into the suit alone and muddle-headed could take twice that, assuming it was even possible.

The thought of reclaiming Vinny's body pulled at him, but the vision of dragging Vinny through the air-lock, securing his body, then returning to the flight deck to find Russ and Jess dead quenched the desire.

Mission Control was right. He hated it, but they were right.

Tuck drew a deep breath, stepped to the aft flight deck control station, and took hold of the translation and rotational hand controller for the remote manipulator. This was a two-person job: one controller and one crewman to operate the video cameras in the bay and those on the nine-hundred-pound arm.

He moved slowly, working the articulated manipulator arm and its six "joints."

Sweat dotted his forehead and his heart felt encased in concrete.

"Dear God, what went wrong?"

"*Say again,* Atlantis."

"Sorry, Rick, but I wasn't talking to you."

"*Understood, Tuck. There have been a lot of those conversations down here.*" A pause. "*PDRS shows manipulator arm activity.*"

Not far from where Rick sat in MCC, the Payload Deploy Retrieval Systems monitor recorded and relayed everything Tuck did.

With hands on the controls, Tuck closed his eyes and forced his breathing to slow. A familiar sensation oozed through him: detachment—a common emotional state for those who routinely faced dangerous situations. He had learned it in pilot's school; his father had learned it in the fire department.

The thought of his father calmed him. The distance between them might be great, but Tuck could still see the old man: gray hair, wrinkles forged in the furnace of life, and eyes that still danced.

Tuck opened his eyes, gazed out the aft view windows, then turned his eyes to the video monitors at the right. He had already selected two of the six available cameras to help him guide the massive arm back into the payload compartment.

One of the questions Tuck had answered a dozen times in his many talks to students dealt with zero gravity. Truth is, he would explain, there is no such thing as zero gravity. There is always some measure of the force, even in what appears to be empty space. What astronauts experienced was microgravity—gravity at such a low level that its force is difficult to experience.

The companion myth dealt with weightlessness. Many assumed that a weightless environment made something massless, and that was dangerous thinking. The arm that Tuck manipulated weighed nearly half a ton. Without appreciable gravity, it could be moved easily and extended in a way that couldn't be done on Earth. However, it still possessed its mass, and if Tuck were to lose control and bring the robotic arm in too quickly, he could seriously damage *Atlantis* and possibly kill everyone on board—those who were still alive.

Having reminded himself of those facts, Tuck began the retrieval and stowage procedure. His eyes moved from aft window to video monitors to the instrument panel with its switches and digital display of yaw, pitch, and more. He moved with caution, doing a two-person job by himself.

As the arm retracted, Vinny's lifeless body wiggled in a macabre dance, its inertia resisting the movement of the mechanical device. His arms moved up and down and his torso twisted at the waist. The unnatural motion reminded Tuck of the time Vinny, well lubricated with Italian wine, tried to teach his fellow astronauts the Macarena. That had been at Jess's birthday party. The memory stung.

The white space suit was Vinny's cocoon. It protected him against the 500-degree shifts in temperature that anything in space experiences. In direct sun, the suit fended off 250-degree heat; in shade, it shielded him from 250 degrees below zero.

Odd, Tuck thought, that Vinny died not from the many threats outside his suit, but likely from something he wore on his neck.

Foot by foot, then inch by inch, Tuck brought the arm in until it settled in its latches. Engineers had not designed the RMS arm to be docked with something attached to its distal end. Tuck had to twist the platform on which Vinny's feet were attached ninety degrees to the resting arm. It tore at Tuck to do so. He felt like he was securing a stray piece of equipment rather than one of his crew. The thought of Vinny riding through reentry in the payload compartment threatened to shred Tuck's mind. He had no idea what it might do to Vinny.

Tuck closed the payload doors.

FOUR

Tuck finished putting on the gloves of his orange launch/entry suit, or LES. The LES was a vital safety element, designed to pressurize should the cabin suddenly lose pressure during liftoff or reentry. It also served as an anti-G suit, a contraption that helped crew face the increase in g-forces endured during the trip back to Earth. If all went well, they would experience only two Gs, but for crews who had spent several days in microgravity, two Gs could be a lot. Unfortunately, Tuck could not dress his unconscious crewmembers in the suits.

Tuck had done all that had been asked of him. He had secured everything that needed securing, checked on Jess and Russ again, checked the five-point harness system that held the crew to their seats, and done something never done before. For a complete autoland, Tuck had to string a cable from avionics on middeck to the flight deck. That data cable allowed control of items such as the air-data probes and the landing gear— work the crew would normally handle.

Tuck was now a passenger.

The only good news came with Jess and Russ. While they had showed no improvement, they had also showed no decline. For that, Tuck was thankful.

He felt the OMS fire and saw the indicators on his panel. The Orbital Maneuvering System consisted of a pair of six-thousand-pound thrusters at the aft end of the orbiter that provided the final boost into orbit. They also slowed *Atlantis* for de-orbit. *Atlantis* had already been flipped to the correct reentry attitude. As it turned, Tuck saw the Department of Defense satellite they had come to repair—the satellite Vinny had worked on. Tuck had no idea if Vinny had finished the work, and he didn't care. The Department of Defense could wait.

"Houston, *Atlantis*."

"*Go ahead,* Atlantis."

"I see DOD 63 off our starboard side. How close have we been to that beast?" The surveillance satellite was the size of a bus. Tuck, in the midst of drug poisoning, had forgotten about the device.

"*It was never a problem.*"

"Houston, let's have an understanding. I want you to keep me fully apprised of all things. I don't want any of that John Glenn garbage."

During John Glenn's *Mercury* mission, an instrument light at MCC indicated Glenn's heat shield had come loose. If true, Glenn would die on reentry. Mission Control kept the information from him. Something Glenn took exception to—loudly.

"*It was never a problem, Tuck.*"

Tuck looked at the satellite. A fender-bender collision with it would have meant disaster—greater disaster.

"Just so that we're clear, gentlemen."

"*OMS burn is good. Attitude is good.*"

"Roger that, Houston."

Tuck leaned his helmeted head back and gazed at the starry sky. There was little for him to do. Normally the intercom would be full of chatter from slightly nervous crew who waited to ride the meteor. No voices came over the headset.

The OMS burn had slowed *Atlantis* by only two hundred miles an hour. Not much compared to the Mach 25 she was traveling.

Soon the craft would dip into the atmosphere and begin its guided plunge to Earth.

"Four hundred thousand feet. Guidance looks good."

Atlantis was dropping into the atmosphere but was still more spacecraft than aircraft. The computers kept the forty-degree nose-up attitude, preventing Tuck from seeing anything but black space. Before him, a monitor showed the orbiter's descent.

"Rick, is my family there?"

"Roger that, Tuck. They're in the viewing area. They can hear you."

"Dad too?"

"Yup. He's a little put-out with you. Apparently you promised to help him fix his truck."

Tuck laughed. He doubted his father said anything like that, but he appreciated Rick's efforts to keep his spirits up.

"Understood, Houston. I'll try not to get dead."

"You had better come back alive. You know what your wife will do to me if you don't."

A moan came over the headset. Tuck turned his head to see Jess raise a hand to her temple.

Another moan.

"Houston, *Atlantis*, I think Jess is coming to."

A pause. *"Understood."*

"My head. What's wrong with my head?" Jess's words trickled out. She whimpered.

"Jess. Are you with me? Jess?"

"The pain. My head is splitting open." She tilted her head back and opened her eyes. Blinked. Blinked again. "What ... Oh, no. Oh, no." She reached for the control stick.

Tuck shot an arm across the center panel and grabbed her shoulder. "Don't move, Jess. Don't touch anything. We're on autoland."

"Autoland? But ... My head ... Can't think. My heart is trying to escape."

"Just sit still. The pain goes away with time."

"I don't understand." She turned to him. Her eyes widened so much Tuck thought they'd fall from her head. She raised an arm and studied it for a moment, then returned her frightened gaze to Tuck. "Why are you in your LES? Where's mine?" She looked out the window, then at the monitors before her. "This isn't right. What's happening?"

"Jess, listen to me."

She snapped her gaze over her shoulder. "Seat positions are wrong. We can't reenter with seats in on-orbit configuration."

"Jess. Settle down. You've been drugged. The whole crew has. We're on emergency autoland headed to White Sands. Everything is under control. Just sit back."

"But my LES. No one but you is wearing an LES. Why, Tuck? Why only you?"

She teetered on hysteria, something foreign to Jess, who seldom showed any emotion beyond humor. The drugs in her system were playing havoc with her reason.

"Pull yourself together, Jess. That's an order."

"*Mach twenty-five point two and three hundred forty thousand feet.*"

Jess straightened, started to speak, then closed her mouth, jaw tensed like a clamp.

"Now listen. Our SAS patches were faulty. You've been out for hours. Me too. I came around a couple of hours ago. MCC decided on an emergency autoland. My reflexes made docking with ISS too risky."

"I should be in an LES. That's procedure now. Ever since *Challenger*."

"I know, Jess. I know. But you don't need an LES. Earlier crews didn't use them."

"Gs, what about the Gs? I don't have my anti-G suit on."

"We're on autoland, Jess. Remember that. Autoland. The autopilot will take us in as always, and Houston will take us the rest of the way. If you pass out, it's all right. I'm here, and MCC knows what it's doing."

Tears ran from her eyes. "My head hurts so much."

"I know. I thought mine was going to explode."

"Patches?" She felt her neck. "Mine is gone."

"I removed them."

"The others? Are they still out?"

Tuck hesitated, then answered. "Yes. Still out. There'll be doctors at White Sands."

"You know they only land you at White Sands if they expect you to break apart on the runway."

"That's not true, Jess."

"It is true."

Tuck looked at the readouts. Maybe he could keep her mind engaged. "Mach twenty-four point eight ... two hundred forty thousand feet."

"We're heating up." Jess looked through the overhead ports. "I can see the plasma ribbon." She stared at it. "So pretty."

As the air around *Atlantis* heated to extreme temperatures, superheat stripped ions from the air, creating slithering snakes of light. They flashed and flickered, bathing the flight deck with flashbulb bursts of light.

"Entering first bank." Tuck kept his voice calm and low. The computers tilted the Shuttle into the first of several seventy-five-degree banking maneuvers meant to extend the distance the craft would fly before reaching the landing area in New Mexico.

Tuck's greatest desire was to take control of the craft, but to do so would mean disaster. Forty-five miles above the surface and speeds that most people couldn't fathom made human control impossible. The nose-up attitude prevented anyone from seeing a runway; that, and the runway waited several thousand miles away. Their lives were in the hands of silicon chips and wires, in accelerometers and computers.

"Mach twenty-two; two hundred twenty thousand feet. Pulling a half-G."

"We see the same thing."

"We're still with Rick?" Jess asked.

"I doubt dynamite would get him out of his chair. Heaven help anyone who tries to move him."

"Dieter still Flight?"

"Same crew."

"This all happened in one shift?"

"At least your brain is still working. I guess I'm no longer the smartest astronaut on board."

"Were you ever?"

"Ah, that's the Jess I know and love."

"Tuck?"

"Yes."

"I can't see. I'm blind."

Tuck's head snapped around. Jess looked straight ahead. "I thought you said you could see the plasma ribbon outside."

She nodded. "Everything went black after that. My headache has decreased. You know what that means?"

"I said it would go away."

"Not that fast, Commander. Something has given way in my head. I've popped an artery or something."

"You don't know that."

"I think the plasma lights may be the last thing I ever see."

"Negative. The docs will fix you up."

She moved her head from side to side. "I don't think so, Tuck. We're going to pull two Gs before we're wheels down. That can't be good for bleeding in the head."

"You don't know that you're stroking."

"Makes sense, Commander. Makes sense."

Tuck thought he heard slurring. "Houston, *Atlantis*."

"Go ahead, Atlantis."

"Jess is . . . Jess says she's blind."

Several moments passed. "Atlantis. *Surgeon says the medical folk at White Sands will be notified.*"

"That's it?" Tuck said. "That's the best they can do?"

"Of coorse it iz, 'mander. Nothin' you . . . can dooo."

Jess's speech indicated a stroke. A new avalanche of despondency crashed on Tuck. Jess could die in the chair with him strapped down and watching.

The cabin was quiet, the ride smooth. Tuck knew that the deeper in the atmosphere they descended, the louder things would become. Right now, he couldn't hear a whisper that would betray their great speed.

"Count usss ... down, 'mander. I don wan to miss ... thing ..."

Tears streaked his face.

"Will do, Jess. Will do." Tuck's voice betrayed his emotion. "Mach twenty; two hundred eight thousand feet; twelve hundred miles out.

"Mach eighteen; two hundred thousand feet; feeling one G.

"Mach fifteen point four; one-and-a-half Gs."

Atlantis began to shudder and wind noise worked its way through the hull.

"Speed brakes deploying. Ten minutes to landing.

"Mach five."

It was time to deploy the air-data probes, and Tuck reached for the switch, then stopped. The probes were already activated and feeding refined information to the guidance system. Tuck had to remind himself again that he was just a passenger, that he had to keep his hands to himself—something no commander ever had to do.

"You still with me, Jess?"

"Yef. 'Till her."

"Hang on, kid. Don't leave me. That's an order. You stay with me. Got that?"

"Yef, 'mander." Her head tilted to the side, her neck no longer able to hold the weight of it.

Let her live, God. Let her live. Husband and kids at home. Please, let her live.

Wind noise continued to increase as *Atlantis* plunged through the thick atmosphere. It sounded like an out-of-control train.

"Mach three point five; one hundred thousand feet."

The nose of the craft lowered as the speed decreased, improving Tuck's vision.

"I've got the runway in sight. Did you hear that, Jess. We're almost there."

No response.

"Jess. *Jess.* Talk to me."

Nothing.

"Mach one point zero; forty-nine thousand feet."

Atlantis shivered as shock waves that had been trailing the craft overtook it.

"Two hundred ninety-five knots; eight hundred feet ... five hundred feet ... two hundred ninety knots ... four hundred feet ... landing gear is down." *Don't leave me, Jess. I've lost too many. I can't lose another.*

"Fifty feet ... forty ... two hundred thirty knots ... ten feet ... touch down two hundred knots."

Tuck could imagine the chute deploying behind them to slow the speeding craft. He removed his glove, reached across the center console, and placed his fingers over Jess's wrist hoping to feel a pulse.

He found none.

Atlantis's forward movement stopped.

"Wheel stop."

"Wheel stop."

"I need help in here. I need it now."

Tuck released his restraints and moved to Jess. He tried several times to find a pulse but came up empty. He moved to Russ and repeated the action. No pulse there either.

He stepped to Jess again and released her harness, then pulled her from the seat.

In the cramped space of the flight deck, Commander Benjamin Tucker began CPR—praying between every breath forced into Jess's mouth and every compression made on her chest.

"One, two, three, four." *Please, God ...*

FIVE

ONE YEAR LATER

Tuck banked the Corsair F4U into a sixty-degree left turn rounding the Marine Air Station in San Diego. The WWII bird responded like a dream, the G-forces pressing him in his seat. The Pratt & Whiney R–2800 engine roared as he goosed the throttle, increasing speed in the turn and aligning the nose of the plane with the center of the runway. Below, thousands of eyes gazed at him as he put the gull-wing fighter through its paces.

At the moment, Tuck gave little thought to the crowd and even less thought to the events of the past year. He was doing the thing he loved most, flying at the edge of the envelope, pushing the sixty-year-old aircraft to its limits.

Applying more power, Tuck pulled the plane into a steep climb, its engine singing with the strain. The Corsair had a distinctive sound. The Japanese called it "Whistling Death."

The deep blue of the sky replaced the distant hills Tuck had seen a moment before the plane began a steep climb, its propeller clawing at the sky, pulling against thinning air.

Higher. Higher.

Tuck fixed his gaze on the canvas of blue before him and his mind added miles and miles of altitude. If only he could keep climbing, keep stretching until the blue of the sky dissolved to black and the Earth receded into a huge blue ball. If only ...

But one did not toy with gravity. The powerful pistons pounded out all the energy they could but the plane slowed its climb, reaching its maximum altitude.

"A little more, baby. Just a little more."

Tuck had no idea of his altitude and he didn't care. Aircraft like these were flown more by feel than instruments. The Corsair began to vibrate with the strain.

"Come on, sweetheart. This is what you were built for. A couple hundred feet more."

The creators of the Corsair had designed it for speed. During the war, pilots learned a new technique for finishing a dogfight: run. The manual instructed pilots in trouble to apply full power, climb, and head home. Nothing else in the air could catch it.

Then the jet age arrived and craft like the Corsair yielded to a new era. Still they served in World War II with distinction and made themselves known in the Korean Conflict. Now the plane was an oddity, a gull-winged used-to-be that once knew courage, strength, purpose, and glory.

An important used-to-be.

Just like Tuck.

Before the engine stalled, Tuck rolled the plane and started a dive that drew goose bumps over every square inch of his skin. Blue sky was now behind him, Miramar Marine Air Station below. He could see the crowds gathered for the annual air show, each a lover of aircraft or related to an enthusiast.

Tuck pulled back on the stick to flatten his descent. He was about to give the audience a sense of what it was like to be the object of a strafing run.

His air speed climbed so quickly that he could use the hands of the altimeter gauge as a fan. It was hyperbole, but the image made Tuck smile. Something he didn't do often anymore.

From the pilot's perspective, the ground rose at shocking speed, but Tuck knew he was the one moving fast.

Fifty feet above the runway, Tuck pulled the Corsair flat and raced the length of the concrete strip. From the corner of his eye, he saw the crowd raise hands and pump fists in the air. He almost wished he could see it himself.

As he reached the end of the runway, he took the plane high again, but this time just enough to allow a safe turnaround.

His part of the show had come to an end and a vague depression—a constant companion over the last thirteen months—invaded him again.

Reality returned.

Tuck despised reality.

He had been warned by the NASA docs—specifically, the NASA shrinks—that depression was likely. They told him of the deep melancholy felt by Apollo astronauts after returning from the Moon. They knew they'd never top the experience. Everything else would be second rate.

Of course Tuck's gloominess didn't stem from a great achievement he could never do again; it came from a massive failure. No matter how many times investigations declared him guiltless, no matter how often the world treated him as a hero—he knew the truth.

He and he alone survived the *Atlantis* mission. The rest of his crew rested in the ground. Dead.

The landing gear lowered smoothly and Tuck brought the blue beast down gently on the runway. His speed reduced quickly and he began the zigzag taxi maneuver every Corsair pilot learned. On the ground, the steep angle of the plane from nose to tail prevented the pilot from seeing forward. The long cowling also limited vision. Tuck moved left then right, left then right, taking sightings out the side of the cockpit.

A Marine stood to the side and guided Tuck to his place on the tarmac with hand signals.

Tuck killed the engine and exited the craft. He did so with a confidence and bearing that fit a fighter pilot/astronaut. A year ago, that confidence and bearing had been real.

"Spit-shine spectacular, Commander." The crewman stepped forward and shook Tuck's hand. He looked too young to be a Marine. Of course, they all looked too young to him now. "If you're up to it, there's someone who wants to talk to you."

"I'm not in the mood, Sergeant. I'd rather catch a cup of coffee."

"I don't think he's here as part of the audience." He stepped closer and lowered his voice, even though no one stood close enough to overhear. "It's Ted Roos."

Tuck blinked. "Am I supposed to know the name?"

"Well, yeah ... I'm mean, yes, sir. Ted Roos created *The Cube* and *New York Underground*."

"I don't follow."

The man looked puzzled. "He's the hottest game designer on the planet."

"Game? Video games?"

"Exactly, sir. *The Cube* sold a bajillion copies, and *New York Underground* is the best shooter game ever created."

"Did Mr. Game Fantastic say what he wanted?"

"No, sir. Just so you know. He's mega-rich. Got more money than God."

"I doubt that. Where is he?"

"He's on the other side of the barrier by the flight line."

"Thanks. Take care of my baby." Tuck patted the wing.

"She's in good hands, Commander. Listen. Do you think you can get his autograph for me?"

"No."

Tuck walked away.

• • •

Tuck didn't know what he expected, but Ted Roos wasn't it. He wore his I-just-crawled-out-of-bed hair proudly, and his chin hadn't seen a razor for several days. He stood five-eight, and bore maybe 165 pounds on a straight frame. His eyes were a blue that looked like they wanted to be green but couldn't pull it off. There was, however, a detectable intelligence behind those eyes.

"You Ted Roos?"

"That's me, Commander."

Tuck ducked under the nylon ribbon that formed the barricade. He was surprised to find Roos here. It was off-limits to the public. "This area is limited to support personnel, Mr. Roos."

"I'm not here as a spectator, Commander. I'm here with a proposition."

"Doesn't explain how you got here."

"I know people, Commander. I have money. I have connections. No big whoop."

"No big whoop, eh? What kind of proposition?"

"Business."

"I already have all the business I need."

Roos smiled in a way that made Tuck think he was the butt of an unspoken joke.

"Something funny, Mr. Roos?"

He shook his head. "I don't mean to offend, Commander. I just know the business you're in and I don't imagine you find it all that satisfying."

"I'm not sure you know that much about me."

Again, a smile. "I've arranged a room where we can talk. Shall we go there?"

Tuck's first inclination was to walk away, but something about Roos hooked him. He was young, maybe early thirties, but he had the confidence of an older, more experienced man. "Lead the way."

The room Roos mentioned was a conference space with a battered table and chairs in the center. Someone had shut the thick Venetian blinds. Another man rose from his seat when they entered. Roos gave a nod and the man departed. He left a laptop computer on the table.

Tuck and Roos were alone.

"Do you want to sit?" Roos motioned to one of the chairs.

"I prefer to stand."

To his credit, Roos remained on his feet too. "I take it you're a straight-to-the-point kinda guy."

"Yup. You said you know my business?"

"No, I said I know the kind of business you're in and that you're probably not satisfied."

Tuck removed his pilot's gloves. "That's a pretty bold statement."

"Let's see if I'm right. In the last year, the year since the accident, you've been traveling around the country shilling for NASA, doing air shows, talking to schoolkids. Right so far?"

"Shilling is a harsh word."

"But accurate. Let me ask a pointed question. When do you plan to go into space again?"

"That's hard to say."

"No it's not, Commander. It's not hard to say at all. NASA isn't going to put you up again, are they?"

"It would be inappropriate for me to discuss any future missions I might have."

"Then I'll discuss it for you. You've been grounded. Not formally, of course, but the suits aren't going to put you back in orbit. Too many questions." He raised a hand. "I know you've been cleared of any wrongdoing or error. In fact, the world thinks you're a hero. They should. I do too; otherwise I wouldn't be here right now."

"Still, it's pretty cocky to say you know what NASA will or won't do."

"Have you been getting odd looks from others on the astronaut corps? Do they look at you like you're a Jonah?"

Tuck didn't answer and he hoped his face didn't tip his hand. He would never admit it to anyone—never admitted it to himself—but he had caught a few questioning stares. Worse were the fleeting looks that broadcast doubt or pity.

"I know your kind is the best and brightest. You're not only superjocks but brainiacs too."

"You may be exaggerating." Tuck tossed his gloves on the table.

"Only to a point. Let's face it: you guys breathe a different air than the rest of us mortals."

"I'm just a man like you, Roos. I have a family. My back hurts if I work in the yard too long."

Roos laughed. "Three times you let them harness you into a vehicle strapped to thousands of pounds of explosive fuel. Before that, you flew fighter jets. In between you were a test pilot." He laughed again. "Yeah, I'm pretty sure your kind is different."

"Normally, I'm a patient man, Mr. Roos—"

"I want you to work for me."

Tuck's mind chugged to a stop. "What?"

"I want you to quit NASA, retire from the Navy, and join me on the front lines of space. I want you to help turn humans into a space-faring people."

It was Tuck's turn to laugh. "NASA has been doing that for decades."

"One time, maybe, but not so much now. Look, Commander ... they call you Tuck, right? May I call you Tuck?"

"No."

"Fine. Have it your way, Commander. You know as well as I do that NASA has been tasked to go back to the Moon and then on to Mars. President Bush laid that down in 2004. All well and good. And they're planning to do it in the same fashion they've gone about everything else, chained to big businesses as contractors. They will spend billions upon billions. The estimated cost of sending astronauts to Mars is five hundred billion dollars."

"And you don't think we should spend that kind of money."

"Of course we should. I think we should spend more. It's not as if NASA is breaking the US budget. Their percentage of the national budget is little more than a sliver. Less than seventeen billion dollars. The National Institute of Health gets twice the funds."

"Most people think NASA gets too much money."

"I'm not one of them. Let's get down to it, Commander. The Shuttle program is on the way out. In a few years, its budget will be less than 1 percent of all NASA dollars. How many orbiters do you think will be riding the flame into space? Not many."

"Work on the ISS continues and will continue."

"Sure it will, but who cares? It took thirty years and a hundred billion dollars to get it to this point. For NASA, low-Earth orbit is passé. Good work has been done. Worthwhile experiments have been performed. But near-Earth work is now on NASA's back burner."

"There's plenty of excitement with the effort to reach the Moon again and Mars."

"Like I said, I'm all for it, but with the end of near-Earth missions, a vacuum has been created. If you'll pardon the pun."

"And you want to fill it?"

"Me and others like me. I plan to put people in space."

"Rich people." Tuck knew where this was going.

"At first, but the dream is to make space available to almost everyone: carpenters, educators, and business people."

"Sounds noble but not practical."

Roos leaned forward. "More practical than you think. Spaceports are already being built. Last count, there were eighteen such efforts underway, including those in New Mexico, Alabama, Washington, Russia, Singapore, Tasmania, Australia, and Canada. Space tourism is almost here. I need someone like you to make sure we lead the pack."

"So I just up and quit. Do you realize what you're asking?"

"I do and I can make it worth your while. If you agree, you'll sit on our board of directors. I'll arrange for you to sit on the board of a few other corporations linked to entrepreneurial space travel. Your income will be in the solid six figures."

"So I sit in a boardroom from time to time?"

"You'll do much more than that, Commander. You'll work with our engineers developing innovative flight tech. You'd also be our public face. I don't make a good spokesperson. I prefer the background."

"Still, I'd be flying a desk."

"Which is pretty much what you're doing now. However, you'll do more than fly a desk, Commander. I want you to be our first pilot."

Tuck didn't know whether to laugh or not. "You want me to fly a homemade spaceship? Into space?"

"Suborbital at first, then orbital. And *Legacy* is hardly a homemade spaceship."

"And you think that comment should make me feel better?"

"When you see it, you'll know I'm right."

"I can't decide if you're mad or laboring under the self-delusion of genius."

"Commander, you know this can be done. It has been done. Burt Rutan's company Scaled Composites won the X-Prize in 2004 by flying into space twice within fourteen days. *SpaceShipOne* reached three hundred twenty-eight thousand feet. Earned them ten million bucks. Michael W. Melvill was sixty-three when he reached space."

"I'm aware of all that, Mr. Roos, but I'm just not interested."

Roos pulled a card from his front pants pocket. Unlike most business cards, this one was made of plastic. "I hope you change your mind."

"I doubt I will." Tuck took the card.

"Oh, one other thing. Lance Campbell signed on last week. You're my choice for lead pilot, but if you decide to stay your course, then I'll offer him the position."

"Campbell? You're kidding, right?"

"I know you two have a bit of history, but I figure you can work it out."

"History? Yeah, you might say we have history."

Roos smiled. "Odd, he said the same thing."

SIX

Grass had covered the gentle mound, its boundaries marked off by a border of flowers. A six-foot-high black marble monolith stood like a sentry over the spot, casting a long, thin shadow that bisected the manicured spot and fell upon the man who stood at the other end of plant-bounded ground.

Had an observer been present, he would have seen no more movement from the man than the stone marker. Overhead, a coagulated bank of clouds stumbled across the sky. A churning breeze tugged at the man's leather newsboy cap. The cap refused to yield its spot. The wind did manage to brush the white beard that hung from sagging cheeks and pointed chin.

Protected by a black leather coat and thick corduroy pants, the man ignored the wind. Other images filled his mind. Images of a spaceship, of a man in a space suit, of a funeral.

Vincent Pistacchia clenched his fists, released them, and then clenched them again as if each were a slowly pumping heart.

It had been a year and more since they brought his son home from space, dead and cold. He arrived on Earth, not like the other astronauts, but in the cargo bay, his feet still strapped to that blasted mechanical arm.

"All dead but one." He spoke to the grave as if its contents could hear and reply. "I told you flying was not the work of men. Space travel? Never should be. We men have enough to do here on the ground."

Tears rolled, twisting and turning as they followed the crags of the seventy-year-old's face.

There had been a big funeral in the United States. Leaders from around the world went to the memorial service; many others visited Arlington to stand by the graves of the dead astronauts. Funerals for heroes.

Not Vinny. Not his Vinny. Pistacchia insisted his son's body be returned to Italy where he could bury him on the property of the Pistacchia estate, the largest in the small country.

NASA offered to pay for the trip, offered to fly Pistacchia to the US so he could return with his boy's body. He would have none of it. He didn't need their charity.

"They said it would pass, Vinny—that the pain would go away and life would go on even though you lay here in the ground. I knew then they were wrong. I knew ..." More tears. "A year, my son. A year and now all the investigating is over and they say it is an accident—a mixup in the medication on that patch they forced you to wear. No one is guilty. No one, they said."

He turned his head and spit on the ground.

"Criminals investigating criminals. Murderers pretending to care."

A light rain began to fall, each drop whispering a sound as it struck the grass-shrouded ground. The wind picked up. The old man didn't move.

"I grieve for you, Son. Day and night, I cannot forget what happened. I have been robbed of you. First your mother so many years ago, and now you. Dead and in the ground. A man should not live beyond his only son."

The image of Vinny trapped in his space suit, dead and brought back to Earth in the payload bay like a sack of onions dug at him, chiseled his granite heart like the mason had chiseled the black marble that bore his son's name.

"There is more to be done, Son. What days I have left, I will spend making sure the responsible pay."

Soft footsteps approached from behind. A gentle, polite cough. Pistacchia didn't bother turning. "This is what I wanted you to see. This is what I want you to avenge."

"I understand." The voice came in a calm baritone. "Are you sure this is what you want?"

"Yes. He is out there—the one who did this. I will have my payment. Do you understand?"

"I do."

Pistacchia tilted his head enough to see the man who stood by him. Tall, thick, head shaved, and eyes dark as a moonless night. He gave a short bow, then left.

A tiny flame of regret sparked in Pistacchia's soul. He looked back at the grave. The flame died.

• • •

When Garret Alderman first met Diane Melville, CEO of MedSys, he thought of Lauren Bacall. Not the lithe, give-a-man-shivers looker from the old Bogart movies, but the aged beauty that time had created. Diane Melville wore her hair parted in the middle, letting the gray locks frame her lined face, and still projected a hypnotic beauty that mesmerized even a midthirties man like Garret Alderman. Today, she exuded that same beauty, but he could also see the anger simmering behind her tired blue eyes.

"Sit down, Garret," Diane said. She motioned to the foot of the table in the large board room. Seated to her left was the short, balding president of MedSys, Burt Linear.

Garret sat as ordered. He knew the drill. Diane was a master of dominating her space and using everything, including furniture, to gain an advantage.

"I received your message. You found him?"

"No, not specifically. I think I know his basic location." Garret placed a small laptop computer on the table and opened it. "As you know, this guy is as slippery as an eel—"

"And far more dangerous." Linear looked nervous. Perhaps eager. It had been ten months since MedSys hired Garret's security firm to track down the man responsible for making alterations in the drug composition used on the dermal patches that killed all but one of the *Atlantis* crew and nearly brought down MedSys.

"As you know, he set up a false ID, false bank accounts, false names, and more. What he did took a lot of planning, and unlike most people of his ilk, he planned a nearly foolproof escape plan."

"But you kept telling us that you could find him." Diane leaned forward.

"Indeed, I did." Garret adjusted his glasses. He knew he looked like a dot-com geek. He cultivated the image. Corporate security involved more electronic work than muscle these days. "I'm confident to the point of cocky and I'm highly motivated."

"Five million should be motivation for anyone," she said. "You still must locate him—down to the address."

"I understand. We've been over this." Garret regretted the words as soon as he spoke them.

"And we'll go over it every day if I so choose. One man almost ruined fifty years of pharmaceutical business." Diane's words were as hard as ice cubes. "My father put his life in this company and so have I. Millions of people are better off because of what we do here. I will not let one mistake doom us."

"With all due respect, it's more than one mistake. Your personnel department hired a man who used a false identity. A better background check might have saved you a lot of money."

"All old news." Linear's jaw tightened. "You can be replaced."

"Yup, you could do that." Garret didn't flinch. He never showed weakness. Bad for business. "In fact, feel free to do so." He closed the laptop and rose. "If you want to bring in one of my competitors, then just tell me. I'll disappear and let you explain to the new guy how you've covered up a crime committed on your premises, how that crime led to the death of some really good people who Americans consider heroes, and how you managed to cover it up. Oh, don't forget to tell them the man responsible has been running free for the last year."

"You want more money, is that it?" Diane's frown deepened, something Garret thought was physically impossible.

"No. The retainer you pay every month is adequate and the five-million-dollar carrot you keep dangling keeps me interested."

"It also keeps you from milking the 50K retainer we pay, not to mention the massive expenses."

"If I could have nabbed this guy the first week, I would have. Now, do I leave or stay?"

Silence hung heavy in the room. "Sit down, Mr. Alderman. We don't want to bring in anyone else." Diane leaned back. "It wouldn't be prudent."

Garret returned to his seat and reopened the laptop. "I know it's been a rough year for you. Frankly, it's never taken me this long to pin anyone down. Your man is smart. Worse, he's clever and apparently has monetary resources. No one can hide for long without a way of sustaining themselves."

Garret already knew a lot about his target. The man had been a troubled teenager but showed enough promise to make it into a four-year college, finishing in only two years. He had spent three years in the Navy before his superiors booted him out. Free of the military, he returned to school. Several misdemeanors later, he left with a BS degree in biochemistry.

Alderman had yet to understand what drove the man. For years, he seemed a model citizen working at some of the best research facilities and companies in the country—not as a scientist, his credentials didn't allow that, but as a master technician. He knew how to make the machinery and electronics do what was demanded of it.

Something in the man drove him to do more, and that "more" puzzled Alderman. He had become a "biohacker"—a term that didn't exist ten years ago. What Alderman learned about biohackers from his clients and his own research chilled him.

Biohacking was a new term. Ask a group of a hundred for a definition and maybe one or two would have an answer. Computer hacking was well known; biohacking was almost invisible.

Among biologists and medical researchers, a debate raged. Synthetic biology promised what all edgy science offered: cures for diseases like AIDS, malaria, and more. Synthetic biology researchers based their ideas on engineering principles and thinking. Researchers approached DNA as a mere string of building blocks they could separate and recombine to do new things or—maybe someday—make new creatures. Many believed they could repair genetic disorders and extend life by rearranging genetic matter in ways Nature hadn't. Food products could be improved by such strange engineering processes as taking "antifrost" genes harvested from a squid and mixing them with tomatoes, making them more resistant to cold snaps.

It was brave-new-world thinking at its best, but all such dreams have dark corners where nightmares reside.

Those dark corners chilled any thinking person. Any virus customized to help could be customized to harm. Just like a computer virus spread between computers on a network, so a bioengineered product might spread through a population of humans, weakening or even killing entire communities. A runaway, artificially created organism might not make as much noise or generate as much heat as a nuclear bomb, but the devastation in lives could be several orders more severe.

The kicker for Alderman, the thing that made his blood thicken with cold, was that someone with minimal training could create such things. Just like computer hackers and computer virus creators need not be computer scientists, so a biohacker may have nothing more than a basic college education. An especially bright person might not even need that. All that the would-be terrorist needed was access to a synthesizer.

This guy had the brains; he had the experience; and he had the mental illness to do great harm. He already had.

Linear interlaced his fingers. Garret could see the knuckles whiten. "You said you had a location."

"I have an area. He's moved across the country. I've had men on his trail from the first week you contacted me. Unfortunately, he had a head start and covered his tracks well."

"What's changed?"

"I believe our man has taken a job in southern California. He either needs money or ..."

"Or what?" Diane prompted.

"He's planning on doing it again."

"How do you know this?" Diane shifted in her seat. The news had made her as uncomfortable as it had made Garret.

"Few work in his specialty. Synthetic biology isn't a crowded field. A skilled technician who knows his way around a DNA sequencer is gold. Companies would hire him for the same reason you did. I've had operatives monitoring companies that have purchased the devices or advertised for the appropriate techs. We've been able to look at some of the applications."

"How did you arrange that?" Linear narrowed his eyes.

"Don't ask. What you don't know won't land you in jail. Then we got lucky. One of the firms is a new client. That gained us some access to their computers."

Diane licked her lips like a hungry woman. "What now?"

"Now I fly to southern California and pin this guy's ears back."

"When do you leave?"

"This afternoon. Oh, and I'll need your corporate jet. Say, three-thirty."

Ten minutes later, Garret walked into a cool fall afternoon and slipped into the limo that awaited him, knowing that his life had just gotten a whole lot more interesting.

SEVEN

Quiet conversation mixed with muted music and the jingle-jangle of silverware and dinner plates. Café Orleans was anything but a café. Not the most expensive restaurant in Houston, it was still a place one went only for special occasions—like a son's birthday party.

The restaurant had been Tuck's choice. He had long since given up on asking the children where they wanted to eat. The very question stoked the fires of sibling rivalry, each trying to outlast the other so they could contradict the first choice. "I want chicken," would be countered with, "Well, I want pizza." "You always want pizza." "So?" Best not to put that flame to the fuel.

Café Orleans would never be the first choice of the children, but they never complained when they ate there. The staff treated the family like royalty, something they did for all the astronauts and key NASA executives. The restaurant, which specialized in New Orleans cuisine, also offered dishes borderline teenagers could enjoy.

A long rack of baby back ribs rested on a plate in front of Tuck. Sharing the plate were collard greens stewed with spicy sausage and grits with cheese. Myra had settled for something more sensible: a plate of pulled pork, roasted corn on the cob, and coleslaw.

Gary ate like a twelve-year-old, moving food down his gullet like a vacuum sucked up dirt.

"Ease up, boy," Tuck said. "There's more food where that came from."

"Yeah, slow down, you little freak." Penny managed to squeeze more annoyed whining into her words than Tuck thought possible. *Fourteen years old, but she is still a child in so many ways.*

"Penny, don't call your brother a freak. It's his birthday. Wait until tomorrow."

"Daaad." Gary stopped chewing and tried to look hurt, but he couldn't hide the smile.

"Okay, okay, I'm sorry, birthday boy. Can you forgive your old man?"

"I don't know. You're pretty old."

"Watch it with the old cracks, bub. I know where you live."

"Yeah, but will you remember tomorrow?"

Even Penny laughed.

"Okay, wise guy, I have a question for you. We'll see how smart you are. I met a man in San Diego. I never heard of him, but someone said a guy your age would know all about him. His name is Roos, Ted Roos."

Gary stopped mid chew. "You met Ted Roos? Really? In the flesh?"

"I take it you've heard the name." Tuck glanced at his wife. She seemed amused.

"Well, duh. He's only the best video game designer on the planet. Tell me you got his autograph. Is that my birthday present? You got Ted Roos's autograph, right?"

Tuck felt ill. He had no idea that Gary would be so enamored. "I'm sorry, Son. I didn't get his autograph."

"Oh, man. You're kidding. You didn't even ask for his autograph?"

"I didn't know you collected autographs. If I did, I could get signatures from the really famous astronauts and test pilots."

"It's not the same, Dad. We're talking Ted Roos here."

"I got his business card; does that help?"

"Maybe. Not much." Gary's face revealed his disappointment.

"Let me see if I can't make it up to you. I have his number. Maybe I can talk him into mailing an autograph."

"That'd be great."

Gary's smile warmed Tuck's heart, but the memory of the conversation with Roos chilled it again. He had not been kind to the man. "I can't make any promises other than to try."

"I'm still lost," Myra said. "How did you meet this famous game designer?"

"At the air show. He was waiting for me after my flight. I tried to brush him off, but he was determined we talk."

"Talk about what?"

"Nothing really. He wants me to retire from the Navy, quit the astronaut corps, and go to work for him."

"Oh, is that all?" Myra looked puzzled.

"He wants you to design video games?" The look on Gary's face was priceless. "You don't play video games."

"Sure I do. We just call them something else—like flight simulators."

"Not the same thing. You don't know anything about video games."

"He doesn't want me for his video game business, Gary. He wants me to help another company he formed.

He's one of those guys who wants to commercialize space."

"What's that?" Penny interrupted.

"In a nutshell, kid, it's a private company that wants to make money taking tourists into space. Roos wants to send passengers into low-Earth orbit."

Myra furrowed her brow. "So you'd be an engineer or a consultant?"

"That's right. Well, he also wants me to pilot the craft."

For a moment, Tuck thought the air conditioner was stuck on high. He watched Myra and the kids exchange glances.

"What did you tell him?"

"I told him I wasn't interested." Tuck saw them relax. "I'll admit he has a persuasive way about him. Still, I have my work ..."

"What?" Myra matched his gaze.

"Nothing. Just something he said." Tuck waved a dismissive hand.

"And that was ...?"

"He said NASA would never let me fly again. Not in space anyway."

"I hope they don't."

"Penny!" Myra snapped.

"Well, I don't. It's not fair to us. You know that, Mom."

"Back up, Penny." Tuck's words were soft. He touched her hand. "What's on your mind?"

"Your last flight ... it's not fair to us. Every time you go into space ... every time you get in that stupid Shuttle ... it's like dying, Dad. It's like dying. Last year ... I thought we lost you." Tears welled in her eyes.

Tuck looked to his wife for support, but she offered none. Gary refused to look at him. "But you didn't lose me, kiddo. I'm still here."

"This time. The others ... the others had children too."

Tuck's heart deflated like a punctured balloon. That fact never left him, haunted him, as did the faces of his dead crew.

Penny rose from the table. "Excuse me." She walked in the direction of the restrooms, her head down, letting her hair hide her tears from the other patrons. Gary mumbled something and went after her.

"What'd I say?"

Myra shook her head. "It's not what you said, sweetheart; it's the work you do. The last year has been hard on them."

"They haven't shown it." Tuck rubbed his eyes.

"Sure they have. You haven't seen it." Myra's words bore no anger.

"So now I'm insensitive?"

Myra took Tuck's hand. "No. The problem isn't insensitivity. The problem is you're a man. Guys like you don't see the little clues kids give."

"They're overreacting."

"No, they're acting like normal kids who love their father—a father who came close to dying a year ago. They don't want to go through that again."

Myra rose from the table, leaned over Tuck, and kissed him on the forehead. "I'm going to check on them."

"What should I do?"

"Order cheesecake. Cheesecake fixes everything."

• • •

He was a dark man: dark skin, dark hair, dark eyes. His eyes remained fixed on the BMW SUV as it moved down Gessner Street in the Bunker Hill Village area west of Houston. His eyes skipped up to the rearview mirror, then back to the vehicle fifteen yards in front of him.

The SUV fit the upscale neighborhood. The man was glad that he had rented a luxury Lexus. A cheap car would stand out in this neighborhood.

The SUV turned onto Stoney Creek Drive. It wouldn't be long now.

The driver followed the SUV around the corner. He had to be careful. Too close would alert the driver, and she no doubt was packing a cell phone. Too far behind and he could miss the house where the woman and her cargo of children would end their journey. If they parked in a garage, then he would never identify the house.

The key was patience.

The SUV slowed and turned into the driveway of a large two-story home. Here's where the professional separated himself from the amateur. The temptation, almost overpowering, was to look at the target car and its passengers as he passed. He didn't. He kept his eyes forward and drove on at a speed just a hair above the residential limit.

Draw no attention to yourself. That was the first and abiding rule for people in his line of work. The second was confidentiality. He was good at both.

Continuing down the street, he pulled a U-turn at the next intersection, killing his lights before he finished the 180-degree turnaround. He moved down the street thirty or so yards and parked along the curb. An abundance of trees made it almost impossible to see the house, but he planned to pull closer in a few minutes. Give them time to get in the home and about their business. He killed the engine, then drew a cell phone from its place on the passenger seat.

He punched in a memorized number.

"I have another location for you." He listened for a moment, then pushed end. He wasn't finished with the phone. Using the keypad to activate the phone's menu, he erased the record of the call.

EIGHT

A round shape on the space side of the bulkhead rose until the whole of it filled the window. A helmet. An astronaut's helmet rose like the Moon over a horizon, the reflective gold shield mirroring the window. Tuck could see his own face reflected from the curved surface.

"Vinny? Vinny!"

Tuck pressed his face close.

Vinny's gloved hand rose and pushed back the protective shield.

The face. Twisted. Marred. Eyeless sockets. Mummy-like grin. Thin lips screaming, *"Don't leave me out here."*

Tuck bolted upright in bed. Sweat dripped from his forehead and into his eyes. His heart tripped and tumbled and skipped. A second later, he sat on the edge of the bed, his bare feet touching the oak wood floors. Air came and went from his lungs like a bellows.

Myra touched his shoulder. "You were dreaming."

"Yeah ... yeah, I know. Sorry."

He had to force the words out. Dream or no dream, it had been real to him. The image of Vinny bore into his brain like a worm into fruit.

Several deep breaths later, his heart slowed and the pressure in his head eased. "Sometimes I think I'm losing my mind."

The bedroom remained dark as Myra crawled across the bed and sat next to her husband. She took him in her arms and he let her. He wanted her to hold him. He needed her to hold him. In any other moment, at any other place, Tuck would have assumed the manly role, telling himself that everything remained fine and he still controlled his future. Not now. Besides, his wife knew him too well.

"The same dream?"

"Yeah. Always the same dream. Different details. Same terror."

"It's been awhile." Her voice was soft, soothing, her skin warm and welcome against his own. She kissed him on the side of his head.

He gave her bare leg a pat. "Sorry to wake you."

"A few extra moments awake are fine with me, as long as I get to spend them with you."

"I'm afraid your husband is a bit damaged."

"Not in my eyes." She rested her head on his shoulder.

"I thought this nonsense was over. I thought I was done with it. It's been a few weeks since my last one."

"I know, baby. I know. Maybe it'll be even longer before the next one. Maybe this was the last."

"From your mouth to God's ear."

"It has been."

"Thanks, kid." He took a deep breath. "Listen, you go back to bed. I'm going to get a glass of milk and watch some television. It's going to take me a few minutes to shake this."

"It's amazing how real dreams can be." She paused. "I'll stay up with you. I'll make cocoa. It won't take long."

Before he could answer, Myra was off the bed and making her way through the dark room like a cat. He looked at the clock on his nightstand. Blue numbers shone 1:03. A lousy time to be awake.

• • •

"Last call, folks." The bartender's voice rolled through the dingy bar, falling on the ears of the last hangers-on. Most had been in Chucky's Bar since early evening. All had entered chattering and telling jokes, but hours of drinking had left the remainders a maudlin bunch gazing into their drinks like a fortune-teller hovering over a crystal ball. But where the psychic boasted of seeing the future, these men saw only the past.

Ronny Mason knew this because he had been one of the dopes who spent their evenings seeking the company of people worse off than they. After losing his truck-driving job because of back problems, Ronny had begun a consistent regimen of self-medication in the form of shots of whiskey. Ronny's change came in the form of an ultimatum from a wife he loved more than life. "Get over your problems, get a new job, or get a new wife."

The prospect of returning home to an empty house frightened him. It was one thing to lose a job, but to lose a woman like Betsy was nothing short of criminal.

Ronny's solution: buy the bar. Chucky's became his two years ago, and he had been sober each day of those two years. His back still hurt and he needed help lifting cartons, but he got by.

"Did everyone hear? Last call." He rubbed his ample belly then began the final cleanup behind the long wooden bar. When everyone was out, he'd lock the door and spend the next hour sweeping the floor, wiping tables, and closing out the register. Then it was home to a warm bed and the smell of his wife.

"Aw, come on, Ronaniro, don't nobody care if you close late."

"State of California does, Mikey. If they closed me down, then where would you go every evening?"

"Um, the place down the street."

"You know they don't let the likes of you in their place. They cater to a better class of losers."

"Ain't no better class, Ronjamite. We is the best lot of losers ever knocked back a beer."

"True." Ronny gave a little laugh. Some of these men he considered family. "And I love you all like brothers. Now finish your drinks and get out. Any of you need a ride, best let me know now. I know you do, Mikey."

"Not me, pal. I'm sober as a judge on Sunday."

"Right. I think you had better hand them keys over now. I'll call you a cab."

"Hey, everyone, the Ronster thinks I'm a cab."

No one laughed. The joke had been played too many times.

Ronny moved down the bar, wiping up spills, salt crystals from pretzels, and shells from peanuts. He stopped when he reached a young man with thick brown hair, bloodshot eyes, and a puffy, awkward-looking ear.

"How about you, young man? You need a cab?"

"Nah, I'm fine, and I'm not that young. I'm almost thirty."

"Almost thirty, eh? Well, when you've got fifty-five in your rearview mirror, then almost-thirty is young." Ronny paused and studied the man. This was his first night in the bar, and he stuck out like a palm tree on a glacier. "You okay?"

"Never better, old man. Why?"

"'Cuz you been tossing shots of Wild Turkey like Kool-Aid."

"So?"

"Nuthin'. Just that most people who hit the juice that heavy have just lost a job or someone's died."

"Well, you're wrong about me. And I don't appreciate your barroom psychology."

"Have it your way, buddy. I just pour 'em. You can drink for whatever reason you like. Don't mean nuthin' to me."

"Smart man."

"This boy giving you trouble, Ronny?" It was Mikey.

"Naw, he just likes his own company. Nothing wrong with that."

"You want me to toss 'im, Ronny? I'll toss the young punk if you want."

The new guy grinned. "You? Toss me? Listen, you old booze hound, you can barely stand. Take a step back before I have you licking dirt off the floor."

"What makes you think you can talk to me like that? I was whipping guys like you when I was in junior high."

"That's enough, Mikey."

"Hit him, Mikey. Hit him good." The voice came from an old man in the back.

"Shut up, Henry. Finish your drink and go home. I'm not going to have a fight ten minutes to closing. That goes for you too, Mikey. Finish your drink and call it a night."

"I can take him, Ronster. I can take him good."

The man began to slip from his stool but before his foot could touch floor, Ronny had removed a Louisville Slugger from beneath the bar and pointed the business end between the two men.

"This ends now, gentlemen. First guy to throw a punch goes home with a goose egg on the side of his head courtesy of me. Got it?"

No answer. The two men eyed each other. If a fight broke out, then Mikey, who had more sheets to the wind than New Guy, would be sobering up in the emergency room. If he hadn't been so certain of that, he might have let Mikey lay a couple of roundhouses to the young guy's noggin.

"I ain't kidding around here, gentlemen. Once I crack a skull, I have to fill out a great deal of paperwork with the police, and I don't like paperwork. Cool it. Cool it now."

"All right, Ronster. I'll step away, but if this pencil-neck geek gives you any more grief, you let me know. I'll take him outside and school him in some manners."

"I'm ready, old man."

"Go sit down, Mikey." Ronny tapped his friend's chest with the bat. Mikey backed away.

New Guy sat down and took his glass in his hand. "I'd have killed him. He can't be serious about taking me."

"Don't fool yourself, friend. Before Mikey took up drinking, he did some serious boxing. Had promise. I seen him put more than one man on the mat."

"What? Fifty years ago? I did some work in the ring myself. How do you think I got this ear?"

"You gonna finish that drink or try to dry it up with all yer talk?"

The customer knocked back the drink in a single gulp. "Answer your question?"

"Yeah, now I got one more. You know how to work a door?" Ronny kept the bat in his hands, ready for action.

The man looked at the door. He got the hint. Slipping from the stool, he started for it, then stopped and sighed. He returned to where he had been sitting. Ronny saw him catch a glance of Mikey, who had yet to take his eyes off the stranger.

"Look. I'm sorry. I'm new in town and I'm not used to sitting around bars. You're right. I lost my job last week and I'm trying to find work. I guess the depression and the booze got to me. How much time until closing?"

"Five minutes." Ronny eyed the man. Something didn't feel right. He watched as the man reached for his wallet and removed a ten and two fives. The bills were folded in the middle, the ten resting inside the fives. He dropped the bills on the counter.

"Buy Mikey another and keep the change for yourself." He tossed the bill on the bar, returned his wallet to his back pocket, then inserted his hands into his front pockets. Ronny could hear keys jingle and paper rustle.

"No hard feelings."

"Thanks." The man waved at the handful of customers clinging to the last few moments in their home away from home, then exited the bar.

"That guy was weird, Ronny-boy. You should have let me pop him one."

"Weird is right. He bought you another drink."

"Did I say weird? I meant friendly."

Ronny snatched up the bills and studied them. The ten looked real. He massaged the paper. Felt real. Since he'd already closed out the register, he shoved the bills in his wallet. It was his bar; he could do what he wanted. *A man can't steal from himself.*

"Don't dawdle, pal. That door over there is going to be locked in five minutes and all of you are gonna be on the other side."

• • •

"Are you going to tell him tomorrow?" Myra snuggled deeper into the crook of Tuck's arm and rested her head on his chest. He gave her a squeeze and felt thankful for the feel of her, the smell of her, the sound of her. Somehow, he always felt more alive when she was around.

"Tell who?"

"You know who. Dr. Celtik. Your favorite flight surgeon."

"First, that's today. It's already Tuesday, kiddo." Tuck fixed his eyes on the old black-and-white movie showing on the TV.

"Okay. Are you going to tell him?"

"I don't know. Haven't given it any thought."

She patted his stomach. "That's your avoidance mechanism. Don't think about it."

"Oh, I see. You got a psychology degree while I was at work?"

"Nope, but I do have a Mrs. degree in Benjamin Tucker Junior."

"I don't want to tell him. He's one of those by-the-book guys. A little something like this could make him uneasy."

"A little thing? You've had recurring nightmares for a year, honey. It's not a little thing."

"It doesn't affect what I do."

Myra didn't respond. Tuck said, "Aren't you going to tell me how it's my duty to tell the doc?"

"No one needs to tell Commander Tucker what his duty is, certainly not his wife. Besides ..."

"Besides what?"

"No matter what I tell you, I lose. If I encourage you to reveal the dreams to Bob and he grounds you, then I'll feel responsible. If I tell you to keep it a secret and they send you back up and something goes wrong ... I'll feel responsible. So I'm going to take the safe road and leave it all up to you."

Tuck kissed her on top of the head. "I married above myself."

"Boy, you got that right." Myra sat up. "I'm going back to bed. Come soon. I don't sleep well without your window-shaking snoring."

"I don't snore."

"Ha. How would you know? You're asleep when you do it."

Tuck watched the thinly draped form of his wife pad barefooted across the carpet. Her form in the dim light provided the exclamation point to his earlier statement: he had married above himself.

"Don't forget to rinse the coffee mugs. Chocolate is hard to clean when it has dried."

"Yes, Master."

Myra disappeared into the bedroom and Tuck returned his gaze to the television. On the screen, a commercial had replaced the movie. Tuck closed his eyes, leaned his head back, and tried to drive out the nightmarish vision that stained his memory.

They were stubborn ghosts, not easily exorcised. He needed help to evacuate the still stinging emotions, and watching TV wasn't cutting it.

Tuck rose from the sofa, took the two mugs into the kitchen, and rinsed away the brown cocoa residue. He then moved into a bedroom that he had converted to an office and turned on the banker's light perched on his desk. It put out just enough light. From one of the shelves in the built-in cherry bookcases, he removed a Bible and opened to Psalms.

Since his return from the failed mission, he had sought comfort from the Bible. Each time he did, he realized how far he had wandered from the faith. At first, he blamed God for it all. But time had dissolved some of the initial bitterness, and Tuck had begun a slow flight back to belief.

In the wee hours and after a soul-dicing dream, he needed some comfort and wisdom.

He opened the book and moved the pages, letting his eyes fall wherever chance put them. He had no destination, just a hunger.

> *Where can I go from your Spirit?*
>   *Where can I flee from your presence?*
> *If I go up to the heavens, you are there;*
>   *if I make my bed in the depths, you are there.*

The room provided a perfect reflection of his mind: dim and full of shadows. Still, a faint light refused to yield to the darkness.

He read psalm after psalm, but the sense of despair would not leave. Tuck felt as if he could see the end of his world from where he sat.

He closed the Bible, went to bed, and watched the clock count off the minutes to dawn.

• • •

Mikey hung around longer than the others, ostensibly to help Ronny clean the bar, but the bartender knew his friend was nursing the last drink of the night. He couldn't blame him. Ronny had a home with a wife and a warm bed; Mikey had a studio apartment with no one but the occasional cockroach to share the space.

Ronny swept while Mikey placed chairs on the tables to make room for Ronny's broom. A bead of sweat ran from the bartender's temple and dripped to the floor.

Mikey saw it. "You're workin' too hard, Ronny. Not much in this world worth sweating over—certainly not a little dirt on the floor."

"I ain't workin' any harder than I did yesterday. Don't know why I'm feeling so winded. This is nuts. Feel like I ran around the block."

"You feelin' okay? It ain't your ticker, is it?"

"Nope. Heart is fine. I just feel a little light-headed and warm. You know."

"Yeah, I know. I feel the same way if I go too long without a drink. You back on the juice?"

Ronny shook his head. "Haven't had a drop in two years. Not a single drop. Me and the booze are on the outs forever."

"Good to hear."

Mikey's words carried the same sincerity as one smoker telling another how proud he is of his friend's determination to desert the flock.

Ronny stopped sweeping and took several deep breaths. "You know what? I'm gonna call it a night. Finish up that glass you been tending. I'll come in early tomorrow and finish this."

"Okay. You da boss. I'll call a cab. I'm a little too lit to be behind the wheel."

"Don't bother. You're not that far off my path. I'll drop you by your place."

"I don't want to be no trouble, Ron-man."

"Won't add five minutes to my trip." The sentence took more out of him than he thought it should. "Let's get going. I think I'm getting a headache."

"Whatever you say, boss-man."

Five minutes later the two had seated and belted themselves in Ronny's Toyota sedan and headed toward the I-8 freeway. Even at this hour, the wide roadway had too many cars for Ronny's liking. Such was life in southern California.

The car accelerated along the on-ramp and eased onto the freeway. Overhead, a gibbous Moon added its lights to the yellow cast of the streetlights. To Ronny, the city looked jaundiced. He started to say so, when a pair of bright lights stabbed his eyes.

"Idiot."

"Who? Me?" Mikey sounded worried.

"Not you. The bozo behind me. Can't figure out how to dim his high beams."

"Maybe one of his low beams is out so he's keeping his brights on. I've done that a few times."

Ronny flipped the lever on the rearview mirror to dim the glare.

"I already got me a world-class headache. I sure don't need some moron to make it worse." He looked forward. The red lights of the vehicles in front of him blurred and ran together. Ronny squinted.

Sweat ran down his face. His heart began to race as if attached to the accelerator.

He shook his head. "Man, I think I got the flu bad."

"Maybe I should drive. I've had too much but I can't do worse than you — *look out.*"

The warning came too late. Ronny's sluggish brain recognized the back end of an eighteen-wheeler that looked like a wall before him.

He slammed on the brakes. Except the pedal he slammed to the floor was not the brake — it was the accelerator.

He heard it first, then felt it. The impact plowed the Toyota nose down. Ronny snapped the steering wheel to the right.

He felt weightless for a moment as the sedan flipped. Mikey screamed. Ronny's head hit the driver-side window then the ceiling as the force of the tumbling vehicle crushed the roof into the passenger compartment.

Noises: squealing tires; blaring horns, crunching of metal; breaking glass; impact thuds of metal to asphalt.

When the car stopped its terrible gymnastics it rested upside down against the concrete divider that separated eastbound traffic from westbound.

We flipped clean 'cross the freeway. It was the second-to-last thought Ronny had. The last one he saved for his wife.

• • •

"What happened? I mean, I didn't cut him off. I couldn't have. I looked. I know I looked, and I signaled. I signal longer than any trucker. How could I cut him off?"

The truck driver held his hands to each side of his head as if trying to keep his brains from expanding and cracking his skull like an egg.

"Take it easy, buddy. I saw the whole thing. It wasn't your fault. The guy was all over the road. Nothing you could have done." Edwin Quain lowered himself to the upside-down car. Behind him, traffic backed up like water at a new dam. Most cars weaved through the lanes, too busy to let yet another accident on a California freeway bother them.

"Are they . . . ? I mean, surely someone has called for an ambulance." The truck driver was a barrel of a man; gray stubble forested his face.

"An ambulance isn't going to do them any good. They're dead."

"You a doctor?" It was a new voice, younger, cockier.

"Nope. You?"

"Then how do you know they're dead?"

Quain stood, dusted the dirt from his hands, and looked at a guy who couldn't be out of college. Even in the dim light, Quain could see his watery eyes and pinpoint pupils. Apparently he'd been having an evening of fun and drugs. "Take a look for yourself."

He did. Swore, stepped to the concrete barrier, and tossed everything he had ingested that evening.

"I'll take that as agreement."

"I don't believe this. This is horrible. It's tragic. I'm minding my own business and driving my rig and a man ends up dead."

"Two people," Quain corrected. "There's a passenger."

The driver leaned against the buttress and began to weep. "Twenty-five years driving open road and not a single accident. Not even a fender bender. Now this." The tears came in wet sobs. "I had the best record in the company. Now this. I killed them."

"Nonsense. They killed themselves." Quain looked over the tangle of metal that had once been a pretty decent car. He felt satisfied. No doubt about it: he was getting better.

"Smells like a brewery in there," College Boy said.

"They were drinking?" the trucker asked.

College Boy nodded. "Oh, yeah. Big time. Trust me; I know the smell of liquor."

Quain shook his head. "I bet you do."

"What's that supposed to mean?"

"Nothing. Go back to your puking."

Quain started toward his car.

The trucker drew a sleeve across his damp face. "Hey, where you going? I need your information. The police will want to talk to you."

"I know. I'm going to get my ID. I can't do anything for the men in the car."

"Oh. Yeah. Good idea."

He walked along the freeway. He had thought far enough ahead to pull over after he passed the wreck. If he had parked behind it, he could be stuck for hours. From behind him, a distant and shrill whine of a siren cut through the night.

Quain slipped into his car. Waited a moment, then started the engine. A moment later, Edwin Quain drove down the road again.

Behind him, two men rested in death. One drunk and too full of the sauce to hold his tongue, and one a bartender who dared raise a bat in Quain's direction.

That twenty was quite a tip and the bar a good proving ground.

NINE

Doctor Bob Celtik leaned to the right, resting his elbow on the arm of his desk chair. His casual thanks-for-stopping-by-for-coffee pose didn't fool Tuck.

"And what about Gary? Is he still plunging headlong into adolescence?" Bob's voice reminded Tuck of a radio DJ: deep, smooth, silky. It didn't fit the fifty-five-year-old medical man.

"Yup. He had a birthday yesterday." Abruptly, Tuck changed the subject. "Bob, let's bottom line this." Tuck spread his legs and leaned forward, not feeling as confident as his pose suggested. "What did the shrink say?"

Bob leaned over his desk, opening a colored folder to scan the pages inside.

"I'm assuming you've already read that, Bob. Just say it."

"Most indicators are good, Tuck. Dr. Bennack states that you've shown the proper journey through grief. Your emotional state is stable and your social interaction indicates good mental healing."

"You're dumbing this down for me, aren't you?"

"Yeah. I am. The fancy terms won't mean much to you."

"So if I'm doing so well, then what's stuck in your craw?"

"The dreams. You're still having the night terrors."

"Nightmares. Let's not exaggerate their intensity or their frequency."

Bob met Tuck's eyes as if the doctor could read thoughts printed on the gray matter. "When was your last night terror ... nightmare?"

Lie. Just tell him a lie. You wouldn't be the first astronaut to fudge the truth about a medical matter.

"Last night."

"And?"

"And what? It was just a dream. I've had them before and I might have a few more. Dreams are just dreams."

Bob shook his head. "No, Tuck, they're not just dreams. What you went through would drive most men mad. You're military. You know the effects trauma has on a man. When I did my psych rotation in med school, I met World War II vets still grieving buddies lost in battle."

"I'm not them." The words came out hard as bricks.

"No, you're not. You're Commander Benjamin Tucker Junior, Navy jock pilot, three-time veteran of Shuttle missions, and hero to the world. You're also made of flesh and blood; your brain is made the same way as the rest of us."

"You're washing me out?"

"No. You're still part of the astronaut corps, but I'm taking you off the flight roster."

Tuck didn't flinch, but his jaw tightened like a clamp. "This is an overreaction, Bob. You know it is."

"I know no such thing. You know as well as I do— scratch that—you know *better* than I do that space travel is not the same thing as flying a plane. If we were just talking air flight, I'd tell you to keep seeing the psychiatrist until the dreams disappeared, but I'd let you fly. Shuttle missions put you in space for days. You sleep up there. I have to think of the rest of the crew." He paused. "Of course, it's all academic, really."

"It's more than that. It's personal."

"It's not personal, Tuck. It's academic because you've already made three flights. You'd be out of the rotation for a while anyway, maybe for good. Who knows?"

"Then clear me to fly and I'll fight the schedule battle with the suits later."

"I can't do that, Tuck. I can't clear you just because I like you. I have to make a medical judgment."

Tuck leaned forward and rested his elbows on his knees. His eyes fixed on the linoleum floor but he saw none of it. He was lost in the vacuum of his mind. Bob's announcement had cored the life out of him. He had walked in a confident pilot and astronaut; now he sat as a shell of a man.

"I take no pleasure in this, Tuck. I didn't sleep a wink last night. I've washed other men out, but this is different. I've always considered you a friend."

"A friend?" Tuck wanted to say more, something harsh, something that would inflict pain and drown the man in guilt. The best he could do was to move his head from side to side.

"Look, I know you didn't want to hear that and you're not going to like this any better, but I had to consider your family as well."

"What have they got to do with this?"

"Everything, Tuck. They came close to losing you a year ago. They know the families of those who did die, and every time they see them, they are reminded how close they came to living the rest of their lives without you."

"You don't know my family that well, Bob." The comment failed to prevent Penny's words of last night from reverberating through his soul.

"I know them well enough, and to be blunt: you didn't see their faces while we were trying to bring you in. You heard your wife over the com system, but I had to look her in the eyes, then your son, and your daughter. I had a few nightmares about that myself."

"So that's it. I'm finished."

"Of course not. The work of NASA isn't confined to a flight deck. We have the new human exploration projects; there's still engineering, still training—"

"Do you know what Leonardo da Vinci said about flight, Bob?"

"Not really."

Tuck quoted, "'When once you have tasted flight, you will forever walk the earth with your eyes turned skyward, for there you have been, and there you will always long to return.'" Tuck rose. "I'm not sure you can understand that, Bob."

"Why? Because I'm not an astronaut?"

"Exactly."

"Why do you think I work for NASA? Do you believe it's because of the money? I make a third of what I could in the outside world. I walked away from a lucrative practice so I could participate in the exploration and utilization of space. So don't tell me I don't understand. I'll never get to do what you do. It wasn't in the cards for me. Nonetheless, I plan to do whatever I can to be a part of space exploration so jockeys like you can do what I can't."

"You can't understand, Bob. You can't. You've never flown in space."

"To my knowledge, neither did da Vinci."

A hot sword of regret pierced Tuck. "I'm sorry, Bob. I'm ... I didn't mean ..."

"Go home, Tuck."

• • •

Mark Ganzi felt ill at ease. He had spoken to the man and had done five grand worth of work for him, so why should he be nervous about meeting him at the airport? He had no answer. Not one to speak often of instinct, he knew a private eye wasn't much good without it. His instinct had just found fourth gear, and each minute that passed pressed the accelerator a little closer to the emotional floorboard.

The George Bush Intercontinental Airport buzzed with activity. In the area where non-travelers bided their time waiting for friends, family, or coworkers to arrive, Ganzi tried to blend in. Several people held signs with names prominently displayed. He had been told not to do such an obvious thing. Instead, he had been told to wait near the back wall with his arms folded.

The flat-screen monitor showing departures and arrivals indicated his client's plane had landed on time. Another stream of travelers started down the escalators into the waiting area near the luggage carousels. One slovenly man pushed his way through the crowds chanting, "Sorry. Excuse me. Coming through." He jostled one man and Ganzi was certain bruises were about to be administered. Nothing came of it. No one wanted to spend more time in the airport than necessary.

At the top of the escalator the figure of a tall man appeared. Even though thirty or more paces separated them, Ganzi could see the man's eyes scanning the crowd. When they made eye contact, Ganzi straightened. The man let his gaze linger for a second, then continued to scan the room. For a moment, Ganzi thought he had set his attention on the wrong man.

He hadn't.

As soon as the escalator deposited him on the lower floor, the man took long strides until he stood before Ganzi. Close up, Ganzi could see the man was not only tall, but also thick across the shoulders. Muscles pressed against the sleeves of his tan sport coat.

"You are Mark Ganzi?"

"That's me. You must be—"

"Anthony Verducci."

"Of course. I assume you have luggage." Ganzi stood several inches under six foot, and standing next to his client made him feel all the shorter.

"One suitcase. I prefer to travel light."

"A wise decision these days. Luggage pickup is this way." Ganzi led his charge into the stream of humanity moving to baggage claim. Ganzi expected more waiting, but bags and suitcases were already moving around the metal carousel.

"It's about time." The voice came loud and harsh. Ganzi turned in time to see the same slovenly man elbowing his way through. "Come on, come on. Let me through. I'm late for a meeting."

He brushed by Ganzi and his client, and in his haste stepped on the foot of a little girl. She screamed and dropped to the floor.

The brusque traveler stumbled but caught himself. He spun to face the fallen child. "Stupid kid. Watch what you're doing." He turned to the mother. "Can't you keep your little monkey on a leash? Bad enough I had to hear her yammer all the way from New York."

The mother reached for the child, tears welling in both their eyes.

Verducci stepped next to Loud Mouth, placed a hand on the man's bicep, and began to squeeze. Ganzi knew what was happening. Verducci had dug his fingers into the space between bicep and triceps, pressing the artery and very sensitive nerve that ran from shoulder to elbow. "Let go of—"

"You've been rude," Verducci interrupted.

"I don't have to listen to some foreigner—" He winced. Strong fingers had moved an inch closer to the upper arm bone.

"Don't you think you should apologize?"

"Okay ... okay. I'm sorry, little girl."

"The mother." Verducci's words were smooth. If he was angry, he didn't let it show.

The man gave her a humble nod and said, "I'm sorry. I behaved badly."

The mother glared at him and gathered her weeping daughter even closer.

"Get your bag and get out." The words were so cold Ganzi thought he saw condensation puff from his client's mouth. Verducci dropped his hand, and the man scrambled away.

Verducci squatted next to the little girl. "Hello, child. Are you hurt badly?"

She sniffed. "He stepped on my foot."

"May I take a look?"

She nodded. "You talk funny."

Verducci smiled. "I am from Italy. Have you ever been to Italy, little one?"

"No. Where is it?"

He moved the sock on her right foot down to the top of her small sneaker. A small scrape was visible. "It is far across the ocean. It is the most beautiful place on Earth. Maybe someday you can visit my country."

"That would be fun."

Ganzi watched Verducci. When subduing the impatient slob Verducci had showed no emotion, but with the child, he flashed a smile and displayed genuine concern.

"Your foot looks fine. There is a scrape and it will sting for a little while. Maybe your mother can put a Band-Aid on it later. Can you stand?"

"I think so." She wiped the last of the tears from her eyes.

Verducci stood. "Then give me your hand, little one." She did and Verducci raised her to her feet. She stood on one foot, and then tested the other.

"Thank you," the mother said.

"Make no mention of it. I am glad to be of help."

He put a hand on the little girl's head and gave it a pat.

Fifteen minutes later, they were in Ganzi's rental car and moving through the busy streets. Ganzi split his thoughts between the traffic and the man seated next to him. Verducci struck the private investigator as an oxymoron: willing to inflict pain on the sloppily dressed buffoon at the airport, yet eager to help a stricken child.

Hadn't Verducci hired Ganzi to gather information on the most famous astronaut in the country? Ganzi still didn't know why.

"You want a report now?" Ganzi asked.

Verducci shook his head. "At the hotel. I need to think."

A moment later, Ganzi heard a gentle snoring.

TEN

Tuck wandered through downtown streets then along residential byways. He saw only enough to prevent him from running his car into the back of a truck or into a tree. Normally prone to stretching the restrictions of speed-limit signs, something he referred to as "speed suggestion" signs, this time he kept his foot light on the accelerator, and the Chevy Avalanche pickup seemed grateful for it. The gas pedal in his mind, however, was stuck to the floorboard.

Bob Celtik's words blared like a car alarm, repeating and repeating and repeating. Bob had been as professional and as caring as a man could be, but anger boiled in Tuck. It wasn't Bob's fault. He hadn't made the psych evaluation; he only read it.

He couldn't go home. Not yet. Not with so much venom aching to inflict damage on the nearest clump of flesh and nerves that passed for human.

He had felt blessed his entire life: reared in a great family, guided by fine teachers, graduated the naval academy, given wings in flight school, and inducted into the astronaut corps. Only a handful of men could boast of such things. He was married to a woman he'd marry again in a heartbeat, and his children ... his children ... The thought of Penny and Gary drained the fury from Tuck and replaced it with scalding regret. Although he had never said it aloud, he drew an impossible-to-measure sense of satisfaction each time his children said, "My dad is an astronaut."

"They can still say that." The voice bubbled up from deep in his brain. At least a part of his gray matter remained connected to reality.

Despite the reassuring voice in his head, one undeniable fact stoked the coals of his regret: he wouldn't be a "flying" astronaut, and flying defined him.

Sure. He could train incoming astronauts, oversee one NASA project or another; he could continue to speak at schools, colleges, and civic groups; he could make the rounds to the contractors who assembled parts of space-going vessels. He could do that and still be one of the most admired men in the country.

Maybe saying good-bye to NASA was the thing to do. Return to active Navy duty. He shook his head. Myra couldn't handle that. Having him gone six months at sea would be unfair to a family that had already endured so much.

Minutes became hours and with little recognition of how he got there, Tuck was home.

The house sat empty. No sounds of children, no radio, no television, no smells of cooking, no laughter, no sibling arguing. His mind had been so full of self-pity that he had forgotten that the kids would be in school and Myra would be working at her part-time real estate career.

Tuck's home was twenty-five-hundred feet of clean, organized, self-decorated bliss. Now, it seemed a well-furnished tomb. He decided tomb was the right metaphor. After all, something had died—his career. He knew the time would come when space travel would no longer be available to him, but he always assumed it would be because he had grown tired of it. One didn't fly the Shuttle every week, or even every month. The time between flights could span more than a year, but just knowing that his name was on the list for upcoming missions satisfied him. He would never feel that satisfaction again.

He slipped into the kitchen and removed a small bottle of orange juice, twisted the lid off, took a draw, then moved back into the living room. A suede sofa became his perch. Leaning forward, Tuck rested his elbows on his knees and peered into the half-empty juice bottle as if the answer were floating somewhere within.

Thoughts that normally fell into line like soldiers in a parade resisted any attempt at organization. Instead of soldiers at attention, his thoughts swirled aimlessly.

Life wasn't over. He knew that. He just didn't *feel* it.

His gaze rose and fixed on a long open box in front of the cherrywood entertainment center. The box rested empty on the charcoal gray carpet. Next to it rested the long narrow contents: the skateboard he and Myra had bought Gary for his birthday. The sight of it brought a small smile to Tuck's face.

The thought of Gary stimulated another memory. His son had been stunned when he discovered his father had met Ted Roos and didn't know enough to ask for an autograph.

Ted Roos. He had given Tuck a business card. What had he done with it?

More from instinct than memory, Tuck set the juice on the coffee table and reached for his wallet. There it was, tucked just behind a twenty. He studied it. The card was simple translucent plastic with black ink, nothing indicating great creativity or marketing savvy: just the name Ted Roos, a phone number, an e-mail address, and a webpage URL. Straight and to the point. Tuck thought it odd that there was no physical or mailing address. Oversight or plan?

It didn't matter. Tuck reached for the remote phone that rested on a side table and dialed the number.

One ring.

"Roos." The voice sounded distracted. Tuck could hear the soft *click-click-click* of fingers putting a keyboard through its paces.

"You answer your own phone?"

"You taking a survey? Who is this?"

"Benjamin Tucker. We met in San Diego—"

"Yes, Commander. Of course, I remember. It's great to hear from you."

"I'm sorry to bother you at work ... you really answer your own phone?"

"For an astronaut you sure are old school. We don't have a company phone number. Every employee gets a cell phone. We have one number that goes to an answering service—a computer really. We give that number to salesmen."

"I see. So the number you gave me rings on your hip."

"Night and day, Commander. Night and day."

"I have a favor to ask. If it's not something you do, just tell me."

"Ask away."

"I have a twelve-year-old son. Actually, he just turned twelve yesterday."

"Congrats." Keyboard noise continued to flow across the line.

"The point is: I told him I met you and he thought I'd lost my mind because I didn't ask for an autograph."

"Ah, he must be an avid video-game player."

"Isn't every boy his age?"

"I hope so. I have a huge mortgage and guys his age keep it paid for me. So you want an autograph."

"If it's not too much trouble." Tuck felt awkward.

"No trouble for me, but it might be for you."

"How's that?"

The keyboard clicking stopped. "Here's what I'll do. Not only will I give your boy ... what's his name?"

"Gary."

"Not only will I give Gary an autograph, I'll give him an advance copy of *Tower Terror*."

"I can't say I've heard of it."

Roos laughed. "I'd bet good money there are a lot of video games you haven't heard of. This one doesn't hit the stores for three months. Gary will be the only one in Texas and one of the few in the world to have it."

"You don't have to do that, Mr. Roos."

"It's Ted. I know I don't have to, but it's the boy's birthday. That's what makes it a gift, Commander. If I had to give it to him, then it would be an obligation."

"There's a hitch to this, isn't there?"

"Yup. You have to come to California to get it. Bring your boy."

"You want me to fly to California to pick up an autograph and a video game?"

"Nope. I want you to fly to California because I want to show you what I'm doing. The autograph and game are unabashed bribery."

"At least you're upfront about it."

"That's me. I'm transparent as glass. I'll even send the corporate jet to pick you up." The *click-clack* returned. "How about tomorrow morning?"

"I'd have to take him out of school for the day."

"Sweet. He'll love it. My dad used to take me out of school to go fishing with him. The school hated it but he didn't care. Come to think of it, neither did I. How about it? Think NASA will unhook the leash for you?"

"That won't be a problem."

• • •

Verducci stepped from his hotel room looking refreshed and showing no signs of travel fatigue. The fact that he was now in a country on the other side of the planet rather than where he had been the day before apparently had not fazed him. He wore white slacks and an eye-blurring geometric print shirt. He looked every bit the wealthy tourist.

Ganzi also wore casual clothing: a dark aloha shirt, crisp new jeans, and New Balance sport shoes. Somehow, Ganzi felt underdressed. Perhaps it was the height difference; perhaps it was the fact that Verducci looked like a Roman statue come to life; maybe it was the air of quiet danger that surrounded his client. He couldn't shake the idea that being next to this man was akin to sitting on a volcano overdue for eruption.

"How was your nap?" Ganzi asked. He had been waiting outside the door. Verducci told him to be ready at 5:35, of all things.

"I rested well."

"And the room is to your liking?"

"It will do."

Ganzi nodded. "Then to dinner. We will talk there." The elevator from the sixth floor released them at the lobby adjacent to the atrium. The place buzzed with activity. The hotel hosted a complimentary manager's reception, and men and women dressed in their best business garb washed away the stress of the day with sips of wine and swallows of beer.

"If the place is too crowded for you, we can go to another place or order room service."

"This will be fine. I've had my fill of airplanes and cars. There's an empty table in the corner." Verducci led the way. Minutes later they each had a drink in front of them and had ordered meals.

"Let me see it." Verducci held out a hand.

Ganzi handed a leather folder to his client. "If you don't mind me saying so, I expected a thicker accent."

"Much of my schooling was done in the US. I not only learned your language but your manner of speaking. I've found it useful."

Tempted as he was, Ganzi didn't ask what that meant. He doubted he wanted to know. Instead, he rested his arms on the table and fingered the glass of Samuel Adams in front of him. He assumed Verducci would have gone for a red wine or similar. Instead, a wide glass of Chivas Regal scotch rested by the open folder.

"You've double-checked this?"

Ganzi nodded. "Every place, every distance."

"It doesn't show the whole city."

"Of course not. Houston is the largest city in Texas. Shoot. It's the largest city in the south, fourth largest in the country. I gave you what I thought was pertinent to your project, what little I know of it."

"I'll decide what is pertinent." He didn't bother looking up. "This will be fine. I see you've listed the hospitals, fire stations, police stations and ..." He flipped through the pages. "I don't see the locations for FBI offices. Why?"

Ganzi had been expecting this. He took time to knock back a third of his beer before answering. He was stalling and didn't care if Verducci knew it. The next words would be hard.

"Look. I appreciate the work and the more-than-generous fee. I don't mind tracking someone down. PIs do it all the time. I don't mind gathering information on a person. That's half my business income. But when someone starts asking for the locations and photos of government buildings, I get a little touchy."

"You think I'm a terrorist?"

"Mr. Verducci, everyone is suspected of being a terrorist. We live in a frightened society now. We doubt everyone and everything."

"Mr. Ganzi, I assure you, I'm no terrorist. Last time I looked, my country and yours were on the same side."

"Then why request this information? Why do you want to know about the Houston police substations, hospital locations, and the like?"

"You will see, Mr. Ganzi."

The waiter brought the food. Steak and potatoes for Ganzi; red snapper for Verducci. When the plate was set before him, Verducci ordered a glass of red wine. The server left.

"Aren't you supposed to drink white wine with fish?" Ganzi didn't care, but he thought the question might lighten the moment.

"Not where I come from." Verducci finished the scotch and pushed the glass aside. They fell silent waiting for the waiter to return with the wine. The moment they had the table to themselves Verducci pressed his fork into the fish and asked, "Are you licensed to carry a weapon?"

"This is Texas. My dog is licensed to carry a weapon."

"Good. If you ever see me do anything that makes you think I'm going to blow up a building, shoot me in the head."

"I would, you know."

"That's why I hired you."

ELEVEN

I can't believe Mom let you do this. I have to be bleeding from the eyes for her to let me stay home sick."

"Where do you get phrases like that? Bleeding from the eyes? You're a sick puppy."

"I am my father's son."

Tuck looked at Gary, who sat opposite him in the Cessna Citation business jet. When the boy spoke, he barely looked up from the handheld video game he had been wearing out since they took to the air. "Your mother taught you to say that, didn't she?"

"I'll never tell."

Tuck smiled. His boy did sound like him and each month *looked* more like his old man. Twelve wasn't old, but he seemed to be maturing fast—maybe too fast. If pride were alcohol, Tuck would be forever inebriated.

"So flying in expensive business jets is old hat for you, eh?"

"No way. I ain't never seen one ... I mean, I've *never* even seen one before. This is way cool. Off the hook."

"Yet you play a video game instead of spending quality time with your pops."

"It's called multitasking, Dad."

"It's also called rude."

Gary turned the game off. "Sorry. I forgot you don't like video games."

"I didn't say that. I've played plenty of video games. My generation invented them."

"Pong doesn't count. Neither does Donkey Kong."

"Oh, is that a fact. Now you're a game snob. How about flight simulators? Big, honkin' projection screens, real aircraft controls."

Gary faked a yawn.

"Oh, that's how it is, is it?" Tuck undid his seatbelt. "I bet I can still tickle you until you beg for mercy."

"I'll cry child abuse." His grin lit up the dark part of Tuck's mind.

"Once the judge meets you, he'll give me a medal." He rose from his seat.

"Okay, okay. You win." Their laughter filled the passenger cabin. The cabin could seat six more, but Tuck and Gary had the place to themselves.

"This is about more than a video game, isn't it? Not that I mind."

"What makes you say that, Son?"

"Nobody sends a private jet from California to Texas to pick up a kid and his dad so he can give them a video game—cool as that is. Are you going to take the job, Dad?" His eyes took on a hint of fear, although it was clear he was trying to be brave.

Tuck turned his eyes to the scrolling ground thirty thousand feet below. "You know what, Son? We've never had a man-to-man talk. You're getting old enough for such things now and you're smarter than your age."

Gary waited, his eyes on his father.

Tuck took a deep breath. "They're taking me off the mission rotation. I won't be doing any more Shuttle missions." Tuck dropped the bomb and waited. Gary gave no indication of what he felt.

"Really? Why? Because of last year? That wasn't your fault."

"They're not blaming me for what happened. They just don't think I'm fit to fly anymore."

"Does that mean you're fired or something?"

"No, just that I won't be commanding any more missions."

Gary nodded. "How do you feel about it?"

"That's a very mature question. I'm more concerned with how you feel."

He shrugged. "I dunno. I mean, I worry when you go up, but I know it's important to you. Mom said it defines you."

"She did? She told you that?"

"Yeah. She didn't mean anything bad."

"I know, Son. I know. I'm just surprised that she's been talking to you and Penny about such things."

Gary looked sad.

"What?"

"Nothing."

"Come on, buddy. What's eating you?"

Gary shifted his eyes to the window, but Tuck was certain he wasn't seeing anything except what was in his brain. "She talks to us because we can't talk to you."

"What does that mean? You can talk to me about anything."

"Not about your work. Not about flying in space."

"Why not?" The words came out harsher than Tuck intended.

"Because, Dad, we just can't. Being an astronaut means everything to you. We don't want you to know how it scares us. We know you need to think about the mission, about your work."

Tuck felt like a candle in an oven. "Gary, there isn't anything in the world you can't talk to me about, and as time goes on—the closer you come to being an adult—the more we need to share. You're my pal. You're my boy. You, Penny, and Mom mean everything to me."

"I know, Dad. I didn't mean that we don't trust you. It's just ... I don't know ... hard."

"I'm sure it is."

"Have you told Mom?"

"Not yet. I want to think about it some more. I'm not sure what to say or how to say it."

"Sheesh, Dad. Just tell her. She'll read your mind if you don't."

"Read my mind?"

"Come on, Dad. She's a mother. She always knows what I'm thinking. Creeps me out. I love her and all, but it really creeps me out sometimes."

Tuck laughed. "I know exactly what you mean. Come to think of it, the way she knows things creeps me out too."

A tinny voice floated from the cabin speakers. "Commander Tucker, we're beginning our descent. Please make certain your safety belts are buckled. We'll be landing at a private runway so there will be no delays."

"Ready to meet your hero?" Tuck looked at the belt around Gary's middle—buckled and snug.

"He's not my hero, Dad. He's just way cool. You're my hero."

"Thanks, bud. That means a lot to me. Wait until I tell your mom you think I'm as cool as Ted Roos."

Gary shook his head and frowned. "I didn't say that. I just said you were my hero."

"What? I should come over there and—"

Gary wagged a finger. "Sorry, Dad, we're on descent. The pilot said you have to remain buckled."

"You little sneak."

"That's me."

• • •

The business jet touched down lightly and began to slow. There was nothing to do but wait for it to come to a stop. When it did, Tuck popped his belt latch and stood as straight as the low cabin would allow. The sleek craft continued to move along the tarmac. The motion was smoother than Tuck expected for a private runway.

He looked out a port side window and saw flat, brown desert dotted with sage, juniper, and odd trees that looked like something from a sci-fi movie: scraggly, gnarled, with bent branches like arms reaching for the sky.

"Are those trees?" Gary's face was as close to the window as it could be without leaving nose prints.

"Yup. Odd-looking things, aren't they. They're called Joshua trees."

"Joshua? Like Joshua in the Bible?"

"Yes. When the Mormons were traveling through they saw the trees and it reminded them of the biblical story of Joshua raising his hands to heaven."

"They look like monsters holding pom-poms."

"Those pom-poms, as you call them, are the leaves, except they're not like the leaves of other trees. These are sharp and pointed, like narrow spearheads. Back into one and you won't forget it anytime soon."

"How do you know all this?"

"Edwards Air Force Base is thirty or forty miles east of here, in the Antelope Valley. I did test pilot work there before you were born."

"This isn't Antelope Valley?"

"Nope. Victor Valley. Actually, we're north of that."

The sparse terrain scrolled past the windows. "There must be a building or two around here somewhere."

As if fulfilling Tuck's request, a large metal building with a curved roof came into view; next to that stood the building's twin. Next to that a concrete tilt-up sat like a large white refrigerator box glistening in the sun.

The Citation turned toward the tilt-up and came to a stop. Over the PA the pilot announced, "We're here, folks, you can release your safety belts." Tuck and Gary exchanged glances. The pilot was several minutes too late with the announcement.

The copilot exited the flight deck and stepped to the door. "Enjoy the flight?" He looked at Gary.

"Yes, sir. Very much."

The copilot held out his hand to Tuck. "Let me say again what a pleasure it has been to have you aboard. You're a hero in my book."

Tuck's stomach twisted. "Um, thanks."

"Okay, it may be September, but it is still hot out there. We've been having a warm spell and temps have been scratching at a hundred. So prepare yourself."

He opened the door and lowered the airstairs. For a moment, Tuck was certain the man had opened the door to an oven.

"Yuck," Gary said.

"You can say that again."

"They tell me it's a dry heat." The voice came from the pilot, who stood just behind his crewman.

"That just means your bones bleach faster." Tuck moved to the stairs and took the few steps that bridged the distance between cabin and ground. Gary followed close behind.

The pilot had pulled within twenty yards of the tilt-up. "Just head toward the door. Someone will let you in."

The building was the pale gray-white of naked concrete. A concrete wall made sense in an area known for wind as much as heat. Tuck could see no windows in the wall. The sound of a large—probably several large—air conditioning compressors drifted on the hot, thick air. A single three-foot-wide metal door stood at the middle of the wall. It opened the moment Tuck and Gary started forward. Ted Roos held the door.

Gary looked over his shoulder. "They went back in the jet."

"Nothing to worry about. They need to refuel, and I bet one of those metal buildings is a hangar."

"I wasn't worried. It's just that I left my video player on board."

"I'm sure it will be there when we fly back."

They crossed the distance between jet and building in short order. Sweat was already forming on Tuck's brow.

"Come on in. Get out of the heat." Roos's hair still looked as if he had combed it with an eggbeater and his face still needed a shave. He wore a pair of khaki shorts, sandals, and a T-shirt two sizes too large.

"You must be Gary." He held out a hand. Tuck expected a polite professional handshake. Instead, he saw a choreographed shake-grasp-palm-slap maneuver that looked like it would take a week to learn.

Roos held a hand out to Tuck.

"I'll take the old-fashioned handshake, if you please."

"No problem, Commander. I remember how to do that."

Roos led them through the gunmetal doorway and into a reception room that would make a Spartan soldier feel deprived. A simple metal desk butted next to one of the walls. A large flat-screen monitor dominated the desktop. Behind it sat a blonde woman of maybe twenty-five years. Her eyes were bright and she wore a simple smile that made her face glow.

"This is Audrey Hull, heartthrob of SpaceVentures, Incorporated. Audrey, this is the famous Gary Tucker and his father, Commander Benjamin Tucker."

Roos was playing to Gary, and the boy seemed to be enjoying it.

"Pleased to meet you, Gary. Thanks for bringing your father along."

"I had to. Couldn't put up with his whining."

"Hey, I know where you live, kid." Tuck put a hand on his son's shoulder. The boy had picked up his father's quick quips and it filled Tuck with a sense of pride only a father could appreciate. Tuck said he was pleased to meet Audrey, then added, "As far away from the public as this place is, I'm surprised you need a receptionist."

Roos looked confused for a moment. "Ah. The room. Audrey isn't the receptionist; she handles scheduling for material delivery and keeps the lines of communication open. This room may look like a receptionist's foyer, but it's not. We don't have many offices at the complex. Everything is open. Consequently, things get noisy."

Audrey nodded. "Since much of my work involves the phone, I needed a place away from the Chimps."

"Chimps?" An image of the early days of space exploration flashed on his mind. "You send animals into space?"

Audrey laughed. So did Roos. "No. The Chimps are the on-site workers and engineers. No one knows how the name came to be, it's probably because we work in isolation like a colony of chimps."

"Not many engineers would put up with that," Tuck said.

"Not many engineers have the kind of vision these guys possess. One doesn't do work like this unless they're a little whacked."

"I can believe that."

"You'd fit right in, Dad."

"Yet another jab at your old man. I may have to ground you for twenty or thirty years."

"You guys hungry? I got leftover pizza, snacks, some type of Mexican food, soda. Or I can send out for something."

"Send out to where?" Tuck asked.

"Let's see, Victorville is to the south, Barstow is to the north. It could take a little time. Maybe an hour or so."

"We're fine for now."

"I'll take a root beer," Gary said.

Roos smiled. "We have a fine vintage of root beer."

Audrey stood. "I'll get it."

"This way, gentlemen. Let me show you the dungeon." Roos walked to the rear door and held it open. Tuck and Gary crossed the threshold.

"Wow." Gary stopped so fast that Tuck almost tripped over him. "This place is huge."

Tuck had spent time in hangars that dwarfed the one he was in, but the size of the place still impressed him. The place was far more cavernous than he expected from a small enterprise.

Half a dozen things caught Tuck's eye. A long brown curtain separated a quarter of the space from the rest of the open area. In one corner of the space sat a young man talking to his computer and running a finger along the monitor. He wore khaki shorts and a white T-shirt decorated with holes in the fabric. He nodded, shook his head, rocked back and forth then side to side, stood, sat, and mumbled. The distance separating them made it impossible to hear what the man said. When the man sat, he typed on the keyboard; when he stood, he paced.

Another man about the age of Roos stood at one end of an acrylic Ping-Pong table. The opposite end of the table stood vertical to provide a wall for the man to bounce the plastic ball against. He was playing a one-man game. The *clack-plack* of the ball filled the massive space. He wore jeans, a long-sleeve dress shirt, untucked, cuffs rolled up. He started a short volley then abruptly stopped and stared into the distance. The ball dribbled from the table to the naked concrete floor and rolled toward them.

Gary raced to pick it up and returned it to the player. The player didn't look down. He stood like a marble statue. Gary placed the ball on the table and backed away.

"Is he okay?" Gary sounded frightened.

Roos laughed. "He's fine, buddy. That's Chancy Tyler, our resident computer and software genius—and I mean 'genius' literally. He doesn't live on the same planet as the rest of us mere mortals."

"But what's he doing?" Gary asked. "I don't think he knew I was there."

"He didn't. He's thinking. You might assume he's wasting time at the Ping-Pong table, but he's not. He thinks on his feet. When he works on a problem, he moves about. There are days when he doesn't sit at all."

"But he's not moving."

"His brain is. That's what matters."

"Smart people can be a little weird, Son." Tuck placed a hand on Gary's shoulder.

"Smart isn't the word, Commander. We've come this far because I've found people who are not only intelligent, but also creative. Creative people are weird."

"I work with the most creative minds in the world," Tuck said. "I don't find them all that weird."

"I don't want to be a rude host, but I'm not very good about standing on ceremony. First, you don't work with the most creative people. Creative and intelligent to be sure, but the *most* creative people can't work in a government environment with set hours, committee meetings, forms to fill out, reports to write. You guys would be two decades further along if you'd cut the marionette lines."

"I don't think you know that much about NASA and how we operate."

"I know enough, Commander."

"We have thousands of engineers and scientists working on projects. I have an engineering degree."

"Tell me about your latest engineering creations." Roos smiled, but Tuck could tell a genuine smile from a mere concession to civility.

"My work is focused on training and flying."

"I'm not trying to insult you, Commander. I am trying to make a point. Creativity is at its best when you take the boundaries away. We've achieved amazing things with a handful of people."

"How many work for you?"

"About seventy-five full-timers. You'll only see a handful here at any one time. Most of my people are spread around the world."

"Just a handful is right. I had the impression that your firm was much larger."

"That would be counterproductive. Fewer works better. Bureaucracy, whether in government or business, is the bane of creative endeavor. My people come and go as they please. They can work here or in their own offices or homes. I don't care where they work or if they do it on a computer or blackboard. All I care about is innovative production. I have people who have worked three days without sleep, not because I demanded it, but because they couldn't let go of a problem. I've had employees slip out of contact for weeks only to appear on my doorstep with a revolutionary idea."

"Still, to put people in space requires the work of thousands."

"Nonsense. Burt Rutan and his group won the X-Prize by making two manned launches within weeks. He doesn't have a staff of thousands; he has a staff that does the thinking of thousands."

Audrey walked into the bay. "Sorry this took so long. I had to raid one of the refrigerators in the other building." She handed Gary a can of root beer.

"Thanks." Gary popped the top and a tiny amount of brown foam escaped. He slurped it. "Mr. Roos, what's behind the curtain?" He pointed at a thick drape hanging from the laminated beams two stories overhead.

"The future, Gary. The future. Come on, I'll show you what only a handful of people have seen." Roos started forward, then stopped. "Um, I need to ask a favor of you two. What I'm about to show you is a secret. I've invested a fortune in this, and this is a very competitive business, more so than most know. I need you to promise not to describe what you see to anyone else. Can you keep it a secret, Gary?"

"Absolutely."

"What about you, Commander? Will you feel compelled to tell your superiors at NASA or the Navy?"

"Does it present a threat to national security?"

"Of course not."

"Then you don't have to worry about me talking to others." *Having just been grounded, I don't feel like talking to anyone, especially NASA.* The bitterness of the thought surprised him.

Roos walked to the wall near the curtain and pressed a button. The curtain moved, drawn along by nearly silent electric motors.

Ten seconds later, Gary said, "Wow. That is so off the hook."

Tuck tried to remain stoic. He lost the battle. A broad smile crossed his face.

TWELVE

As a teen, Tuck liked nothing more than reading science fiction. Some of those stories pushed him along the course from child to astronaut. Before him stood a craft that could have appeared on the cover of any of those books.

"Gentlemen," Roos said, "this is *Legacy*."

"Cooool." Gary's eyes widened, and a smile tried to wrap itself around his head.

Roos laughed. "Gary, only a handful of people have seen this, and no one your age has laid eyes on it."

Tuck's trained eye drew in the details. In many ways, *Legacy* looked like a scaled-down version of the Space Shuttle but with much sleeker lines. Like the Shuttle, it had a fuselage, wings, and a clearly identifiable cockpit area. Unlike the Shuttle, which looked much like a brick with wings, the *Legacy* bore rounded lines that tapered aft to what Tuck assumed was a rocket motor system. The wings were also larger and looked as if they might be able to pivot.

Two other distinctions made the craft stand out. On the Shuttle, the only windows were associated with the flight deck: front windows for the commander and pilot, two overhead windows, and a set of aft windows that overlooked the cargo bay. The *Legacy* had a line of windows that swept up the midsection of the craft. Tuck counted three teardrop-shaped ports on one side as well as those of the cockpit. He could also see the edge of windows running along the top of the vehicle.

Gary noticed them too. "The Shuttle doesn't have windows like that."

"You're right, Gary." Roos put a hand on the boy's shoulder. "That's because the Shuttle fleet and *Legacy* have different purposes. NASA designed the Shuttle as a space-going delivery truck. Even the mission designations show that fact. STS—"

"Space Transportation System," Gary interjected. "I know. My dad flies them."

"Of course. Sorry. I get a little excited every time I see this thing. Anyway, engineers designed the Shuttle to carry materials for the construction of the space station as well as deliver satellites and the like. *Legacy* has only one purpose: to take people into space."

"For a short time and for a price," Tuck said.

"Exactly. Two hundred thousand dollars per person, and the flight only reaches the edge of space. No orbits. Not yet. *Legacy 2* is in the works and will provide orbital flight to passengers and scientists."

"Why is it orange and white?" Gary had yet to take his eyes from the spacecraft.

"It's easier to track with ground-based telescopes during takeoff and landing. We tape everything and give every passenger a DVD of their experience. Who wants to look inside?"

Gary didn't hesitate. "I do."

"Wait." Tuck held his ground. "How about some details?"

"Ah, ever the engineer. I can respect that." Roos took a short breath and began what sounded like a well-practiced spiel. "*Legacy* is the passenger unit of a two-part lifting body transportation system. It is a three-thousand-kilogram passenger-bearing craft. As you will see, *Legacy* carries four passengers and two pilots. The second part of the system is a craft we named *Condor*."

"So *Legacy* rides piggyback?"

"No, she rides beneath *Condor* and is carried as high as the new GE engines will take her. *Legacy* then frees herself to reach space. *Condor* returns home."

"Didn't Burt Rutan build his own carrier aircraft for *SpaceShipOne*?"

"Yeah, he did. It's a beauty. I have to give him that. He was several steps ahead of us. That's his advantage. That and he's a genius. Ours operates on the same basic principles. Of course, we've used some proprietary research that makes us unique. When I first got into this business, I thought I might be one of two or three people crazy enough to dump time and money into the commercialization of space. Turns out you can't swing a cat without hitting someone trying to be the first successful space tourist business."

"So you're behind," Tuck said.

"No. You're not listening carefully. I said Burt Rutan *was* ahead of us. We've made great strides. Come on. You need to see the interior. Oh, and Gary, leave the soda behind. Just set it on the floor." This time Roos didn't wait but marched to the opposite side of the vehicle and climbed a set of metal stairs that led to an open hatch just behind the cockpit area. Gary wasted no time following. Tuck couldn't help smiling. It was good to see his son excited about space.

Tuck was the last up the stairs and before he reached the last step, he heard his son's voice. "Oh, wow. Serious cool."

This Tuck had to see. Although he wouldn't admit it as readily as Gary did, what he saw impressed him more than he'd expected. The same design sentiment that led to the sleek science fiction design of the exterior had carried to the interior. To his right were four seats that reminded Tuck of a streamlined dentist chair complete with headrests and support for everything from feet to head. An aisle separated the two seats on the left from the two on the right.

At each seat was a teardrop window near where the head of a passenger would be. Tuck noticed an additional window behind each seat and overhead. The port behind the seats puzzled him for a moment, then it hit him: the seats reclined.

"Look at the back of the seats, Commander. In fact, you and Gary should have a seat."

Tuck and Gary moved to the two rear seats and sat. "Comfortable. Wide."

"The width is necessary. Each passenger will wear a partial pressure suit much like your orange LESs but with much more style."

"Of course."

"The cabin is pressurized for the entire trip. The suit is for the unlikely event *Legacy* loses pressure."

"What are these screens?" Tuck asked, pointing to two four-by-six-inch plastic panels stacked one atop the other in the back of the chair in front of him.

"All of this is about customer experience, Commander. We want our clients to experience everything they can."

"A nice goal since they're forking out two hundred grand."

"Exactly. Those screens allow the passenger to see everything that happens during liftoff and reentry. The top one receives video feeds from the ground and from outboard cameras. The lower screen displays information the passenger might find interesting: speed, altitude, and Gs pulled." Roos tapped a small protrusion mounted to the interior wall just in front of the first seat. "Since the first row doesn't have a seat in front of it, we've provided the same displays in these consoles."

"Seems you've thought of everything."

"Oh, I haven't even begun to describe everything. Come up here and sit in the pilot's seat. Come on, Gary, you can sit in the number one chair."

Gary was out of his seat and moving forward before Roos had put the period on the sentence. Tuck followed more reluctantly. He knew when someone was working him.

The first thing Tuck noticed: there was no bulkhead and door separating the two-person crew from the passengers. He reminded himself that these would not be typical commercial flights. The rules were different.

Gary plunked down in a chair that was twice the size he needed. It reminded Tuck that his son was still a boy, and the reminder was welcome.

"How high does it fly?" Gary wondered. To Tuck's relief, Gary touched nothing.

"The lift plane will carry *Legacy* to an altitude of fifty thousand feet, then start a maneuver that will help it gain additional speed. After that, *Condor* pulls up to an angle of forty-five to fifty degrees. *Legacy* will detach from the aircraft and wait a few moments for it to bank clear, then the pilot hits the Go button. Next thing you know, the rocket fires, you're pressed back into your seat, the sky outside turns black, and in a few minutes you're seventy miles high, weightless, and out your window you see the curved horizon of Earth."

"Man, that would be great. Just like what you've done, Dad."

Roos spoke before Tuck could. "Not quite. Your father and astronauts like him fly much higher—two hundred miles—and stay in orbit for much longer. Someday, my company will offer that. Right now, we're just trying to reach the edge of space."

Tuck took the remaining flight seat. "What about reentry?" Tuck laid a hand on the control stick between his knees.

"*Legacy* faces much less stress than the Shuttle. First, what we offer is in essence a six- to seven-hour elevator ride. Since we don't have to maintain an orbit, our speeds are much less than the eighteen-thousand-miles-per-hour you boys fly. We won't get anywhere close to that kind of velocity. We have two ways of landing *Legacy*. First is a dead-stick glide. You're familiar with that, Commander. It's the way the Shuttle lands. The second landing protocol won't be new to you either, since NASA did a good bit of research on the technique."

"Parachute?"

"Yup. Delta wing, steer-capable parachute. Lands like a mother setting her baby in a crib."

"You've tested it?"

"Several times."

That made Tuck suspicious. "I keep up on most things involving space travel, Mr. Roos. I don't recall reading about any such tests."

"That's good to hear. You're not supposed to. We tested outside the US. Unlike my competitors who work as publicly as possible, we work under the radar."

"You have secrets?"

Roos laughed. "Of course we do. So does NASA. So does any business. Look, let's say you want to run for Congress but you're facing a squeaky-clean, longtime officeholder who the pundits say is unbeatable. You can announce your run to the media, let them do a few pieces on you, and maybe win a few votes."

"Or?"

"Or you can work behind the curtain, privately lining up funds, positioning key volunteers, mapping your strategy, and waiting for the right time."

"My opponent would know I'm running because I have to file election papers and documents."

"True, but you don't have to respond to him or to the media until you choose to do so. Now, let's say you're good at what you do; you can kiss babies and shake hands with the best of them. Your opponent has already written you off. After all, there have been no campaign speeches, no position papers, no media buys. He thinks you're just some bozo who wants to see his name on the ballot. In the final month before the election, you open the floodgates. You buy enough media to make a splash, then hit the campaign trail in a full sprint. You catch your opponent off guard and force him into a defensive posture. Now he's playing catch-up. Add to all that the mystique your secrecy has created. People are now interested in you."

"So you plan to just appear on the space tourism front?"

"Exactly, and when we do, the spotlight will shift to us."

Tuck frowned. "Surely word is out about what you're trying to do."

"We've had traditional and Internet media sniffing around, but so far we've kept the lid on."

"What about employees?" Tuck pressed. "One of them could let the cat out of the bag. Some people can be bought."

"*Most* people can be bought, Commander. I know that and I've taken precautions. For one, I deposit a large chunk of cash in an escrow account. Each employee will share in that money if he or she helps keep things under wraps. Each stands to make more money than anyone would offer as a bribe. So far, it's worked magnificently."

"Sounds like you've given this a great deal of thought."

Roos smiled. "Thinking is my superpower."

Gary giggled. "Superpower. I like that. I want a superpower."

"Most people have one or more unique powers. Take your dad; one of his superpowers is courage—courage and skepticism." He looked at Tuck. "Yes, I said skepticism. It's a great defense mechanism."

"What is my superpower?" Gary asked.

"I'm just getting to know you, buddy, but I know courage is one of them. Just like your dad, you have massive amounts of courage."

Gary's smile evaporated. "I haven't done anything brave."

Roos squatted to look into the boy's eyes. "Have you watched your father fly into space?"

"Yes. Every time."

"How did you feel?"

He lowered his head. "Scared."

"But you watched anyway, right?"

"Yeah."

"Listen, Gary, in my book, the only people more courageous than astronauts who fly rockets into space are the families of astronauts. Watching that takes more guts than anything I can think of."

Tuck met Gary's eyes but said nothing. He knew both their minds had raced back to their earlier conversation.

Roos stood. "Come on. I'll give you a tour of the rest of the facility, then I believe I promised an autograph and game for someone who recently had a birthday."

"Yeah. That'd be me." Gary's smile returned.

Tuck smiled too, and then let his eyes trace the graceful lines of the interior of the strange little spaceship. She was a beauty, all right.

THIRTEEN

The news had come over the seventeen-inch color television in Garret Alderman's Holiday Inn hotel room in San Diego. A woman with soft Asian features delivered the story on the local morning news. Her face showed well-practiced sadness as she told of a mysterious death.

Alderman turned up the volume.

"Cindy Sellers died this morning at the county coroner's office. Ms. Sellers, twenty-five, had just completed her first year as a medical examiner's assistant. As yet, no cause of death has been given. Prior to her death, fellow workers said she seemed confused and complained of nausea and headache. Results of the medical examiner's report are pending."

The young woman's symptoms were too familiar to Alderman. They were also further proof that he was in the right city. Alderman had tracked Edwin Quain across the country and narrowed his search to San Diego, but that wasn't narrow enough. Quain was a biotechnician with skills that laboratories and pharmaceutical companies demanded. The problem rested in the size of the biotech community in San Diego. Over eighty companies had set up shop in the county, making it the largest repository of such businesses in the state and one of the largest in the country. Alderman had, using techniques he refused to reveal to his Med-Sys bosses, found a firm that had hired Quain under a different name. He worked only three days and disappeared—a day before Alderman arrived.

The camera switched to the woman's coanchor, a middle-aged man with just the right amount of gray and a square jaw. "Another tragedy struck on our city's freeway when a car lost control and collided with a big rig." The video image of emergency workers at the site of the accident filled the television screen. "CHP said Ronald Mason, a bartender, swerved into the semi on Interstate 8. He and his passenger died instantly. One witness said the car and driver seemed fine one moment, then became erratic. Officers at the scene said the strong smell of alcohol has made them suspect the driver of drinking and driving, but couldn't confirm the suspicion until after the autopsy."

"We have video taken by an onlooker shortly after the accident." A grainy image appeared on the television. Alderman studied it.

The reporter continued. "Here you can see several people gathered around the car to help—"

"Quain!"

The video ended and the newscasters moved on to the next story.

Alderman switched off the television and started his computer. Within minutes he was searching the Net. First, he found the website for the local paper. Fortunately, the *San Diego Register* maintained an active Web presence, and he located the story of the accident. His eyes vacuumed the facts from the screen, his mind committing every detail to memory, including the names of the dead men in the car and the truck driver.

Alderman Googled the names of all involved. He found a citation for the ME tech at the county website, then something struck him. Could the dead bartender and his buddy be related to the tech's demise? Wouldn't the authorities transport the accident victims to the county ME? He did a search for the bartender's name but found nothing. He discovered the truck driver's name listed on his company's website, but it offered very little information beyond his experience and training. He spent the next twenty minutes scouring the Net for more details, and then tracked down the address and phone numbers of the men. Fortunately, they had not taken precautions to maintain their privacy. He used several sources for the address, knowing that online white pages information could be, and often was, out of date.

Alderman left his hotel room.

• • •

"I'm sorry to bother you, Mr. Hammond. I know you've had a difficult time."

Dick Hammond's thick, barrel-shaped body filled the doorway of his small post-war house in Linda Vista. Despite his fireplug build, he looked fragile, like a huge egg in a vise.

"How can you know what it's like?" The trucker forced the words.

"Like I said, I'm an insurance investigator. I see tragedies like this every week."

"How do I know you are who you say you are? Maybe you're another reporter."

Alderman shook his head. "This is old news to reporters." He reached into the pocket of his dark blue sport coat and removed a business card. "As I said, my name is Oscar Tillman. I'm with the National Insurance Consortium for Highway Safety."

"Never heard of it."

"That's good to hear," Alderman said. "We like to work beneath the surface."

"So what? You here to put the blame on me? Those guys were drunk and caused the accident. There are witnesses and the Chippers said so too."

"I've read the CHP report, Mr. Hammond. They hold you blameless. Besides, we're not an insurance company in the usual sense. I'm not here to assign blame. My organization gathers information on deaths that occur on freeways in an effort to influence the various governments to make improvements."

"Someone needs to tell them what to do. I pay a boatload of money in taxes and I don't see much return on it."

"Exactly our point, Mr. Hammond. Guys like you fork over lots of money then get blamed for accidents that are really the fault of Cal Trans, local and state governments, and even the federal government. Our nonprofit organization is trying to hold the right people accountable."

"Glad to hear it."

"May I come in and ask a few questions? I promise not to take too much of your time."

"I guess. I gotta tell ya, I don't much like talking about it."

"No one does, Mr. Hammond. May I call you Dick?"

"Sure, if I can call you"—he looked at the card—"Oscar."

"That'll be fine." Alderman stepped across the threshold and entered a living room dark as a cave. *To be expected. The man is trying to shut out the world.* The room was tidy and well organized. The furniture looked to be less than two or three years old. A tall glass of beer rested on an end table next to a leather recliner. The clock had yet to pass early afternoon. Hammond was trying to take the edge off the shock of having been involved in something that snuffed out two lives.

"Is your wife around?" Alderman asked.

"Died two years ago. Just me now. The kids all moved away. They call now and then. Sit there." He pointed at a padded rocking chair. *His wife's?* Alderman did and Hammond returned to his chair and reached for the beer, then, as if he realized how it must appear, replaced it on the coaster.

"How are you holding up?"

"Didn't sleep last night. I doubt I'll sleep tonight."

Alderman nodded. "Not unusual. Just remember, you did nothing wrong."

"Maybe so, but two men are dead."

"Can you tell me in your own words what happened? Take your time."

Hammond sighed and tears filled his eyes. He started slowly, then gained steam as the telling went on. Alderman listened to every word, sifting through the emotional tale for any helpful clues. He waited patiently. Hammond would have little to offer, but Alderman needed to play the game. Thirty minutes later, Hammond finished.

"You've been very kind to give me your time. I just have one last thing and it's going to seem a little odd." Again, Alderman pulled something from his coat pocket. "I want to show you a photo of a man and ask if you recognize him." He handed the small photo to Hammond.

"I know this guy. I recognize his face. And who could forget that ear. That moron ran off after the accident. Told me he was going to his car to get his ID, and then drove off. Left me standing there to explain everything and that after he told me he had witnessed the whole thing. Good thing for me there were other witnesses who stayed around. Who is this guy?"

"I wish I could tell you. We think he might be part of a truck piracy ring. He may have been following you."

"You said you are with some insurance company, but now you're talking like a cop."

Alderman shook his head. "I'm not a cop. We're not even sure this guy is involved in anything nefarious. It's just that he was at another accident and left. My people thought it might be a good idea to ask around. Looks like we'll be turning this guy's activity over to the police."

"You really think he was tailing me?"

"Maybe. Or he may just be a very shy Good Samaritan. We don't know. It will be up to the police to find out. In the meantime, I'll file my report. I appreciate you taking the time to help us."

"No problem."

"Sure it was. To tell the story is to relive it. You're a brave man, Dick. Stay brave. Don't let this alter your life. Remember, you're one of the victims, not the perpetrator."

More tears filled the man's eyes. "Thanks. I ... just thanks."

Alderman rose and shook the man's hand. "Guys like you don't get enough credit. Stay strong. I'll see myself out."

As he closed the door, he thought of Quain. "I'm coming for you, chum. I'm coming hard and fast."

FOURTEEN

For the second time that day Alderman pulled a card from his coat pocket and handed it to the man in front of him.

"Private investigator, huh?" The medical examiner was unusually tall, but too thin to have ever played basketball. "You're not expecting me to be impressed, are you, Mr. Scofield?"

Alderman laughed. "Not at all. I gave up expecting that the first year I opened up shop."

The ME wore a white lab coat with the words Dr. Kenneth Short, ME, stitched over his left breast pocket. Life was ironic. "Your card says you're based in San Francisco. I did my med school up there. Where do you live? In the city?"

Alderman was glad he developed backstory for his "professional personas."

"No. Too ritzy for my tastes, not to mention my wallet. I live in Daly City and have an office on Market Street. The rent is killing me."

"And here I thought all you PIs were rich."

"The broke PIs made famous in dime novels and old movies might be cliché, but it is also accurate. I do all right, and so far I haven't had to resort to following wayward spouses."

"Good for you. Too bad I'm not going to be able to help you. The autopsies are still pending."

"I'm not looking for an autopsy report, just a few answers to some simple questions."

"Who are you working for, Mr. Scofield?"

"Call me Julian, Doctor. I'm working on a class-action suit for a well-known San Fran attorney. Of course, I can't give you his name just yet or the details of the case. The guy would skin me alive and hang my carcass in the sun to dry. You know lawyers."

"Believe me, I know lawyers. So what can you tell me about the case?"

"Only that a half-dozen people are suing a pharmaceutical firm for wrongful death. One of the men who died in last night's auto accident appears on the list of prescription recipients. Ronald Mason is his name. His sudden death may be related to the other wrongful deaths. If so, there might be substantial money due his widow—not that that will lessen her sorrow."

"But the money would be good for her. It's hard to lose someone." Kenneth Short looked sad.

"I guess seeing death every day doesn't make you immune to personal tragedy." Alderman hesitated. "I'm assuming you've lost someone dear?"

He nodded. "A son. Motorcycle accident sixteen months ago. He was being stupid. Speeding in and out of freeway traffic. A car merged into him."

"I'm sorry. I can't begin to imagine what it's like."

"I hope you never find out."

Alderman said nothing. He had been a loner all his life. No family. Few friends. He liked it that way. A man couldn't grieve the loss of something he never had.

"How's your stomach?"

The question caught Alderman off guard.

"Your stomach. You're not queasy, are you? Some people find this place unsettling."

Just because there are stacks of dead people around here? "I'm pretty stable."

"Follow me, please."

Short led Alderman from the lobby into a pale hall that smelled like an ill-kept hospital. Metal tables populated the room, each one butted to a sink. Alderman tried not to think about what swirled down those drains every day. At three of the tables stood an ME, each hard at work on various body parts.

Short moved to the nearest table. The body of a naked male lay before them, unblinking eyes staring at the bright lights overhead. He looked to be in his midforties; the battle with middle-age belly bulge was well under way, and he had been losing. The side of his head was concave, and blood matted his hair.

"This is Mr. Mason. I was getting ready to crack him open before you arrived."

Alderman studied the dead man then looked at the tools of Short's trade: scalpels, scissors of various types, and a host of items that looked like they belonged in the garden section of Home Depot.

"I won't stand in your way then. All I need to know is if he showed any symptoms before dying."

Short picked up a clipboard. "Ronald Mason, forty-four, six-foot-one, two-hundred-twenty-five pounds, average musculature for a man his age; no signs of recent wounds; described by family and friends as being in decent health; last medical examination was four months ago. His last exam revealed his blood pressure was slightly elevated, but his blood chemistry came back normal."

"So he hadn't complained of recent illness?"

"I asked his wife when she came by earlier and she said he seemed fine. I asked about medications and she said he took vitamins and the occasional aspirin. Come to think of it, she didn't mention any special meds like you suggest."

"Not unusual. I'm sure if you visit the house, you'll find a bottle in the medicine cabinet."

"You know everything we discuss here is off the record. You'll have to petition for an official report."

"I understand. I just want to see if I'm on the right track here. I appreciate your cooperation. You may be saving more lives or at the very least helping families get some recompense for their losses."

"What do you want to know? I can't let you observe the autopsy."

"No problem there. I'd just as soon skip that." He paused. "The news said he might have been driving drunk."

Short shrugged. "I doubt it. He owned a bar, but his wife said he had been sober for several years. Of course, I drew blood for chemistry and that will tell us if he had been sipping on the sly."

"But you doubt he was drunk?"

"I've cut open a lot of dead drunk drivers. They usually reek of the stuff when they arrive. My best guess is—and it's an educated guess—that Mr. Mason was sober. His friend, on the other hand, smelled like the inside of a whiskey barrel. I'm pretty sure his blood test will show significant alcohol content."

Short read from the clipboard again. "Paramedics pronounced both men DOA. The fire department removed the bodies after the cops documented the scene."

"This is going to come out of the blue, Doctor, but I heard on the news that one of your staff died last night."

"Early this morning. About five o'clock. We're not certain because she was working alone."

"Doing what?"

"She's one of our techs. Part of her job is prepping bodies for autopsy."

"She would be the one logging in personal effects?"

"Yes. Why?"

"Was she working on Mason's body?"

Short didn't answer. He didn't need to. Alderman saw the answer in the man's face. "Are you implying there's a connection?"

"So you still have whatever he had on him at the time of the accident?"

"Yes. After the autopsy we release personal effects to the family unless it's been tagged as evidence."

Alderman shifted his weight and thought. He had worked himself into a bind. Short was no dummy. If given more information, the ME would begin to put pieces together. Alderman didn't want that. On the other hand, he didn't want others to become ill, maybe die because Quain had somehow contaminated the driver's possessions.

"I think you had better talk to me." Short narrowed his eyes. "This has to do with more than medication-induced wrongful death, doesn't it?"

"Not to me. So far there's been no one death connected to another, just to the medication."

Short frowned. "And what medication did you say this was?"

"I didn't and I'm not allowed to disclose it, the manufacturer, or the names of other victims. I'm afraid I need this job."

"If a contagion is involved—"

"I know of no contagion. I just find it interesting that Ronald Mason and your tech died the same day. If there is some connection, then it's news to me. Only your autopsy can make a link if there is one."

"How am I supposed to check for the presence of a new drug if I don't know what it is?"

"Well, you got me there. I tell you what. I'll call my client and see what I can do, but before I do, where does your tech prep the bodies?"

"In here. The bodies come into a receiving room. We tag them and place them in the cooler. Before we do, we remove their clothing and bag it. We inventory all personal items including money, jewelry, and the like. Then the deceased is put in the rotation for examination unless there is some pressing reason to move them to the front of the line."

Alderman knew he was going to have to be careful. Short was acting like a man with newfound suspicions. "One of the things I have to do is verify the identity of Mason."

"I can affirm that the man on this table is Ronald Mason."

"Thank you, but ... Look, the attorney I work for is a real bear. His firm makes millions of dollars because he sues and sues big, if you know what I mean. That means he has to face off against a whole squad of lawyers bought by the pharmaceutical companies. He likes to have every *t* crossed and every *i* dotted."

"I deal with lawyers all the time. Your man can't be any more aggressive than some I've dealt with."

Alderman shook his head. "I imagine you handle them very well, Dr. Short, but I'm telling you, my guy asks nicely but only once, then he bulldozes his way through until he gets exactly what he wants. I've seen him go after county supervisors, city council members, coroners, police chiefs, anyone. If he had to, he'd drop a case of law books on a little old lady who had the misfortune of walking her dog past the front door of this building."

"Are you threatening me?"

"No, sir, I am not, nor would I consider it. I'm trying to do a professional courtesy. I'm trying to keep him off your back. He'll make a media thing out of it if he has to."

"But that would reveal information you're telling me he wants to keep secret."

Again, Alderman shook his head. "He's keeping things under wraps for now, but it's all going to hit the media soon."

"So what do you need to confirm the identity? Fingerprints? You want me to drag his wife down here again and have her identify the body once more?"

"No. Definitely not. My client may be a bull in a china shop, but he does care for his clients. Most likely, Mrs. Mason will join the class-action suit. He wants to help her, not hurt her."

He frowned. "So how do I get rid of you?"

"Just let me take a quick look at his personal effects. You know: his wallet and ID. Then I can tell my client that I double-checked the identity. My client will be happy, and I'll be back on the road to San Francisco."

For a moment, Alderman thought Short would call his bluff. He didn't.

"This way."

Moments later, Alderman stood in a room with a wide table. A young woman stood at the battered surface neatly folding clothing Alderman assumed belonged to a new arrival: jeans, a T-shirt with a pink heart over the right breast, white sport shoes, blue panties, a bra, and a white smock. She wore latex gloves. The woman wiped away a tear with her sleeve as he and Dr. Short entered. She seemed embarrassed.

"Kelli, I thought you'd be done by now," Short said softly.

"I'm sorry. I should be. It's just taking me longer to ... I mean ..."

Short stepped to her and put an arm around her shoulders. "I understand. It's different when it's a friend."

"She was so kind and always upbeat. I couldn't stay depressed around Cindy. She was such a light to everyone."

"We're all going to miss her greatly." Short gave her a quick squeeze. "Take a few minutes to yourself. I'll package the rest of this. You've done more than you should have to."

"I can finish—"

"I insist. I have to look for something and I'll only be in your way. You have everything organized. It'll only take me a few minutes to finish up."

"You're the best." Kelli slipped from the room.

"Putting away the belongings of the deceased is work for the strong of heart. When it's a friend or family, no one is strong enough."

"They must have been close."

"Kelli is a little shy. Cindy brought her out of her shell, even played matchmaker for her."

"It was kind of you to give her some space." Alderman paused and watched Short stare at the clothing and other items on the table, clearly moved. "Your son was about the same age?"

"Yeah." Short moved the items to the end of the table, then turned his attention to a large metal locker. Labels with dates were visible on the front of the doors. Before opening anything, Short stepped to a cardboard container that reminded Alderman of a facial tissue box and removed a pair of latex gloves. He tossed them on the table. "Put those on, Mr. Scofield."

Alderman did and watched as Short did the same. He didn't bother to tell Short that he had a pair of gloves in his pocket. The ME then opened one of the lockers and removed a small plastic package and set it on the uncluttered end of the table.

Alderman had slipped into the gloves but knew better than to reach for the package. *Patience.* "You said the police don't consider this evidence."

"They don't. You're wearing gloves to protect you from any latent bio material—any overlooked blood and guts or bodily fluids."

"I appreciate it." *And for more reasons than you know.*

"Everyone is supposed to wear these. Unfortunately, not everyone does. Some people have allergies to the latex powder. I was always on Cindy about it."

Alderman said nothing. Short was offering information. The fact that no latex gloves were with Cindy Sellers's belongings indicated she might have been avoiding the gloves. Certainly she would have worn them while working with the body, but to record and package personal effects she may have skipped the protection.

Short proved a meticulous man. He removed each item in the bag one at a time and set them on the table as if setting them in a grid only he could see. Keys, a penknife, and a wallet.

"I assume you want to see the wallet." Short clipped his words.

"Yes. If I could just look at it for a moment, I need to take a photo of any identification and medical cards. My cell phone has a camera. So part of Ms. Sellers's work was to file all this away?"

"Everything has to be inventoried. More than once, a family member has tried to get the best of the county by accusing us of stealing rings or money. So we log everything." He looked at the material on the table. "Make it quick; I have work to do."

"It will only take a moment. I'll be done before you have Ms. Sellers's stuff bagged."

Short looked at the clothing as if they had slipped his mind. He moved to a cabinet and removed a large paper envelope that looked like a mailing envelope on steroids and turned his attention to the clothing.

Alderman took the wallet, opened it, and spread its contents across a bare area of table. He lined up Mason's driver's license, a medical insurance card, and several credit cards. He also removed all the money from the bill compartment: a ten and two fives. Removing his cell phone from his belt, he began to take pictures. He had no interest in anything but items Quain could have passed to the bartender. The only thing that fit was the money.

He took photos then returned the phone to his belt. He picked up the wallet and returned the driver's license and other items to their place. He picked up the money, opened the wallet, acted as if he was placing the money in the bill compartment, but before releasing the paper, he deftly folded it in half and palmed it like a magician doing a coin trick. Using the bag to conceal his next move, he crumpled the three bills until he concealed them in one hand.

After dropping the wallet into the item bag, Alderman replaced the keys and penknife. He closed the bag. He turned to the locker from which Short had removed the material. "You want me to put this back?"

Short had paused his activity, allowing his gaze to rest on the clothing of his dead workmate. Alderman placed the bag into the locker and removed his gloves. "Yeah, thanks."

"I'm sorry for your loss, Dr. Short. I wish I could say more."

Short nodded. "I'll show you out."

"No need, Doctor. I can find my way. At the moment, you have more important work to do."

Alderman gave the tall man a pat on the shoulder, then left.

FIFTEEN

There you go, buddy, one officially autographed *Tower of Terror.*" Roos handed the small plastic-wrapped copy of the video game to Gary. "And so you don't have to destroy the signature by opening the package, here's another one for you to use."

"This is too cool, Mr. Roos. Thank you."

Tuck thought he could see Gary swelling with joy. It was late afternoon, and they were seated in a small, sparsely furnished office just off the foyer they had passed through when they first arrived. Tuck sat in a cheap fiberglass chair. Gary did the same. Roos leaned against an old metal desk. No art hung on the walls, and the white paint looked freshly rolled on. A thin window in the concrete exterior wall let in a stream of late afternoon light. To one side of the office was a drafting table with rolls of plans resting on its surface.

"You have a sister, don't you?"

Gary seemed surprised. "Um, yeah."

"Well, since she didn't get to come along, I have a gift for her as well." He rounded the desk and opened the large drawer that most people used for files and extracted another plastic-wrapped game package. "I don't know if you know this, but selling video games to females is far more difficult than selling to males. Most tire of shooting things."

"That's because they're girls."

Roos laughed and looked at Tuck. "I take it your boy hasn't rounded the corner."

"Any day now." Tuck smiled.

"What are you guys talking about?" Gary frowned.

"Just that your opinion of girls is going to change soon." Roos winked. "Anyway, my company has designed a new game aimed at teenage girls, and I would like her opinion." He removed a second game from the desk and stepped close to Gary. "This one is for her and this one is for both of you. Here's what I'd like you to do: Review both games and shoot me an e-mail about what you think. Be brutally honest. If it stinks, then it stinks. I'll pay each of you two hundred bucks."

"Two hundred dollars?" Gary's mouth dropped open.

"Mr. Roos—," Tuck began.

"Don't say it, Commander. I'm not bribing your kids. I pay my consultants. 'A workman is worth his hire,' my father used to say. He said that was from the Bible. I don't know anything about the Bible, but the words made sense and have served me well in business." He looked at Gary. "Deal?"

"Deal!"

"Just be sure you both understand that I want the truth. Don't tell me what you think I want to hear; tell me what I need to hear."

"Sound advice," Tuck said.

"I'm glad you agree, Commander." Roos pushed himself up on the desk, using it as a chair.

"How so?"

"Because I'm going to tell you what you need to hear instead of what you prefer to hear." His gaze shifted to Gary. "Do you mind if I have a word or two with your dad? Audrey can take you over to the lunchroom. We have a few arcade-style video games there—a couple of old-school games as well as two newer ones. I promise we won't be long."

Gary looked at his father, and Tuck gave a nod. A few moments later, Tuck and Roos were alone. Tuck expected him to assume the position of the dominant executive, plopping down behind the desk. Tuck had seen the suits at NASA do it many times. Instead, Roos turned the seat Gary had just vacated to face Tuck, sat, then leaned forward, resting his elbows on his knees. He looked more like a man about to confess his sins to a counselor than the head of a billion-dollar company and CEO of a leading space tourism firm.

"Listen, Commander, I imagine you've seen through my little ploy to get you out here. I could have sent the games and autograph by Fed Ex."

"It's a little transparent."

"That's the way I am, Commander. I don't like pretense and hate putting on airs. I am what you see and not much more."

"I admire that." Tuck knew what was coming. "You want me to reconsider your offer."

"You've seen what we're doing. You've seen things no one outside the firm has. I've not asked you to sign a nondisclosure agreement or anything else to keep you from broadcasting to the world what you've seen. I know I'm asking a lot of you—"

"You're asking me to resign NASA and my Navy commission. Yeah, I'd say you're asking a lot."

Roos straightened, and for a moment, Tuck thought he had offended his host. He thought that until he saw the smile. "Three months from now we will do our first full test of *Legacy*. I want you on that flight. Not long after that, we'll take our first passengers into space."

"That seems a tad fast."

"It's not. As I've said, we've already had several successful tests. When you come on board, I'll show you the video and test results."

"*If* I come on board."

Roos's smile broadened. "At least you're thinking about it." He paused and the smile dissolved. "So far, I've been very good at guessing the results of events I haven't seen. I'm no psychic but I am incredibly insightful. Things have deteriorated for you at NASA. Am I right?"

"I'm not free to discuss such things."

Roos nodded. "I understand. Let me cut to the chase. I don't think you'll ever fly for NASA again. I think they've grounded you, either formally or informally. In either case, you're about to be strapped to a desk. Here, Commander Tucker, you could be flying in three months. Three months."

Tuck didn't respond, didn't show a flicker of emotion that might reveal his hurt and anger.

Roos pulled his mouth tight and his eyes narrowed. "Commander, you can lead the vanguard or you can let them retire you to flying an easy chair."

"You assume too much—"

"Of course I do. Do you think a spaceship like *Legacy* gets built by someone who cares about what other people think? Do you honestly believe that a normal man would undertake the impossible and sink his personal fortune into the task? I've faced the facts about myself a long time ago. The world sees me as borderline crazy, a risk-taker beyond all risk-takers. They're right—absolutely, spot-on right. I care nothing for the standard approach. I want to be on the edge of things. For guys like me, that's where life is—on the bleeding edge. Tell me you're not the same kind of man."

Tuck said nothing.

"You can't, can you? If you're not reaching beyond your grasp, then you're unhappy, unfulfilled, hollow."

"You don't know me that well."

Roos swore and stood. "Of course I do, Tucker. Life has cut us from the same cloth. Granted, the cloth is burlap, but who cares. Look at your life: Annapolis, flight school, combat pilot, test pilot, astronaut. A lesser man would have gone to a standard four-year college, and if he wanted to fly would have taken private lessons and ended up chauffeuring airliners around the country with paying customers crammed in the back of the aluminum tube."

"Nothing wrong with being an airline pilot."

Roos dropped in the chair again. "Look me in the eyes, Tucker. Look me square in the eyes and tell me you'll be a complete man sitting at a desk or behind the yoke of a commercial airliner."

Tuck didn't blink. Again, he held his tongue.

"You can't, Commander, can you?" Roos lowered his voice. "I can't offer you the Moon, but I can offer you the edge of space now and later much more. I've already told you that the money will be good. You'll sit on the board of several cutting-edge companies, you'll speak at packed venues around the country, you'll rub elbows with the wealthiest people in the world, and you'll fly high once again."

The image of black space caressing the blue curve of Earth flooded his mind, and for the first time in his life, Tuck wished it hadn't.

SIXTEEN

Garrett Alderman argued with himself all the rest of the afternoon. No words came from his mouth, but the dispute warred in his skull nonetheless. He had returned to his hotel room, inserted the bills stolen from the medical examiner into a plastic bio bag, sealed it, inserted it in a padded mailing envelope, and sent it to MedSys in Houston via Fed Ex.

He then sent an encrypted e-mail to his employers. The encryption was foolproof, but the fact that such concealment had been undertaken would raise eyebrows should any of this get out.

Getting information out was the catalyst that fired up the internal debate rattling in his brain. By most factors, Alderman was an honest man who valued justice. For twenty-five years he'd served honorably in Air Force intelligence. Then, itching for a change, Alderman retired early with a full pension. His monthly check gave him enough to live on while he started his security business, an enterprise tailored to Fortune 500 companies. He was just forty-three. Now at forty-nine, he was the head of an operation that made him several million every year.

Twenty-five people called him boss, each with very special skills. Some jobs, however, demanded his personal touch.

It was during his days in Air Force intelligence that he learned that ethics rode a sliding scale. Things were said and done that not only affected business executives but many innocent people who worked for them, not to mention stockholders.

Here Alderman's conscience ran aground on the unyielding reef of practicality. MedSys was a publicly held company. If the world learned that one of its employees slipped a cog and poisoned an entire Shuttle crew, then the business would fold faster than a house of cards. The lawsuits could last a decade, government oversight organizations would close the business down, and thousands of investors would lose their money. In the end, everyone lost. He understood the need for secrecy, and once the journey down that path had begun, more secrecy became imperative. If they were discovered, jail sentences loomed for the key execs and probably for Alderman as well.

Still, a part of his mind argued the converse: not only were five astronauts dead because of Quain, but now a bartender, one of his acquaintances, and a medical examiner's aide were dead as well. And those were just the ones Alderman knew about.

Alderman had used every resource of his firm to find Quain, but he still lagged behind. Quain was as smart as he was twisted, as devious as he was insane. He remained not a step ahead, but miles ahead of Alderman, and that ate at him. Every day the nutcase remained free was another day one or more people might die for being in the wrong place at the wrong time.

Alderman liked to plan. Anticipating problems and creating contingency plans were his greatest skills, and this situation pushed those abilities to new levels. He carried the confirmation numbers for five first-class airline tickets to five cities with connecting flights to five other cities, all in his name. If things went bad, he would kick-start the plan. Five of his operatives would use the numbers and fake ID to travel under his name to Madrid, Berlin, Buenos Aires, Caracas, and Moscow. Authorities would have a tough time following a trail with a five-pronged fork in it.

Of course, Alderman would be on none of those flights. Instead, he would charter a private jet to an overseas city of his choosing, then ultimately make his way to South America. But it was the last thing he wanted to do.

• • •

Myra had arranged to spend the after-school hours with Penny. With the "men" gone, she thought they deserved some girl time. Shopping, a pedicure, and something involving chocolate was on the docket.

"We have about forty minutes before we get our little tootsies done. You want to hit a Starbucks for something sweet, chocolatey, and certain to make us feel guilty?" Myra steered the SUV away from the curb in front of the middle school and into the slow line of cars coagulated in the road.

"Tootsies? You said 'tootsies.'"

"Yes, it's true. My vocabulary is awe-inspiring."

"Um, yeah ... awe-inspiring ... And yes to the Starbucks."

"I've been looking forward to this."

"Me too, Mom. I have to admit, I was a little envious that Gary got to skip school and fly to California."

"You and me both. They get to go off on an adventure and I got to go to the office and you to school."

Myra slowed quickly to avoid bumping the car in front of her. Traffic around the school demanded constant attention. "I can't believe the cars. It seems like things get worse as the year progresses."

"Don't get us killed until after the pedicure. That way the coroner can put the toe tag around our newly painted ... tootsies."

"You have a sick mind, girl."

"I got half my genes from you, you know."

"I contributed sweetness and light; your twisted humor comes from your father."

"Can't argue with that."

"I'm thinking a mocha latte," Myra said. "Heavy on the mocha. What about you?"

"Sounds good."

The road widened to two lanes as they moved into the business district. Myra pulled the car around a slower-moving sedan.

• • •

"Where's the boy?" Anthony Verducci showed no signs of being upset, just curious. Still, it made Mark Ganzi nervous.

"I don't know." Ganzi let another vehicle pass him before pulling the car into the same lane as his mark. "He's only a grade behind his sister. She should have picked both children up."

"But she didn't."

"Maybe he has an after-school activity and she's going to pick him up later."

"Too many maybes. Plans fail because contingencies haven't been considered."

"With all due respect, Mr. Verducci, keeping track of a busy family of four is impossible for one man. If you allow me to form a team—"

"No one else. Just us. We're the team. The more you add, the greater the chance for error and betrayal—and the more you have to divide your fee."

"I agree, but that scenario comes with limitations."

"Limitations are for limited minds."

"If you say so." Ganzi had more to say but kept it to himself.

"I say so. Not too close. No need to tip our hand." Verducci spoke like a man on the verge of a nap. He showed no emotion, no sense of concern about discovery.

"I've tailed people before, including this woman. I know what I'm doing."

"Which is why you're making more money for this work than you've ever made before. Not too close."

Ganzi eased off the accelerator and bit his tongue.

SEVENTEEN

Ted Roos stood at the window in his office and watched the Cessna Citation begin its taxi. From behind him came the sound of his office door opening then closing.

"I was taught to knock before entering a room," Roos said, never moving his eyes from the window.

"You made a mistake bringing him here." The voice belonged to Lance Campbell, one-time NASA astronaut.

"You're the one harboring a grudge against Tucker, not me." Roos didn't need to see to know that Campbell had moved closer.

"You don't need him. There are many good pilots out there that can do the job as well, no, better than Tucker."

Roos shook his head. "I doubt that. I agree there are many good pilots to choose from, but none have the currency he does. The world sees the man as a hero. His name can open doors for us."

"He's no hero. He lost his whole crew." Bile laced the words.

"You know that wasn't his fault. Everyone knows that. NASA cleared him of any wrongdoing. It's not his fault he lived or that his crew died."

"I can walk."

"You're free to do so, but I remind you of our agreement. You will be held to the nondisclosure contract, and that little loan I gave you will be due the week you leave. That was our agreement. You leave before our first successful commercial launch and the monies come due. Do you have half a mill to pay it back?"

"You know I don't."

"Then I'd say that things are going to continue on just as I planned them." Roos watched the jet take to the air. He turned to face Campbell. The man's black face looked as if it had permanently hardened into a scowl, and a fine mist of perspiration gave his bald head a sheen. Square across the shoulders, he looked as fit as any man Roos had seen. Campbell stood two inches short of six feet, and his dark eyes glistened with intelligence and anger.

"I'm telling you, Tucker doesn't deserve this opportunity. Even NASA has written him off."

"So you've told me and I appreciate that bit of info. Their loss is my gain."

"If they don't trust Tucker, then why should we?"

"We? We?"

"I'm the one strapping myself in next to him, not you."

"Lance, this has nothing to do with the *Atlantis* tragedy. I've done my research. I know you and Tuck have had a thing against each other since Annapolis. He always finished better than you, right?"

"That has nothing to do with it."

"He graduated top of his class and you were what? Second? He outscored you in flight school, didn't he? I believe he also went to Top Gun school and you weren't invited? Let it go, Lance, let it go. I asked you to be part of this team because I believe in you. A smart guy like you should notice that I asked you first. You are my go-to guy." He gave the shoulder a pat. "Now show me what you've been working on."

• • •

The business jet taxied down the runway, gaining speed, and then smoothly made the transition between ground and air. Before long, the craft was cruising at its designed altitude. Tuck looked at his watch and realized it would be dark by the time they landed in Houston. A late dinner then bed sounded good to him.

Gary sat in the seat opposite him. The boy stared out the window. "Well, any regrets about skipping school?"

"Like that could happen."

"What did you think of Mr. Roos?"

"I liked him. He was great. A little weird, but great. I thought he'd be younger."

"You think he's old?"

"Not old like you, but older than I thought."

Tuck raised an eyebrow and watched Gary struggle to stifle a laugh. "I think I'll tell the pilot to let you off at the next corner. You can walk home."

"Mom would kill you."

"Your sister would come to my defense. I imagine she's already a little put out that she had to go to school and you didn't."

"If I'm lucky." Gary's words came with no animosity. He and his sister seldom fought, although he knew a dozen ways to irritate her. "Dad?"

"Yes?"

"Will we have to move?"

"Move? Move where?"

"To the desert. The spacecraft was cool and every-thing, but I didn't like the desert."

"What makes you think we'd move there?"

Gary's gaze rose to meet Tuck's. "He has a space-craft and you're an astronaut. It makes sense."

"I'm an astronaut with NASA."

"You said NASA wasn't going to let you fly anymore."

Tuck blew a silent stream of air through his lips and struggled to find the right words.

"You don't have to talk about it, Dad. I know I'm just a kid."

The words made Tuck's heart stutter. "You're more than that, Gary. You're my son and my pal. You always have been and you always will be." Tuck gave a nervous tug on his ear.

"Mom will be happy for you."

"And you?"

"I dunno. I worry when you're up there, but I know you love it." He looked out the window again. "So will we have to move?"

"No. I haven't decided to take the job. Even if I did, there's no need to move unless the family wants to."

"But then you'll be gone all the time."

"No more than I am now, but I would be traveling a lot."

"You'll take the job."

"How can you be so sure? I've told him no."

Gary met Tuck's eyes again. "Because I saw the way you looked at the *Legacy*. You wouldn't come all the way out here if you knew you'd be turning Mr. Roos down."

Tuck had to smile. "When did you get so smart, kid?"

He shrugged. "Just part of my genius. What will Mom say?"

"Don't jump the gun, pal. I haven't decided anything, and I wouldn't without talking to your mother first."

"She's been praying for you a lot. We all have."

The world lowered on Tuck's shoulders. "Thanks. I appreciate that."

"Do you still pray, Dad?"

Tuck's throat dried in a second. "I still believe in prayer."

"But do you pray? Will I still pray when I get older?"

The question gutted him. "Yes, Gary, you will. For me ..." He stared at his son. Gary had been a constant source of pride. No man could have asked for a better son.

Tuck leaned forward. "It's been difficult, Son."

"Did you pray up there when ... you know, when *it* happened?"

Tuck nodded. "My mind was muddled with the drug that caused the problem, but I can remember praying. I remember thinking of you and Penny and your mom." Moisture filled his eyes. "Yeah, I prayed. I prayed when we landed and I was trying to save ... Well, I prayed a lot."

"But not since then?"

"Not much."

"Are you mad at God?"

"I don't know. Maybe. I don't think about it."

Gary nodded as if he were a psychoanalyst. "I would be mad at God if you died up there. I don't think I would be able to pray anymore either."

A great ache bored through Tuck's chest.

EIGHTEEN

Ganzi checked his watch as the red Chevy Avalanche truck pulled into the driveway of the Tucker family home—7:30. He lowered his hand slowly, not wanting to make any movement that might draw the attention of someone with a sharp eye, and raised a small directional, shotgun microphone. He aimed the rodlike mike at the car. The earbuds delivered the collected sounds with crisp clarity.

He waited, expecting Tucker to pull the car into the garage, but he didn't. Tuck, tall and lanky, slipped from the driver's seat as the passenger door opened and disgorged a young boy who held several items in his hands. Tucker moved faster than the lad and elbowed his way in front then stopped, suddenly blocking the boy's progress. The boy pushed by him but Tucker grabbed him by the collar and pulled him back. The two tussled and Ganzi could hear their laughter.

The sound brought sadness. He thought of his own mostly missing father and the fact that he was a father to no one. For him it had always been work. No time for a family. What wife would put up with the odd hours he kept? Private detective work was nothing like that seen on television.

As he watched, Tuck took a quick step toward the door, but the boy hung on his belt, hindering his advance. In a quick movement, the boy let go and shot around his father, the items he carried now tucked under one arm.

"Hey, you little rat."

"Takes one to know one."

More laughter—the kind of laughter only love could grow.

A soft, golden light washed over them as the front door opened. Tucker and his son came to a halt, the elder thrusting his hands in his pockets and looking at the sky as if studying the stars. The younger followed suit with his free hand and began to whistle.

"What are you two doing?" The light silhouetted the one who opened the door but by shape and voice, Ganzi knew it had to be Mrs. Tucker.

"Who?" he heard Tucker say.

"Us?" the boy replied with artificial innocence.

"We weren't doing anything," Tucker said.

"Just walking up to the door," the boy added. "Yeah, that's it. Just walking up to the door."

"Yeah. What he said."

The woman stepped out, bent over the boy, and kissed him on the forehead. He wasted no time wiping it away. He then shot past her toward the door. "Hey, Penny, Penny, look at . . ." Ganzi couldn't hear the rest.

The two stood staring at each other for a moment, then Tuck crossed the few feet that separated them and took her in his arms. He kissed her once, then again in an embrace that lasted several seconds.

"Oh, yuck. Get a room." The new voice came from another silhouetted figure in the door, smaller than the first woman, but definitely female. She stepped onto the porch. Tuck pulled her in and kissed her on top of the head. The young girl reached both arms around her father's neck and gave him a hug.

"And there goes the luckiest man in the world," Ganzi whispered.

"I feel the need for pizza," Tucker said.

"I'm starving. I didn't think you'd ever get home, and Mom wouldn't let me eat."

"Then you can choose the pizza joint. Now let's see if we can peel Gary's fingers from the video game."

"I can hit him with a rock if you want," Penny said.

"Did he tell you about the little job he scored for you?"

"No."

"Then you may want to hold off on the rock."

They stepped through the door and the wash of light disappeared.

Ganzi lowered the mike and reached for his cell phone. "He's home. They're going out for pizza." He listened. "Will do."

For what must have been the one-millionth time in his life, Ganzi felt dirty.

A few minutes later, Tuck led his family to the BMW and drove away.

Ganzi waited ten minutes before exiting his car, moving to the trunk, and removing a brown baseball cap with the words *Skyline Plumbing* embroidered on it. He lifted a tool case, closed the trunk, and walked to the front door. Once inside the small alcove that protected the porch from the weather, he paused and took a quick look over his shoulder. Certain that no eyes were watching, he drew a small plastic case from his pocket and removed a set of tools from the locksmith's kit. Ninety seconds later, Ganzi crossed the threshold into the Tucker home.

He closed the door behind him.

• • •

Tuck and Myra lay in bed, six inches of cold, silent space between them. Myra had pulled the sheets, blanket, and comforter to her chin as if the fabric could shield her from harm. Tuck had interlaced his fingers behind his head, his elbows sticking out like wings. Above them, the brighter stars of the night sky peered through a large skylight as if watching the drama between the two humans unfold. When they first moved into the house, Myra had taken over the decorating. Every room had her mark on it. Tuck made no complaints and had only three demands: he would choose the size of the television; he would get a part of the garage for a small workshop; and a skylight would be installed over the bed so he could gaze into the night before falling asleep. Myra agreed without hesitation. Now the night sky mocked them.

"I meant for this to be a fun evening." Tuck's words were as soft as the pillow upon which he rested.

"You should have spoken to me first. You shouldn't have sprung it on me like that."

"I didn't spring it on you. I just brought the family into the loop, that's all."

Myra kept her gaze fixed to the scene above. A falling star slipped into view and disappeared a half second later. Normally, such a sight drew a gasp of wonder. Myra let it pass without comment. "You sure you didn't tell us as a group to control my reaction?"

"Oh, come on. When have I ever been able to control you? I'm not that manipulative, and you know it."

She sighed and then sniffed. Something she did whenever tears were about to emerge. "I know, I just ..." She paused. "When will it end?"

"My fascination with space flight? Never. My ability to continue flying ... I don't know. Flying is as much a part of me as ..."

"Me?"

He paused, took a deep breath, and then rolled to his side to face her. "You know me, Myra, flying defines me; it is what I was born to do. That includes space."

"I know. I knew that about you when I married you. I just can't get over what happened. It haunts me." A tear ran down her cheek.

"It haunts me too, every day, sometimes every hour. Maybe that's why I have to take this job. I have to fly one more time."

"You have nothing to prove."

He pursed his lips. "Yes, I do. I can't explain it. I doubt anyone else would understand, but I do have something to prove." He sat up and crossed his legs in front of him. He would have held her hand if it weren't sheltered under several layers of bedding. "I lost my crew, Myra. I lost every one of them. Dead as dead can be. I went up in a spaceship and flew home a hearse."

"No one blames you."

"A lot of people blame me. They walk the halls of NASA. Sure, they smile, they shake my hand, they make small talk, but I see it in their eyes. They're looking at the only astronaut to lose his crew."

"Other astronauts have died."

"I know that. I can name every one of them, but I returned alive and well. Had I died up there, then people, my peers, would honor my memory, but as the lone survivor they question my decision making, my strength, and my resolve in an emergency."

"No, they don't. People flock to hear you speak. The newspapers still call you the heroic astronaut." Another tear, then another formed a rivulet on her cheek. In the dim moonlight that filtered into the room, Tuck could see a damp spot on the pillow, just below her ear, and his heart began to break.

"I don't work with them. I don't work with the press. Their lives have never been dependent on any decision I make. What the world thinks doesn't matter."

"Does what I think matter?"

He hesitated, then whispered, "Yes. More than anything."

She pushed herself up and crossed her legs to match him. She touched his bare knee and the feel of it ran through body and soul. His heart stuttered; his lungs hung on a single breath.

Her words floated just above a whisper. "Each day I ask why. Why did you live and the others die? Why you and not one of them? I thank God a hundred times a day that you're still here with the kids and me. I thank Him repeatedly that I can still touch you, still smell your aftershave, and still pick up your stinky socks from the floor. Every time you laugh, I feel like I won the world's biggest jackpot. Then the guilt returns. I think about Vinny and Jess and the others. I think about their families—fractured, torn to pieces by the world's worst coincidence, and I love you even more. Guilt and relief, guilt and joy, guilt and thankfulness, and this thought keeps coming back to me: no one can be that lucky twice."

Her words scooped the life from him, but he formed a reply. "I don't know why my dad rushed into burning buildings, except he loved his work, and it was his duty. I know I have to fly at least one more time to prove to myself that I didn't leave something in space, that I didn't leave my courage there—that my crew didn't die for nothing, but for the innate dream that possesses someone like me. I don't know why God let me live, but He did. Still, I can't hide from life; I can't hide from me."

Heavy silence swirled in the room. Myra lowered her head. Tuck touched her face. "Tell me not to do it and I won't."

She shook her head. "Telling you not to fly is like telling a whale to leave the ocean. I'll support you in this with all my heart and soul."

"Thank you."

She lowered herself to the bed and Tuck did the same. He took her in his arms and waited for her to fall asleep.

She did.

Two hours later.

• • •

A weary Ganzi picked up his cell phone and placed it to his ear—an ear previously covered with one end of a set of headphones.

"I have something interesting," he said.

NINETEEN

Diane Melville walked through the wide lobby of MedSys ignoring the comings and goings of employees. Her head hung as if weighted by the heavy thoughts that churned in her skull. Too many days had passed without any meaningful word from Alderman. When the security expert last left her office, he had assured her that he was closing in on the deadly former employee. So why hadn't she heard anything?

So much had gone so wrong. Despite her desire, her *duty*, to protect the multi-billion-dollar company, a constant churning sea crashed at the bulwark of conscience. She reminded herself that children with cancer benefited from the designer drugs MedSys made, that diabetics led better lives, that heart patients recovered from surgery faster, and all because MedSys was the leader in synthetic drugs.

She took long strides to the executive elevator at the end of the lobby and inserted her passkey into the slot to the right side, then waited for the elevator cab to arrive. Sure, she should have told the authorities. At the very least, she should have called the local police once she realized what had happened, but she hadn't. They would bring in the FBI, and since the crime occurred against NASA, a government agency, Homeland Security would have been crawling all over the corporation, through its bookwork and peering into the private lives of all the employees, including her. As paranoid as the government had become, they might even classify her and every other exec as terrorists ruining lives and destroying careers for a lifetime. The business would never recover.

The brass-clad doors parted and she stepped inside. She punched the button for the top floor with enough force to make the knuckles in her finger throb. *Easy, girl. Don't take it out on the elevator.* The doors closed and Diane felt entombed.

At first, she had wanted to notify the authorities, but Burt Linear had convinced her otherwise, and she so wanted to be convinced. Now too much water had passed under the bridge, or over the dam, or whatever the cliché said. Bottom line, it was too late to go to the cops. But concealing what had really killed the astronauts one year ago made her an accessory to the crime. She and Burt would be arrested, MedSys would shake and then be crushed under the weight of scandal, several hundred employees would be out of work, as would subcontractor businesses that depended on MedSys for their existence. People who depended on designer meds would go wanting. *What a mess. What a disgusting mess.*

The elevator eased to a stop and a moment later opened its doors. She took a deep breath and tried to sculpt her face into a mask of confidence and normalcy. She had become good at donning the disguise.

It was the fear of prison that bothered her most. Last night, she dreamed she had awakened in a dim, dank, dreary cell in a federal penitentiary. Diane had a cousin whose son did a short stretch in a federal prison. He had complained that the thing that bothered him the most was the noise. Apparently, such places were never quiet. Such an environment would drive her mad.

"Good morning, Dr. Melville." The greeting came from her twenty-four-year-old assistant, Liz.

Diane started for her office located behind Liz's space. "Any messages?"

"Mr. Linear has been by and would like you to call him when you can. Last night's mail is on your desk."

"I don't suppose Mr. Alderman called while I was out."

"No, ma'am."

Diane entered her office. She kept the lighting low and the furnishings dark. Contemporary art hung on the walls, as did her degree from Stanford and her medical license. The latter represented a different era in her life. Medical practice never suited her but research did—and so did business. Twenty years after med school, she was the CEO of the most innovative pharmaceutical firm in the country. At least for the moment.

She set her purse in one of the drawers of her wide desk and sat in a suede leather executive chair. On the desk rested a pile of mail. Most were routine things she had seen a thousand times before, but one caught her attention: a white envelope with the return address for the IRS. The bottom right corner of the envelope read, "Department of Audits."

"Great. Just what we need."

Removing a daggerlike letter opener, she sliced into the mailing with more force than required and snatched the letter from its holder. Like the envelope, it was white and the letterhead read Internal Revenue Service. The paper felt odd, almost oily.

The body of the letter told her that MedSys had been selected at random for a corporate audit. She whispered an obscenity. Then she saw it. The signature seemed wrong. She read it again. It was signed by S. W. Eet-dreams. It took a moment for her to decipher the puzzle. "Sweet Dreams? What kind of joke is this?"

Her chest tightened and the next few breaths came with difficulty. She heard herself wheeze. She sat and read the letter again. On the surface, the Internal Revenue Service form looked legit. Even the address looked right, but something struck her as wrong—something she couldn't put her finger on. The signature could be real. The world had its share of bizarre names, but this seemed too odd. It had to be a joke, but who would go to such extremes?

She set the paper on the desk and rubbed her fingers together. Like the paper they felt oily. She sniffed them but caught no unpleasant odor. Diane picked up the letter and raised it to her nose. No smell. As she drew the paper from her face, the light in the room revealed something on the other side. She turned the document over.

I KNOW YOU SENT HIM AFTER ME. YOU SHOULDN'T HAVE.

"Quain." She had to force the word past her lips. Her vision blurred. Her head pounded like a bass drum.

"Oh, no." *Oh no, no, no.* She tried to rise, but her legs refused to obey. "Liz." She meant it to be a cry for help, a scream heard through the building. Instead, she managed only a croak. Her left eye began to spasm, then her right.

Again she tried to rise but only managed to shift her weight. Thirty seconds later, Diane slipped from her chair to the floor. Two minutes after that the room went dark.

• • •

Liz glanced at her watch. Her boss had arrived nearly sixty minutes before and had shut herself in her office. Not unusual. Diane Melville was an intense woman who worked long hours. Liz hated to disturb her, but she needed to get some signatures and other information.

Liz picked up the phone and buzzed her boss. No answer. She buzzed again. Nothing.

She rose, stepped to the door that separated her office from her employer's, and then, after knocking, opened it. Diane wasn't at her desk. She hadn't left so that meant that she must be in the rest—

Liz screamed.

Diane Melville was not at her desk but under it, her arm and head the only thing visible from the doorway. Her eyes had blanched and a small pool of frothy drool formed beneath the corner of her mouth.

Liz screamed again.

• • •

Burt Linear had just opened the letter from the IRS and was reading it for the second time when the sound of a woman's screams rolled into his office. He rose, still holding the missive in hand. "What the—" He stepped from his office. His assistant Cary Woodland met him.

"Did you hear that?"

"The whole world heard that." He pushed past her and into the corridor. As he crossed the threshold, Liz appeared at the door of Diane's office.

"Help. *Help.*"

He charged forward, brushing past the panicked woman into Diane's office. What he saw froze him in place. It took all of his will to walk forward and place two fingers on the CEO's throat. The skin was still warm. No pulse.

Like Diane, he had trained first as a medical doctor before entering the more lucrative world of pharmaceutical research. His first thought was that she had had a massive heart attack. That assumption melted under the heat of his next discovery: a letter from the IRS resting on the floor near her lifeless hand—a letter identical to the one he held.

"Call 911. Call now." His speech slurred. Liz didn't move. He raised a tremulous hand and pointed at her. "Do ... it ... now."

Liz disappeared into the outer office. No doubt, she thought the ambulance was for Diane. He knew it was for him.

Burt snatched up the letter before he could change his mind, stood, and staggered to the small fireplace in the office's conversation corner. The gas-operated unit was more for décor and seldom used except at the key executive Christmas party. Burt tossed the two letters in and pushed the start switch. The letters burned quickly and Burt switched off the gas and returned to Diane. He wondered if he would look the same in death.

Liz reentered the office. "Paramedics are on the way."

Burt nodded but said nothing. Sweat dotted his forehead, and his heart rumbled. The room began to spin.

"Aren't you going to do anything?"

"No. Nothing ... can be done."

"CPR. Help me do CPR." Liz started past Burt but he grabbed her arm.

"Too late. Don't touch her." He swayed. "Dangerous ..."

"Dr. Linear? Are you all right?"

"Tell para ... tell them ... ccs of epinephrine ..."

To Burt the floor seemed to rise. His head bounced off the carpeted surface.

"Dr. Linear!"

"Don't touch ..."

Blackness flooded his eyes, then his mind.

• • •

It seemed to Liz that a year had passed from the time she had called 911 until the paramedics arrived. When they did show, they went to work quickly, their gloved hands feeling for a pulse, checking for any sign of life. They fired off questions in machine-gun fashion: "Did either party have a previous medical condition ... ever pass out before ... complain of chest pains ... under a doctor's care ... on medication ...?" Liz answered the best she could. Every VP in the building stood nearby waiting for some determination of their leaders' fate, although one look at the corpses had settled that in everyone's mind.

The phone rang and instinctively Liz moved to her office to answer it.

"If that's the press, you know nothing. Got it?" The order came from Wally Thompson, VP of operations. Liz assumed he was taking charge.

She snapped up the phone. "MedSys, Diane Melville's office ..." Speaking her dead employer's name brought her to the edge of tears again. "This is ... this is Liz."

"This is Garrett Alderman for Dr. Melville, please."

"Oh ... um ..." Liz broke into tears. She had met Alderman on several of his visits to the office.

"Whoa, easy. I'm not that hard to deal with."

"Oh, Mr. Alderman, it's ... it's horrible. Dr. Melville died in her office a short time ago."

"What? In her office?"

"Yes, and Dr. Linear too. How could both die on the same day and in the same place?"

Liz couldn't hear what Alderman said. It sounded as if he had removed the phone from his mouth. A few seconds later, he was on the phone again. "Who is in charge there?"

"Several of the VPs are here."

"Who ... wait ... let me think ... Thompson ... Wally Thompson heads operations right? He's medically trained?"

"Yes."

"Get him on the phone. Don't use my name. Just tell him it's important."

Liz said, "I'll try."

She put Alderman on hold and walked to Wally Thompson. She motioned for him to bend toward her so she could whisper in his ear. All she said was, "You had better take this call."

Liz could see his reluctance, but he followed Liz to her office. She stepped away once the phone was to his ear. A moment later, she heard the VP shout, "What?"

• • •

Alderman closed his flip cell phone and set it on the desk of his hotel. Acid burned his stomach. The worst had happened. No, he corrected himself. *Not the worst. Quain is still out there and he could kill thousands if he wanted.*

With the death of Melville and Linear, he no longer had a client. No one to foot the bills and no one in Med-Sys who knew what happened. Things could go downhill fast now. He knew nothing of Wally Thompson. He might be of a different mind about keeping things secret. In his heart, Alderman hoped that was true, but it was too late for that kind of honesty to do him any good. The authorities would see Alderman's stealth as obstruction of justice and more. Things could end up with him in prison, Melville and Linear in their graves, and Quain free to hopscotch around the country killing as he pleased.

The number of variables had reached a point beyond calculation. If he returned to MedSys to discuss matters with Thompson, he might find himself nose-to-nose with the FBI. If he returned to his own office, he might find the same thing. Since he couldn't be certain what Quain had used to infect Melville and Linear, he had to assume it might still be present. To save lives, Alderman had given the *Reader's Digest* version of what had happened and hopefully Thompson had listened and had the room cleared. Unfortunately, such largesse would not keep him from a dozen or more years behind bars.

Alderman rubbed weary eyes and sat on the bed. His mother used to describe any conundrum as being stuck "between a rock and a hard place." The rock had just grown larger and the hard place even harder.

It was time to call his office. Additional contingency plans were needed.

• • •

Edwin Quain drove his rental car through the streets of San Diego. Azure sky, warm air, and the faint smell of salt from the ocean made things seem just right. He thought of his former employers opening letters from the IRS. Everyone opened letters from the IRS. The organization was so frightening that no one would ignore such a mailing. He had received a few in his day, and so it took very little effort to have letterhead and envelopes printed. Any good printer hooked up to a decent computer could do it. Very few people would examine the lettering to see if it measured up to the real thing.

Quain smiled. By tomorrow, he would have confirmation of their deaths. A simple hookup to any wireless network would allow him to search Google News. Their deaths would be mentioned there.

Yup. It was a fine and beautiful day.

• • •

Anthony Verducci hung up the phone and took a deep breath. Things had just become far more complicated and telling his boss had been difficult. More people would now be involved, and every addition was one more link in the chain that could fail. He didn't like that—didn't like it at all.

He picked up the receiver again and punched in the number of Ganzi's cell phone.

Ganzi's words were hushed. "Yeah?"

"We need to talk."

TWENTY

FIVE MONTHS LATER

"So tomorrow is the big day."

"Yup. This time tomorrow, I'll be touching the edge of space. Not as high as a Shuttle mission, but seventy-two miles up is nothing to sneeze at."

Ben Tucker nodded his head, then brushed back a wisp of gray hair. As they relaxed over coffee in the hotel restaurant, Tuck looked at his father and felt the high tide of pride. A brave man who faced all problems head on, even in his senior years, his father remained an impossible force to ignore. Perhaps his strength came from the many years spent as a firefighter, or the equally many years as a deacon in his church.

"And you say the ship flies like it should?"

"It's a dream beginning to end and top to bottom. As you know, I've done two test flights with it, and others have flown the earlier version. Tomorrow we take up our first passengers and make history in the process." A broad smile crossed Tuck's face. "When I was a kid, I dreamed of a spacecraft like this. The Shuttle has a beauty all its own, but *Legacy* looks like something out of the old sci-fi magazines. Actually, it looks better. You'll get a firsthand look tomorrow morning. That's another thing I appreciate."

"What is?"

"NASA has so much security. I could get family tours from time to time, but Roos allows much more intimate tours for the families of his workers. There are some secrets, of course, but at least you can get close enough to see inside and touch things."

"I'm looking forward to it. Have you met the passengers yet?"

"No. I know about them. I've read their files. Lance Campbell has been handling their training."

"I assume there's still bad blood between you two."

"I'm afraid so. He's still arrogant and he still blames me for his finishing lower at Annapolis than I did. Ridiculous."

Ben swiveled his head from side to side. "He accused you of cheating."

"He never believed the decision of the investigation. His allegations were groundless. I graduated in the top five of the class and he a little farther back. I got a couple of choice assignments in the Navy and he got a couple of dogs. Still, he proved himself a capable pilot and sailor."

"That's the problem with some people. They can't be happy at being great as long as someone finishes ahead of them. Is he going to be a problem for you?"

"No. He's let me know that he still resents me. We've had words but nothing too bad. I've only wanted to punch him five or six times. Roos keeps a tight leash on him."

"How did he take the news that you were selected to be the lead pilot on the first flight?"

"Not well, but I'm not fooling myself. Roos gave me that position because of its marketing value. I have higher name recognition—unfortunately, for all the wrong reasons."

"I've never met someone so uncomfortable with being considered a hero."

"We've been through this, Dad. I'm no hero. I didn't even land the Shuttle; they did that from the ground."

"But you did do your best to save lives and fought against crippling illness to do so."

"I did what any one of the crew would have done. I neither deserve nor want the attention." Tuck poured milk into his coffee.

"Didn't the Navy teach you to drink your coffee black?"

"They taught me many things but not that."

The bustle of the late-dinner crowd filled the few moments of silence the men shared. Tuck enjoyed the time he spent with his father. The man before him had earned his respect, not just because he was Tuck's father but because of the nobility in the man himself.

"I appreciate you bringing me all the way out here. I've never been on a fancy business jet like that before."

"The boss owns that. I still prefer my Corsair." Tuck gazed out the window of the hotel and watched the twinkling lights of the Victorville, California, traffic roll by. "You've been at every one of my launches. I can't see any reason to change now. Besides, you're my good luck charm."

"I thought you told me your wife was the good luck charm."

"Can't have too many of those—good luck charms, not wives."

Ben chuckled. "I was hoping you'd clarify that." He sipped his coffee. "How are they doing with all this?"

Tuck returned his gaze to his father. "Just like they always have. They're worried about me, but they deal with it. Myra has resigned herself to having married a crazy man. The kids ... well, the kids know that a man has to do what a man has to do. They're back in the room watching a movie. I'm always a little antsy before a big flight. I appreciate you giving me a little distraction."

Ben looked into his coffee cup as a gypsy fortune-teller looks into a crystal ball.

"What?" Tuck said. "Something swimming in your drink?"

"Nah. I pulled that out a few minutes ago."

"Then what? I know that look."

"It's just that your family isn't dealing as well with it as you might think. Penny talked to me earlier. You were still at the launch site."

Tuck's chest felt empty. "She's had the most difficulty with me flying again. Never got over the *Atlantis* tragedy."

"None of us have. Have you?"

Tuck shook his head. "No. Not *over* it, but *beyond* it. I've compartmentalized it to the past."

"Is that possible?"

"No, but I tell myself it is. So what did Penny bend your ear about?"

Ben looked out the window and waited for the waitress who appeared from nowhere to refill his cup. A second or two after she left, Ben said, "She asked if I was praying for you."

"She has always been the spiritual one."

Ben frowned, and Tuck realized he had offended the old man. "There shouldn't be a spiritual *one* in a Christian family, Son. Are you saying Myra and Gary are less spiritual?"

"Of course not. It's just that Penny is more involved in church than the rest of us. We all attend but she likes to do the other things—with the youth group, I mean."

"Reminds me of a young man I used to know."

The reference was clear. "It's true. I used to be very active in church when I was young, but things change."

"Things don't change, Tuck, people do. You've changed."

"What do you mean?" Tuck said defensively. "I'm still a believer."

"I don't doubt your belief; it's your practice I worry about."

Tuck leaned back in the booth. "Wait a minute, Dad. I've done nothing wrong. I'm faithful to my wife and my family. I don't chase women, I don't get drunk, and I mind my language."

"Is that what you think Christian faith is all about— good morals?" Sadness covered Ben's face. "Then I think I owe you an apology."

"No need, Dad. No harm done."

"I'm not being clear. I'm not apologizing for what I said. I'm apologizing for not having been a better Christian example. Somehow, I failed to get the core idea across."

"Nonsense. No man could have been a better father than you've been to me."

"I failed to instill in you the proper understanding of faith, Tuck. Apparently, I didn't say the right things, didn't do the right things, didn't exemplify what a Christian man is. That's why I need to apologize."

"I believe in God, Dad." Tuck lowered his voice. "I still claim Christ as my Savior. That hasn't changed."

"But your relationship to Him has. Do you still blame God for what happened on *Atlantis*?"

"I never blamed Him. I've never said anything against God."

"Have you said anything *to* Him?"

The distinction shot past Tuck's brain. "What do you mean?"

"Do you pray? Do you worship?"

"I attend church. Perhaps not as much as I should, but I still attend. And I read my Bible from time to time."

Ben pursed his lips. "Look. You're a grown man capable of making his own decisions, but you're still my son. Don't you see? Ignoring God is the same thing as denying Him."

"So what do you want me to do, Dad? Fall on my knees right here?" Tuck pushed his cup away. His tone came harsher than he intended.

"No, Son. I don't. Every Christian father's fear is that his children will depart from the faith. I know you haven't denied your faith, but I fear that it's dying of atrophy. I'm as proud of you as I have ever been. You are the joy of my life and have been since the day you were born. Even then, I knew you were special. I saw it in your childhood: keen intellect, curiosity, and the necessary lack of common sense that keeps the rest of us from climbing on top of rockets."

"I got all that from you. As I recall you used to be the first into burning buildings. You are a legend at the fire department."

"Maybe, but I never went into situations like that without being fully prayed up." He paused, then added, "God didn't kill your crew. An accidental mix of medications did."

"He . . ."

"What?"

"Nothing. Let it go."

"Do you think God doesn't already know what's on your mind? Just say it, boy."

Tuck leaned over the table and whispered the words. "God may not have killed my crew, but He didn't save them either."

"Ah, so that's it. You do blame God for *Atlantis*. Not for killing your crew but for not saving them."

"I don't know. Maybe. I haven't given it any thought."

"And there, Son, is the problem. You need to think about it and think hard." Ben pushed the coffee cup aside and folded his hands. "I'm not going to give you a sermon, Tuck. I never could preach much. I have no talent in that area. Still, I'll tell you this: I'm dying. You're dying. Everyone is dying. Your crew died before your eyes, so that makes it far worse than most of us can imagine, but in the end, it is no different than someone dying in an auto accident. Christians aren't promised trouble-free lives, but we are promised help in the days we have and an eternity after this life ends."

"I know that."

"I know you know it, Son. I'm just not sure you live it."

A heavy pause separated the men and Tuck felt lost. His father ended the awkwardness. "You know I love you, Son. Maybe I'm losing my grip on things. I'm getting close to the end of my life, and I just want to know that your faith is more than a belief held, rather, a life lived."

"You've got plenty of years left."

"No, don't say that, Tuck. No one knows what he or she has left. None of us is promised another sunrise. Tomorrow you go into space again. God forbid that something should happen, but it could. For that matter, something deadly could happen on the way to the launch site. Parents shouldn't outlive their children, but if that happens the only comfort available to me will come from God. He was there for me when your mother died. He's always been there."

"I think I understand, Dad. I really do."

"I hope so, Son. Myra and the kids need to know that as well."

An odd feeling filled Tuck. He was chilled and warmed at the same time. Guilt swirled in his mind and mixed with embarrassment.

The silence returned. Tuck paid the check, and as the two left, he placed an arm around his father's shoulders. "You know, for a really, really, really old man, you're pretty smart."

"A man is only as old as others make him feel."

"Hey, are you trying to lay another guilt trip on me?"

Ben smirked. "No. You make me feel young. Young and proud."

· · ·

"Is there something wrong with your meal, sir?" The waitress was stout and well into her fifties.

"What?"

"Your meal. You've hardly touched it."

The man looked down. "No, nothing is wrong with the food. I'm just not as hungry as I first thought. Please bring me the bill."

"Do you want a container for the food? The rooms all have microwaves. You can reheat it if you get hungry later."

"No, thank you. Just the bill." He fixed his gaze on the two men who left the restaurant.

"The rooms have refrigerators—"

"I'm not staying in the hotel. Please bring me the bill."

"Easy, honey. I'm just trying to do you a favor." She huffed and left.

Anthony Verducci didn't wait for the ticket. He rose, withdrew a twenty from his billfold, and dropped it on the table.

He slipped from the restaurant and into the cold desert night. He walked to a van parked in the lot and entered the back.

"Anything?" he asked.

"No," Ganzi replied. "I've kept my eye on everyone coming and going. The family is still in the suite, and Tucker's old man is in the suite next door."

"Anything on the mike?"

"Not a thing. I can't get much from inside. I even tried the laser microphone, the one that reads the vibrations of the window, but I still don't get much. So far, all I can tell is that the kids and mom are watching some kind of movie. Sorry."

"Don't be sorry. Just be vigilant."

"You know my PI license isn't much good in California."

"That only matters if we're caught. It's worse for me. I'm a foreign national. Imagine what your Homeland Security can make of a nonresident alien with surveillance equipment. Have you heard from your Houston people?"

"Yup. They're bored stiff. Nothing happening in the neighborhood. The Tucker house is tighter than a drum."

"Okay. You're going to be on your own for a while."

Ganzi gave a puzzled look. "Why? Where you going?"

"To the airport. I'm picking someone up."

"Who?"

"My employer. The man who is paying your salary and for all this equipment. His plane lands in about two hours."

"Close to midnight. The red-eye, eh?"

"It's a long flight from Italy."

TWENTY-ONE

Ginny Lin plunked her thin frame in a luxurious leather chair in the media room. Mounted to the wall opposite her hung a large flat-screen television. Although she hadn't turned the television on, she could still see the pretty oval face of a starlet who had yet to see thirty years of age. It was her image reflected on the screen: cropped blonde hair with expertly added highlights, large almond eyes, and a long graceful neck.

"It's not too late, kiddo." Ginny didn't bother turning. She knew her manager's voice all too well.

"Not too late for what, Denny?" She pulled a cigarette from the pack of Virginia Slims she held and inserted the filtered end into her mouth. She fumbled with a gold-plated lighter.

Denny Loft stepped to his charge, snatched the cigarette from Ginny's mouth, and crushed it in his hand. "No smoking in the house. That was part of the agreement."

"What are they going to do, sue me?" She forced her eyes away from him. She found him painfully handsome with his ice-blue eyes, smooth jaw, and sensual mouth. She would have made a play for him long ago if he weren't the same age as her father.

"Look, kid, we're lucky to have this place. The doctor who owns the mansion agreed to rent it to us for the week but made it clear that smoking was a no-no. Besides, smoking ages you prematurely."

"That's why studios have makeup artists." She extracted another cigarette and started the routine again. This time Denny not only took the cigarette but snatched the pack away as well.

"If you prefer," he said, "we can book a room in one of the local hotels, but last time I checked there wasn't a hotel in the high desert that would suit you. Or we can drive out to the launch site. Roos and his buddies have set up some short-term housing for the passengers."

"I'm not staying in a white-trash trailer park."

"They're custom-made modular buildings designed for his guests, Ginny. It hardly constitutes a trailer park. I checked them out myself."

She narrowed her eyes, determined not to let logic and reason spoil a good pity party. "I can't believe people live out here. It's the ugliest place on the planet."

Denny frowned. "Some people find it beautiful."

"They're wrong." She crossed her arms like a disappointed child.

Denny sat in one of the leather chairs facing the large-screen television. He had to turn to face Ginny. "I repeat: it's not too late."

"And *I* repeat: Not too late for what?"

"To back out of this deal. We can get in the car and I can have you back in LA in two hours."

"I'm not backing out. I paid over two hundred thousand dollars for this; I'm not going to walk away from it."

"I know that's a lot of money, but maybe we can get some or all of it back. I'll make up an excuse. You've come down with a cold. They won't let you fly with a head cold. You can express your supreme disappointment. We can then let the attorneys fight it out over the money."

"I'm going into space tomorrow, Denny. I said I would and I will. Besides, you know what it will do for my career." She paused and played with the lighter. "I'm looking forward to it."

Denny laughed. "Look, kid, you're beautiful, talented, and my favorite client, but you are a lousy liar. I can see the fear. In fact, I can smell it. Look at you — you're fumbling with a cigarette lighter. You stopped smoking two years ago and here you are, ready to get into a fist fight with me for a single smoke."

"I'm nervous, not afraid. There's a difference." She turned her face from him.

"All I'm saying is you can still back out. Only you and I will know the real reason."

"My knowing is enough. I've never backed away from anything."

"Backing out now is not quitting; it's an exercise in logic. All it would mean is that you have come to your senses."

"I think you're worried for my safety."

"Of course I am." He leaned forward and lowered his voice. "This is dangerous work."

"Maybe you're worried about losing my fee."

"There are other actresses and actors who want my time, Ginny. I wouldn't even notice the blip in my income."

"So you wouldn't mind if I fired you." Her jaw clenched.

"We've been over this. You can't fire me, Ginny. I'm part of your contract. You owe the studio another picture, and they hired me to help manage your career and to keep an eye on you."

"Did they tell you to talk me out of this?"

"Yes, but I'd try even if they didn't."

He leaned back in the seat. Ginny could see Denny's reflected image on the television screen. "Really?"

"Absolutely, kid. You're not just a client to me."

"Sometimes it feels that way." She turned to him. He didn't return the gaze.

"Yeah? Well, emotions are great little liars. Life goes better when one spends more time thinking than feeling."

Ginny laughed. "And I thought I was a cynic."

"Cynicism has served me well."

Ginny longed for her own bed with its well-used pillows and the smells of her own house. She stood.

"Where are you going?"

"I'm going to bed. Tomorrow is a big day. Besides, you're boring me to tears."

"I can't change your mind?" He stood.

A wry smile crossed her lips. "About what?" She stepped closer to him. "Are you saying you don't want me to go to bed right now?"

"About not taking that stupid flight tomorrow. Don't be coy."

The smile dissolved like sugar in boiling water. "I'll be anything I choose to be." She marched from the room.

"Ginny. Don't go away like this. Don't leave angry."

She raised a dismissive hand and strode to her bedroom for the night. She had made her feelings known. What she kept secret was the fact that she agreed with everything Denny said. She wished she could hop in the car and drive to LA. She knew she wouldn't.

She knew she couldn't.

• • •

The clock read 12:30. Tuck was now officially in launch day and he had yet to fall asleep. Not unusual. He seldom slept well the night before launch. Apprehension, an overactive mind, a relentless rehashing of launch protocols, and two or three hundred other things conspired to keep sleep at bay. Now there was another factor involved: Myra was in bed with him. Before Shuttle launches, Tuck would be in Florida sequestered with the rest of the crew. Not here. Tonight he lay on his side, his wife spooned next to him pretending to sleep and doing a better job of acting than he.

Several times, he considered starting a conversation but feared where it would go. He already knew of her deep anxiety. To hear it in discussion would make things worse. *Anxiety is contagious—you get it from your family.* His own apprehension had grown several orders of magnitude just being around his father, kids, and Myra. He didn't resent their presence. In fact, he loved having them along, but everything about them reminded Tuck how worried they were. It was a difficult thing for a man to learn that he could not protect those he loved from the torture of anxiety and fear. It was worse knowing he was the cause of those eroding emotions.

He took a slow, deep inhalation and let it out in measured breath. Myra wiggled closer and held on tighter. He rolled onto his back and extended his arm in a familiar exercise. Myra snuggled close to his chest and let his arm enfold her.

Streetlights pressed illumination through a thin opening in the drapes, forcing a slice of yellowish light across the ceiling—the only thing in the room Tuck could focus on. From the nearby freeway came the sounds of big rigs and cars plying the asphalt river of the I-15.

His mind drifted to the room next to theirs where Penny and Gary slept. They had been putting on a brave front, something that became more difficult to do as the launch day drew near. Today, Penny had been almost mute and Gary couldn't stop talking. Tuck's father occupied the room to the south. He had remained stoic throughout the three days they had been here. Tuck knew that attitude well and attributed it to a firefighter's discipline. Seeing death often and facing it every workday made such men immune to the emotions that cripple others.

As he thought of his father, he thought of their conversation. The old man had pulled no punches, and each comment had stung like a boxer's jab. In the dark room, the words came back. Tuck had never wanted God to slip from his daily life, had never made a decision not to believe, but his action proved that such had become the case, if not by choice, then by default.

Have I written You off, God? Have I wandered away?

No spiritual voice sounded in his ear, and Tuck had expected none. He had never heard the voice of God and didn't expect to in this life. That, however, had never affected his belief. There was much he had never seen but still knew to be true.

Images, unwanted and disturbing, played on his imagination. He could hear Jess's slurred speech, hear the stress in the voices of Mission Control, hear his own nonsensical response. He could also hear himself praying for Jess to live and then watching her die. The anger he felt toward God but had kept under wraps bubbled to the top.

How could it happen, and why wouldn't the pain of it go away?

How can I not blame You, God? They were all good people and You let them die—and You've made me live with it. I can't help but wonder what You have planned for this trip.

He tried to keep the emotion hot. If he were truly angry with God, then why not be honest about it, honest in a way he could not be with his father?

He replayed the tragic images again, hoping to stoke the coals. He had a right to be angry, and if he was going to be awake all night, then he might as well use the time to clear the air between him and the Divine. But the anger never came.

Still, he told God of his hurt and his fear and his regret and his animosity in a way he had never before allowed himself. He wondered if it was wise to be so frank with God, especially before chauffeuring the first set of civilian passengers into space. His father's words rose to the surface: *"Do you think God doesn't already know what's on your mind?"* Tuck had never been much for formal theology, but he knew what omniscient meant—God knows everything, including a man's thoughts. What was that verse? From the book of Hebrews: "Nothing in all creation is hidden from God's sight. Everything is uncovered and laid bare before the eyes of him to whom we must give account."

For well over a year, Tuck had borne the burden of Atlas: supporting a planet-sized load of guilt on his shoulders. He had been successful in pretending it wasn't there, but he could no more hide the weight from his family than the hunchback of Notre Dame could conceal his disfigurement.

And it is Your fault, God. You were asleep at the stick. For someone who supposedly is on duty 24/7, You snoozed through this one.

Saying the words in his mind brought no anger, no fear, and not an ounce of relief. Tuck was lying and he knew it. He could accuse God all he wanted, but the blame would never stick. His dad had been right. People die. Sometimes they die in their beds, sometimes in their cars, sometimes by disease, other times by accident.

And Jesus died. Died horribly. Died unjustly. Died for others. Died while "on mission."

Tuck tried again to fire up the resentment he felt, but it refused to ignite. He couldn't bring himself to hate the One who loved him so much. At times Tuck's engineering mind clashed with his spiritual sensibilities, but in the end, he always found them to be compatible. Nothing would ever make him feel good about the tragedy. No insight would ever make him say, "Oh, I get it. In that case it all makes sense." It would never make sense. Not tonight as he lay in the soft bed of a hotel in California, while his crew lay in their respective coffins; and not tomorrow when he would carry aloft men and women who, like he—and like those who died on *Atlantis*—had within them an unquenchable desire to fly.

What were the words he memorized at Annapolis? Words by the poet John Gillespie Magee Jr. Words recited by President Ronald Reagan after the *Columbia* disaster in 1986. He struggled to call them to mind, then in the dark of the night and the black of reminiscence, he mouthed in silence the words:

> *Oh! I have slipped the surly bonds of Earth*
> *And danced the skies on laughter-silvered wings;*
> *Sunward I've climbed, and joined the tumbling mirth*
> *of sun-split clouds,—and done a hundred things*
> *You have not dreamed of—wheeled and soared and*
>   *swung*
> *High in the sunlit silence. Hov'ring there,*
> *I've chased the shouting wind along, and flung*
> *My eager craft through footless halls of air ...*
> *Up, up the long, delirious, burning blue*
>
> *I've topped the wind-swept heights with easy grace*
> *Where never lark nor even eagle flew—*
> *And, while with silent lifting mind I've trod*
> *The high untrespassed sanctity of space,*
> *Put out my hand and touched the face of God.*

The story of the author flashed through the emotion of Tuck's mind. John Gillespie Magee Jr. was born in China of missionary parents—his father an American and his mother British. John joined the Royal Canadian Air Force, too impatient to wait for his own country to enter World War II. The Canadians taught the young man to fly and assigned him to the 412 Fighter Squadron, RCAF on duty at Digby, England. That was June 30, 1941. In September, he wrote a poem based on his experiences of flying at thirty thousand feet, then sent the poem to his parents on the back of a letter. In December, he was killed, the victim of a midair collision with another aircraft. In a desperate effort to save his life, he managed to push back the canopy, but it was too late. He jumped but was too close to the ground for the parachute to open.

He was nineteen.

Nineteen.

A clergyman's son.

A soldier with a poet's heart.

Dead after an accident in the air.

The distant sounds of freeway traffic faded as Tuck raised his hand through the midnight of his room, stretching, reaching, extending fingers as far as tendon and muscle would allow and ...

... touched the face of God.

TWENTY-TWO

Theodore Burke moved his head from side to side, forward and back as he stretched muscles in a vain attempt to release the tension that had built in the past few hours. A headache nibbled at his brain. The sound of pulsating engines and spinning rotors worked its way into the marrow of his bones. He shifted his gaze out the side window and watched the desert tableau scroll by bathed only in the ivory light of a half-moon.

Five minutes earlier, he had left behind Edwards Air Force Base. He had spent the day there, having arrived early that morning on Air Force Two. His day had begun at 4:00 a.m. Washington time and he had been on the go since. After his morning ritual of exercise and breakfast over two major newspapers, Burke headed to the office. A few minutes later, he found himself in the Oval Office in his weekly meeting with the president of the United States.

Burke was happy to leave the cold of Washington, DC, behind, but when he left that morning, the coldest place was not the February morning outside, but the Oval Office itself. He was about to do what no other major government figure had ever done—he was about to fly in space.

A former Air Force pilot, Burke's love for the air had not diminished since he entered civilian life so many years before. Not even the fact that he was a card-carrying senior citizen, sixty-two years of age, could keep him from thinking of flight and outer space. During his active-duty days, Burke had done his best to become part of the astronaut corps. He made the applications and took the tests, but he was never chosen. The best he could do was fly transport planes carrying supplies from one military base to another. Those years had long passed.

Every day he looked in the mirror and felt surprised by what he saw: no longer a young pilot, but a white-haired, jowly man. He was still fit and maintained a regimen of exercise that would weary a much younger man, but age was age, and no matter how powerful the man, how high his office, he could not thwart the onslaught of passing years.

After exiting the Air Force, Burke returned to school and applied his formidable intellect to the task of obtaining a PhD in political science. He first thought of running for office, but he soon learned that he had no taste for campaigning. His skills worked best in one-on-one situations. A gifted negotiator, he'd worked in the diplomatic corps, and his skills were soon recognized. Over the years, he rose in prominence and influence, and now he served in his sixth year as secretary of state for the United States of America.

Burke loved the give-and-take of negotiating. He thrived on the planning and the forethought necessary to sway the opinion of world leaders, but he had not lost his hunger for flight. On many occasions, he encouraged the president and the members of Congress to continue what he called "man's greatest exploration— the conquest of space." His appeals went unheeded. There were other needs, and only a limited amount of money to go around. Still, Burke felt a thrill each time the Shuttle launched.

One year ago, he met a man who would change his life. Ted Roos had introduced himself at a five-thousand-dollar-a-plate fundraiser held for the president. Burke managed only a few moments with the young entrepreneur, but in that short span, Roos pitched an idea that clamped on to Burke's imagination and refused to let go.

"Imagine, Mr. Secretary, ordinary folk flying in space."

"It will be a long time before NASA can make such a claim," Burke had said.

"I'm not talking about NASA, Mr. Secretary. I'm talking about flying in space without government aid and without government dollars."

"Commercial space?"

"Exactly, Mr. Secretary, exactly. I plan to build and operate the world's first affordable space-tourism business."

Burke had given a gentle and polite laugh. "I admire a dreamer, but what you're suggesting will cost millions, maybe billions to whoever tries to make such a dream a reality."

"It just so happens, Mr. Secretary, I have billions, and I'm willing to spend them on this project."

It took a few moments for Burke to judge if Roos was serious or just a crackpot. There was something different about young Ted Roos that made Burke believe the man. He gave him a pat on the shoulder and said, "Should that day ever come, Mr. Roos, let me know. I'd be happy to be one of your first passengers."

"I may just hold you to that, Mr. Secretary. I have everything under wraps for now, but when the time is right, I'll issue a press release. I assume you read the *Washington Post*."

"It's required in my job."

"Good." It was all Roos said.

That night Burke stayed up late searching the Internet for information about Ted Roos. What he learned surprised him.

A few months ago, an article appeared in the *Washington Post* describing the successful launch of a privately owned space-going vessel. The man behind it all was a young video-game entrepreneur named Ted Roos.

Later that day, Burke made a phone call. Roos had been expecting him.

Now, Burke was making the short flight by helicopter from Edwards Air Force Base to the spaceport created by Ted Roos. It was not the secretary of state's first visit. He'd been on-site earlier that week to receive a briefing, undergo some training, and receive a final fitting of his flight suit. He made each visit in tight secrecy. Burke insisted that his involvement in the flight be kept in the strictest confidence. Very nervous members of the Secret Service agreed.

"On the day we fly," Burke had instructed, "you can tell the world that the American secretary of state is on board, but not before."

Roos acquiesced but not without heated protest. A hot conversation with the Secret Service had convinced Roos to follow the program. Burke could see Roos did not take orders well, but if he wanted to include the secretary of state on the inaugural passenger flight, then he would have to learn to take some instruction.

Burke knew of another man who didn't like to take instruction—the president of the United States. When Burke first mentioned to his boss that he intended to fly into space aboard one of the first fully commercial spaceships, the president hit the ceiling and delivered a ten-minute unbroken diatribe about the sacrifices people like Burke had to make for the good of their country.

"We can't have the secretary of state of the world's most powerful nation taking a trip to outer space to fulfill some childhood dream. It is not seemly, it is not safe, and it may reflect badly on this presidency."

"With all due respect, Mr. President, none of that is true. It is more than a childhood dream, and although it may not be safe, it is worth the risk to me. And as far as reflecting badly on your presidency, I couldn't disagree more. I believe it will be of great benefit to your legacy and to some of the causes we hold most dear. You know my position on space exploration. It is a duty we have let fall by the wayside. Sure, we are planning new efforts and new manned space trips, but we have done so begrudgingly. It is my opinion that humankind reaches its pinnacle when it stretches beyond its grasp, when it tries to reach what cannot be attained, when it does the brave thing in the face of danger."

Leaning against the large desk near the center of the Oval Office, the president said, "I know this means a great deal to you, but I can't allow you to do it. What would the other countries think?"

"I don't care what the other countries think. Some might think I'm nuts, others might think I'm brave. I don't care either way. You know me, Mr. President; my goal has always been to do the right thing with little concern for appearance."

The president shook his head as if he were dealing with an obstinate child. "Theo, I just can't allow it. I'm still president, and you're still part of this administration."

Burke rose from the sofa and faced his commander-in-chief. "Mr. President, I can have my resignation to you by the end of the day."

"Resignation? You're joking. There's no way you'd walk away from the office of secretary of state for a few hours in space."

"I'm sorry to be disagreeable, Mr. President, but there is a way. If you feel my participation in what has been a lifelong dream is inappropriate and an embarrassment to this office, then I will resign to spare you the awkwardness."

"Theo, you can't be serious. We're just now making headway with North Korea. China is finally opening some doors to help us solve the human rights problem. How can you walk away at such a time as this?"

"The undersecretaries are well briefed, and very capable of handling whatever comes our way. In this role, it only becomes a factor if the worst happens."

"And what if the worst does happen, Theo? What would I tell the country? What do I tell your family? What do I tell the world?"

"You tell the country and the world that I died doing what I've always wanted to do: fly in space. Tell them that I died trying to be part of the opening of a new frontier. As far as my family goes, you won't have to tell them anything. They already know how I feel."

The conversation ended soon after that, and Burke was still secretary of state. But the president was still unhappy about the decision.

The military helicopter skipped along the landscape, the sound of its thunderous rotors echoing back toward the craft. Burke checked his watch: 1:00 a.m. He was used to keeping late hours. It came with the business he had chosen, but this time the lateness of the hour had taken its toll. He longed for sleep. The day had been tedious, much of it spent at Edwards Air Force Base meeting with engineers and technicians from the various NASA groups that called the base home. To the media it would look like a government dignitary had come by to pay a short visit.

"Five minutes to wheels down, Mr. Secretary."

The announcement came over the headphones in the helmet that Burke wore. When he left Edwards, he did so not dressed in suit and tie, his everyday uniform, but in a jumpsuit, partially for his comfort, partially to conceal his identity. Back at the base, Air Force Two sat empty waiting for its passenger to return the next day—assuming all went well.

"Thank you, Captain."

In a few minutes, he would be at one of the world's first commercial spaceports—at least one of the first dedicated to passenger flight. His earlier visits showed him that it wasn't much to look at, but it had everything necessary. It looked like little more than a local community airport. For Burke, the spaceport's appearance didn't matter, but what the spaceport held did. The thought made his pulse quicken.

• • •

Ganzi took another long draw of coffee from a thermos. The night was rubbing his patience thin. The last five months had passed with excruciatingly slow progress. Even now with months gone, he didn't know the ultimate purpose of his work. Verducci insisted on the smallest possible team, and even that had taken Ganzi several weeks of debate to achieve. If Verducci had his way, he and Ganzi would be the only two working. Long hours extended over multiple weeks had taken a toll on both men. Finally, Verducci had allowed the addition of investigators. Ganzi was to keep them all in the dark about the true nature of their mission. This was easy for Ganzi. He was still in the dark himself.

He heard a sound outside and froze. He strained his ears to hear, then came three knocks, followed by two on the side of the van. Ganzi opened the back door and two men entered. Verducci and their employer.

Ganzi eyed the man closely. He was elderly with a white beard, wrinkled face, and eyeglasses that seemed too large for his face. His hair, longer than Ganzi expected to see on a man his age, was as white as sugar. Blue-gray eyes peered through the nearly black interior of the van. The man's mouth hung in a deeply etched frown.

"Mr. Ganzi, this is your employer, Mr. Pistacchia. He has come to check our progress."

Ganzi rose from his small chair in the back of the van and extended a hand to the old man. The hand felt dry and fragile like parchment, and Ganzi felt if he squeezed too hard, the hand might crumble to dust. "Pleased to meet you, sir."

The old man nodded his head. He wore an expensive-looking herringbone sport jacket, a deep blue turtle-neck shirt, pleated tan pants, and a pair of Nikes. By his clothes, he looked like a man who had everything a senior citizen could want. But his face said something else. If life were one hundred miles of bad road, then this man had hit every pothole.

Pistacchia directed his gaze to Verducci, who in turn looked at Ganzi. "Anything to report?"

Ganzi sat again and shook his head. "Nothing. They've been quiet as mice. No movement, no phone calls, no visitors."

Verducci said something to Pistacchia in Italian. Pistacchia replied in a quiet, almost-impossible-to-hear voice. To Ganzi, Verducci said, "I will help Signor Pistacchia with check-in. I should be back in twenty or thirty minutes."

Pistacchia offered no complaint when Verducci helped him from the van. The doors closed quietly and Ganzi was alone again in the darkness. He donned the headset that allowed him to listen to any conversation and noise coming from the Tuckers' room, but his mind was elsewhere. There was something about the old man, something that seemed familiar. Even the name rang a bell.

Mysteries bothered Ganzi. It was what initially drew him to the PI business. Here he sat in the dark well after midnight with little to do but listen to the sound of nothing. His curiosity proved too much.

He pulled out a small laptop computer, set it on the makeshift plywood counter that served as his desk, and cracked open the lid. A few moments later, the computer located the wireless network owned by the hotel. Ganzi chose a room number from one of the occupied rooms and signed in. Several keystrokes later, the private detective was on the Internet. He tried several spellings of Pistacchia. After some research, he discovered that Pistacchia was an extremely wealthy Italian business-man. And not only that. He was the father of one of the astronauts who died on Tucker's last mission: Vinny Pistacchia.

Ganzi had his connection—but what did it mean?

TWENTY-THREE

James Donnelly rolled to his side and pulled the covers up under his ear. By his count, this was the fifteenth time he had done so. It wasn't the bed. Space-Ventures had gone out of their way to provide the most comfortable of beds. The "barracks" rooms were small, but he had expected that of modular buildings.

As a ten-year veteran of field reporting, Donnelly had hunkered down with Marines in Iraq, slept in the tiny confined bunks on a fast-attack submarine, and even dozed in the damp forest of the Northwest while following a group of trackers searching for Bigfoot. Sleep came easy then.

Tonight, however, on the eve of his first flight into space, sleep evaded him. His mind raced through scenarios and a hundred sound bites rattled in his brain. James Donnelly had been hand-selected by Ted Roos to be the pool reporter for this monumental event. Unlike the other passengers, Donnelly had not been required to pay for his seat; he only had to report everything he experienced.

He flopped onto his back and stared into the dark of the room. From the distance arose the aching howl of a pack of coyotes. Their yelps and manic cries sounded demonic in his ears—just one more thing to keep him awake.

Two a.m. It was no use. Donnelly threw back the covers, swung his feet out, and sat on the edge of his bed. Dressed in only a white cotton T-shirt and a pair of boxer shorts, he let the ebony of the lightless room enfold him. He wondered if the space that he would soon fly through would be as black.

He reached for the pull-cord on the lamp next to the bed and gave it a tug. The darkness fled. He ran a hand across the stubble on his chin and pushed his fingers through his black hair. He had just passed his fortieth birthday, but this morning he was feeling much older.

Donnelly stood and stretched his back. He was weary from traveling all day. His trip began with a flight from New York City to Los Angeles, then a commuter flight to Ontario, California. From there, a driver provided by Ted Roos had driven him into the high desert. Delays in flight and delays on the ground had left him longing for sleep, but it appeared he was to be denied that simple wish.

Feeling a little claustrophobic, he dressed quickly, slipping into a pair of jeans, tennis shoes, and a leather bomber jacket. A minute later, he stepped from the room into the desert's biting cold.

When he arrived in the high desert the wind had been gusting, pushing dust and sand into the air, but now only a gentle breeze wafted from the south. Stars bejeweled the night sky, dimmed only slightly by the half-moon. Another light snatched his attention: the dim yellow glow of a Coleman lantern. In its glow sat a man in a thick coat, jeans, and high-top basketball shoes. The shoes were untied.

"Can't sleep?" The voice rode on a heavy Japanese accent.

"Not a wink." Donnelly looked across the short distance that separated him from the man in the folding chair. "What about you?"

"I gave up trying. Jet lag. It is daytime where I live." Although English was not Daki Abe's first language, he spoke it with flair and confidence, and Donnelly was impressed. "I've been conducting business."

"Beats fighting the bed all night." Donnelly glanced around and found a second folding chair. He pulled it to the Coleman lantern and sat a few feet from Daki. The Japanese man was thin but well proportioned. Donnelly knew him to be in his early thirties, but his Asian face and longish hair made him look younger. Lining his jaw was a thin beard, and an even thinner mustache hung just below his nose.

Donnelly had done his homework, including a background check on every passenger. Daki had made billions in various forms of technology and manufacturing. *Fortune* had listed him as one of the wealthiest men in the world, and Donnelly had heard more than one person quip that Daki could buy all of Japan and perhaps half of China.

"Can I ask you a question, Mr. Abe?"

"Only if you call me Daki."

"Have you invested money or resources in Space-Ventures?"

Daki looked heavenward, then said, "I would've thought a reporter like you would have done a background search."

"I did, but there are some things about your life that are unpublished."

"As it should be, James, as it should be." Donnelly watched the man study the stars for a moment and wondered if he should prompt him with another question. Instead, he held his tongue. A few moments later, Daki returned his gaze to Earth and said, "I gave both money and proprietary technology to Mr. Roos to help him in this endeavor."

"May I ask how much money?"

"You may, but you will not receive an answer. Such things are not ready to be discussed. I'm sure you understand."

Donnelly gazed into the dark of the desert. In the distance, he could see the lights of Victorville. As easily as one man might ask another where the best restaurant in town was, Donnelly inquired, "Would it be fair to say that you're a partner with Mr. Roos?"

"I and a few others have a vested interest in the success of this endeavor. It is the same in your country. Sir Richard Branson has invested heavily in a spaceport not that far from here and is building a permanent spaceport in your New Mexico. Jeff Bezos has done the same for a spaceport in Texas. Those of us who believe in space travel for the masses are not separated by national boundaries or ethnic differences."

"So if space travel catches on, do you plan on building a spaceport in Japan?"

Daki frowned. "Please forgive me, James, but like you I've been traveling all day. Perhaps we can do an interview another time."

"Of course, of course. I apologize. I've been a reporter so long now I don't know how not to be. I hope you can forgive me."

A new sound interrupted their conversation. For a moment, Donnelly thought he was hearing thunder, then he recognized the noise. Pounding through the desert air was the *thump-thump-thump* from the rotors of a military helicopter.

"I wondered when he would get here." Donnelly rose and scanned the sky. Daki joined him. It took nearly a minute before Donnelly could see a small white light moving through the sky, headed their direction. He pointed. "There it is."

"He's coming by helicopter? I would have thought that he would have arrived in a big jet like the president."

"No, they're trying to keep this under wraps. Military helicopters fly around here all the time, so no one's going to notice."

Across the fifty feet that separated the temporary housing from the hangars and administration building of SpaceVentures, a door opened, casting a long rect-angular patch of light on the concrete plaza. A single, silhouetted figure appeared in the doorframe. Even at this distance and in the pale moonlight, Donnelly recognized the form of Ted Roos. He watched as Roos pulled his coat tight around him and then made his way to where they stood.

"And then there were three." Roos spoke loudly, a timbre of glee in his voice.

What once had been a single light in the dark sky had become two, and Donnelly realized that he was hearing more than one aircraft. "Two helicopters? How many people are they bringing?"

"Not many," Roos said. "They fly with two helicopters for a reason. First, it's impossible to tell which helicopter the secretary of state is on, thus adding another layer of security, and two, one will do a flyover to make sure the ground is safe."

Daki asked, "Safe from what?"

"Vehicles, debris, terrorists, you name it."

The lights began to separate and it looked to Donnelly like one was holding its position while the other moved ahead. A moment later, he corrected himself—the two choppers were going in different directions, one to the east and one to the west. Two minutes later, the thundering cacophony of the noisy aircraft rained down on the men. Donnelly could feel the force of the rotors in his bones. As a helicopter flew overhead, a light, which seemed to Donnelly to be as bright as the sun, illuminated the area. Roos waved. The noise lessened as the helicopter moved away.

"I wish I could invite you to go with me, gentlemen, but I must insist that you stay here. The Secret Service has some unusual requests. They are a touchy bunch."

"But we get to meet him?" Daki seemed disappointed not to be able to go with Roos.

"Not tonight. The Secret Service will escort him to his room and stand guard all night. You get to meet him tomorrow morning at breakfast."

"I guess that is to be expected." Donnelly sat down again and blinked weary eyes. "I'm surprised that he's going with us at all. It's not every day that you get someone that high up in the government to risk their lives for something like this."

Roos looked shocked. "Risk his life? I don't see much risk in this. I have every confidence that all will go well."

"I don't want to be rude," Donnelly said, "but the best I can tell, you're not riding with us."

The dark made reading the nuances of expression impossible, but Donnelly was certain he saw disappointment in Roos's eyes.

"I would if I could." Roos tapped his chest with a finger. "Bad heart. I couldn't pass the physical. If I could, Mr. Donnelly, I'd be sitting in your seat."

One hundred yards away the helicopters landed, coming to rest on the runway from which Donnelly and the others would take flight tomorrow. "If you'll excuse me, gentlemen, I must look after our new guest."

"Tell him if he wants to play cards, he knows where to find us." Donnelly gave a little salute to Roos, who returned it and walked toward the grounded helicopters.

TWENTY-FOUR

At precisely 6:00 a.m., a black Lincoln Continental pulled into the parking lot of the hotel and sounded its horn. Tuck didn't need a reminder. He had peered through the drapes every five minutes for the last hour and a half. By his count, he slept all of three hours—he felt it was more than he needed. Adrenaline coursed through his veins and his heart rate was running slightly higher than normal. He felt this way before every flight.

"My ride is here." He let the drapes fall together again and turned to face his family, who had joined him in the hotel suite. Myra had ordered up room service for the family. Normally, Gary and Penny would complain about the early hour, wanting to stay in bed until high noon. This morning was different. With NASA, he left days before, but since this time he would not be in space for weeks or even days, there was no need for isolation. If he were about to catch a cold or the flu, it wouldn't matter just as long as he was ready to fly in a few hours.

They had assembled around the table in the suite eating scrambled eggs and toast, drinking orange juice and coffee. The conversation had been light, jokes told, but tension filled the room. Everyone knew the dangers of space flight. Although neither Gary nor Penny said anything, Tuck read the fear on their faces and heard it in their muted words.

"I've got to go." He took Myra in his arms, gave her a kiss, and pulled her tight. He then drew each child in individually, hugging them for long moments, and kissed each on top of their heads. Finally, he embraced his father in a hug that lasted long seconds. Before the two could part, another pair of arms reached around them—they belonged to Myra—then another smaller pair of arms, then another. Another tradition played out.

It had not been asked for, but it came anyway. The long embrace led to bowed heads, and while each one clung to those closest, Benjamin Tucker Sr. began to pray.

"Our heavenly Father, for all things in life, for all the good things we experience, for the love that we share, and for this day, we give You thanks. We ask Your blessing on my son as he undertakes a great task. We pray that You would grant him wisdom and skill, knowledge and understanding, and safe passage through Your space. We pray for his copilot, we pray for his passengers, and we do so knowing that You are with them every second of the journey. And for those of us whose feet are fixed to the ground, whose faces stare skyward, we ask for confidence in Your providence. We as a family ask all of this in Jesus' name. Amen."

The hug lingered and Tuck could hear Myra sniff and knew she was close to tears. The sound came with the softest echo from Penny. Tuck expected this; it was the same every time. He also learned not to dismiss it. The tears were ribbons of love and of concern—and they also reminded him that the greatest courage was not expressed by those flying in space but by those who waited behind.

Tuck hugged each one again and then moved toward the door. "I'll see you all in about four hours. Don't forget to bring sunscreen and your sunglasses. It may be February and it may be cold, but that's still a desert sun overhead."

"We will," Myra said. "You know you don't need to worry about us."

Tuck opened the door and started across the threshold, then came to a sudden stop. He turned and looked into the moist eyes of his family. "Dad, Myra, I want you to know I've been listening to all that you've been saying. Last night ..." He paused, lowered his head for a moment, then raised it again. "Last night I did some serious thinking ... and some serious praying. Me and God, well, we straightened things out."

Benjamin started to say something, but it caught in his throat. Myra didn't bother trying; she just walked to him and gave him another hug and a long kiss. "Thanks for telling us."

Tuck wanted to say more, wanted to explain things to the kids, but he knew the words wouldn't come— not now. Maybe later. Tuck closed the door behind him, walked to the exterior stairs of the hotel, and made his way to the ground level. He didn't look back. He knew he couldn't. When he arrived at the car, the driver had the back door open, and Tuck slipped in.

As Tuck fastened his seatbelt, the driver took his place behind the wheel. He seemed youngish and intense. Tuck also noticed the driver had a malformed ear.

• • •

The drive to the Mojave spaceport took less than thirty minutes. Tuck watched the desert scenery scroll by as the car moved down a two-lane road. The sky still had a deep blue tint from the dark of the night before, and the air was cold, but thankfully, the previous night's wind was gone.

His years of life in the military, his training as an engineer, and his many years at NASA had given Tuck a disciplined mind. The moment the door to the car had closed, he compartmentalized his thoughts and the emotions that had churned up with his family. By the time the car had reached the street and headed toward its destination, Tuck's mind had focused on the flight that would take place in less than six hours. He'd been through all the procedures before as part of his training. He had flown the simulators, and twice he had taken the craft to the edges of space. All of that would be the same, except this time he had passengers, and that made things different.

As a NASA astronaut, he knew every member of the crew had signed up for the mission. He also knew that each had been highly trained, and each understood the risks they faced. Here things were different. Four untrained individuals would climb aboard *Legacy*, strap themselves in, and turn their lives over to three men. It was one thing to face the dangers of space flight for oneself, but it was an entirely different matter to ferry untrained people into an environment where a single mistake could lead to catastrophe. In many ways, he admired the passengers who were willing to undertake such a journey and paid so much money to do so.

The driver turned the Lincoln down a private road. Tuck had traveled it many times since joining Space-Ventures. The road was arrow-straight, covered in fresh macadam, and normally desolate of all traffic. This morning there were at least a dozen cars in front of them, and Tuck turned to see an equal number following close behind.

On one of Tuck's earlier Shuttle missions, Mission Control had diverted them to Edwards Air Force Base for their landing. Bad weather had made a Florida landing impossible. When he and the crew exited the craft, he was surprised to see hundreds of people lining the roads, spectators who had come as close as possible to watch the Shuttle land. It pleased him to realize there were still many people who felt inspired by space travel. Still, seeing the line of cars on this road surprised him.

"We seem to have rush-hour traffic this morning, Commander." The driver turned his head only slightly when speaking.

"Ain't that the truth. And you can call me Tuck. No need for 'Commander' any longer."

"No, sir, I spent a few years in the Navy. Anyone above lieutenant deserves to carry his rank for life."

"Another swab, eh? How did you pass your time?"

"Drove an admiral around. If you want to know anything about Washington, DC, restaurants, then I'm your man. I've driven to almost every one."

"I'll remember that if I'm ever back in DC. So now you're driving around a broken-down astronaut. How did you land this job?"

"I applied for it. I grew up watching the space program and never lost my taste for it. When I learned about this, I did my best to get hired on."

"So this is a temporary job for you?"

"No, sir. I've been hired to handle the transportation department. Mr. Roos thinks after today's successful launch a lot more people will be signing up to fly. When someone pays a couple hundred thousand for a short trip, they deserve some decent transportation and a trustworthy driver."

"I didn't know that."

"No reason you should, sir. You have more important things on your mind."

"I haven't had much dealing with the business side of things. I focus on the flying." Tuck rubbed his weary eyes and wished he had at least a couple more hours of sleep.

"How big of a hurry are you in, Commander? You want me to pass some of these larger vehicles or just fall into step?"

Tuck looked at his watch. "No rush. Take your time. We don't want to run the risk of ticking off some potential passenger."

"Very well, sir. Just let me know if you change your mind."

"Will do." Once again, Tuck's eyes fell to the damaged ear on the right side of the driver's head. "What's your name? It doesn't seem right calling you buddy or driver."

"The name's Quain, sir. Edwin Quain."

"Well, Edwin, I'm just going to embarrass myself and be rude ..."

"You want to ask about my ear, is that it?" Quain turned his head to the side and Tuck could see the crumpled ear clearly.

"Tell me if I'm too far out of line."

"Doesn't bother me, sir. I've lived with it for a lot of years and told the story many a time. What's it look like to you?"

Tuck leaned forward. "I'm no expert, but it looks like a cauliflower ear—the kind of thing a man gets in the boxing ring."

"Exactly right. I picked up this little gem while doing some amateur boxing in the Navy." He tapped the ear with his index finger.

"Took a beating?"

"A bit, but you should've seen the other guy. What about you, Commander? You do any boxing?"

Tuck laughed. "I gave it a try during my third year at Annapolis but didn't much like it."

"Didn't like the sport or didn't like the pain?"

"Didn't like the embarrassment. Got the snot beat out of me by some underclassman. I heard about it for the rest of the year, so I thought I'd save myself any future embarrassment and focus on my studies."

"I understand. It's not everyone's cup of tea. For me, I rather liked it. I never could figure out if I liked receiving pain or giving pain more."

The words struck Tuck as odd, and he tried to conceal his displeasure. He assumed he failed when he saw the driver's eyes shift to the rearview mirror then say, "I'm sorry, Commander. It's a boxer thing. I was full of vinegar then. I spent my younger days on the mean streets of Philly. The Navy was my way out."

"No need to apologize to me, Edwin."

"I just don't want you to think I'm some kind of nutcase. You know how it is; some people get the wrong idea."

"Nah, it's not the first time I've heard such things."

By big-city standards, the traffic on the road wasn't much, but it was enough to bring things to a crawl. Tuck looked at his watch again. "Are you still willing to drive around this mess?"

"Glad to do it. There's no shoulder on the side of the road so I'll have to drive in the oncoming lane. There shouldn't be any cars coming this way. I'll keep an eye out for fast approaching Greyhound buses and eighteen-wheelers." He chuckled.

"Thanks, I appreciate that. My kids tend to get a little upset when I return home all battered and bloodied."

"Yeah, that can be off-putting." Quain pulled the Lincoln into the oncoming lane and accelerated.

Off-putting? Tuck thought the driver's conversation and vocabulary odd and a degree or two higher than he might expect from a professional chauffeur—not that a chauffeur couldn't have a good command of the English language, but it still struck him as out of place.

A few minutes later, they approached a gate manned by two uniformed security guards. The guards stopped each car and appeared to ask for identification and a printed pass. The other guard noticed the Lincoln in the wrong lane and moved to the other side of the gate, the one used for exiting, and lifted the cantilever barricade. Once the bar had reached its full height, he waved the Lincoln in.

"How's that for service?" Quain gave a quick look over his shoulder and flashed a smile.

"As good as it gets. I assume the car has an ID somewhere." Tuck was relieved to be on the grounds; his mind churned with the preparation before him.

"Yes, sir. I'm carrying a small transmitter that identifies me and the vehicle. That's why the guy didn't stop us."

The driver pulled through the gate and turned on a long dirt path that ran behind several rows of parked cars, pickup trucks, and more motor homes than Tuck could count. Spectators gathered in clumps, parents held the hands of children, young couples walked hand-in-hand. From cars and motor homes poured the sounds of clashing music. To Tuck, it all looked like barely controlled bedlam.

"Man, I didn't expect this large a crowd this early." Tuck's head swiveled as he tried to take in the sight.

"There were people at the gate before sunrise. By the time I left to pick you up there must've been over a hundred people present."

"Looks like they came ready for a tailgate party."

"They won't get in your way, Commander. Security has confined them to this one area."

Quain drove slowly through the crowded area, occasionally having to break for careless pedestrians. The road led to two upright concrete posts set in the ground. The posts were twenty feet apart, and a thick chain hung between them. As they approached, a uniformed guard stepped into view, unhooked one end of the chain, and dropped it to the ground so that the car could pass.

Free of wandering enthusiasts and cars looking for parking places, Quain pressed the Lincoln forward, making easy progress to the large hangar next to the administration building. The car stopped a few feet from the front door and Quain exited quickly to open the door for Tuck.

"A man could get used to this," Tuck said. "I don't suppose you'll be doing this for me every day."

"That would be up to Mr. Roos, Commander, but I doubt it."

"I appreciate the ride, Edwin. I can see why the admirals liked to have you around." Tuck shook Quain's hand.

"Thank you, Commander. I'll have the pleasure of returning you to the hotel when the mission is done."

"So what do you do now, Edwin? Do they have other exciting work for you?"

Quain grinned. "I help with security. Sort of the plainclothes guy. A couple of hours from now, I'll leave to pick your family up and escort them to the VIP staging area."

"Don't let my daughter convince you that she can drive—or my son for that matter."

"No worries, sir. I'll take great care of them."

Odd man. Tuck moved from the car to the hangar.

TWENTY-FIVE

Lance Campbell stood beneath the wing of *Legacy*, a large cup of coffee in his hand. The steam from the drink danced in the cool air of the hangar. As Tuck entered, he caught the cold gaze of his fellow astronaut. Dark eyes glowered at him from an even darker brow. He stood as tall as Tucker, but his shoulders were several inches wider, his arms thicker, and his temper thinner. The African-American gazed at Tuck for only a moment, then returned his attention to the sleek exterior form of the *Legacy*.

Legacy hung in its launch position, suspended from the belly of *Condor*, its own underside hovering four feet above the concrete floor. The launch platform was better than twice the size of *Legacy*, and its bulk took up most of the hangar. To Tuck, *Condor* looked like a mother bird carrying one of its young for its first flight. *Legacy* could not take off without the help of *Condor*, which would carry it along the runway and high into the air. On its return, *Legacy* would extend its own landing gear and make its homecoming to Earth all on its own. The sleek, powerful-looking aircraft still impressed him. He doubted he would ever grow bored of its sight.

Standing with Lance was a short man with gray tinted hair and facial lines that declared he had seen a great deal of life. Jim Tolson was a likable man, quick with a joke and a pat on the back. He spoke with a twang that revealed his Alabama upbringing. Jim served as the pilot for the *Condor*. Like Lance, he wore the custom-designed flight suit that Ted Roos had commissioned from a New York design firm: long-sleeved, dark blue, a half a dozen pockets on sleeves and legs, and a large flight patch over the left breast. The patch featured an image of a flying desert condor and a handful of stars. Above it, stitched in gold thread, were the words, "SpaceVentures. *Legacy One*, Seizing Tomorrow."

Tuck approached, his footfalls echoing in the cavernous hangar.

"Good morning, gentlemen." Tuck's voice reverberated in the room.

"Well, look who's here all bright-eyed and bushy-tailed." Jim Tolson extended his hand and Tuck shook it. "You ready for today's big to-do?"

"I was born ready, Jim. What about you? I know you Air Force guys need a little extra time."

Jim laughed. "You just better hope I don't remember that crack when we are more than fifty thousand feet above the planet. An old man like me might forget to flip the right switch or something, and where would that leave you?"

"Taking over, as the Navy always does." Tuck gave Jim a slap on the shoulder. The good-natured digs had become part of their friendship.

"Then we're all doomed."

Tuck turned to Lance and gave a nod. "Morning."

Lance made a point of looking at his watch. "Glad you could make it, Commander. I was preparing to make the flight by myself."

Tuck felt his jaw tighten. "As much as you would like that, Lance, you're stuck with me. Once again I suggest we make the best of it." He paused. "Or do I need to make that an order?"

"You may have held a full grade more than me in the service, but that carries no weight here." Lance took a sip of his coffee as if he'd said nothing more than good morning.

"Look, Lance, I know Roos recruited you before me and I give you some degree of seniority, but he chose me to pilot this mission, and I'm going to do it. His reasons are his own, and if you have a problem with that, then take it up with him."

Lance cast Tuck an icy stare. For a moment, Tuck felt the room chill. He took a step closer to Lance. "You've carried this grudge far too long. It's your privilege to carry it as long as you wish, but I will not let it interfere with the mission, nor will I let it become a factor that may endanger the lives of innocent people. Lose the attitude, pal, and lose it now. When we're back on the ground safe and comfy, you can choose to say whatever you want about me, but not until then. Clear?"

This time Lance took a step closer to Tuck. Not more than two feet separated the men. Tuck kept his relaxed and poised stance, but Lance tensed, one hand clenched into a fist.

Tuck held no desire for confrontation, but he had been selected to lead this mission and to do so properly required command authority and unquestioning obedience from those under his leadership—even if there were only two people answering to him.

Jim Tolson stepped between them and put a hand on each of their shoulders. "Now look at you two, standing here all up in each other's faces like two male elk buttin' heads over some doe." He lowered his voice, and Tuck felt the hand on his shoulder squeeze hard. "Take it easy, boys, and listen very carefully. Here's the deal: you know as well as I do that any one of us can pull the plug on today's flight. Those are the rules Roos set up. What that means is if I don't think you two can get along well enough to make this flight a success, I can sink the whole thing right now. I'm hoping you won't call my bluff, but don't think for a moment I won't do my job."

He lowered his arms and put his hands in his pockets. "Now, I'm not asking that you gentlemen sign up to send each other Christmas cards, but I am insisting that you put any bad blood in the past and leave it there—at least until everyone's back on the ground. Understood?"

Tuck nodded. "I'm good to go."

Lance pursed his lips, then said, "You'll get no problem from me, Jim."

Lance took a step back and raised the coffee cup to his mouth, his eyes tracing every inch of Tuck's form. Tuck knew that Lance would like nothing more than to go a few rounds with him. The copilot turned, started to walk away, then stopped and returned his attention to the two men. He looked at Tuck. "Roos wants us suited up and in his office in fifteen minutes to go over who's going to say what at the press conference. Time to get out of your civvies ... pal."

Tuck surrendered a small smile. "I'll be there with bells on."

Lance walked away.

Jim let out a long, noisy breath. "For a moment there, I thought I was going to have to play referee. I don't know what he has against you, but he's carrying a pretty big chip on his shoulder."

"We've had problems for years. Even in the astronaut corps, he made a point of sitting at the far end of the table whenever we were in the same room. Now that rank doesn't stand between us, he seems to feel freer to say what's on his mind."

"Tell me true, Tuck, are we safe to go on this mission? I don't want you guys coming to blows in the cockpit."

"Nothing to worry about, Jim. Lance can be a royal pain, but I've never known him to be anything other than professional on a mission."

"The question is serious. Would you put your mom on this flight?"

"If she were alive I would, Jim. I'm not eager to die, and I certainly won't let it happen over something as silly as hurt feelings. I've had all the crises in space that I want."

"All right, if you say so, but remember, once I cut the latches loose you two are on your own. You carry some pretty wealthy cargo in the back."

"They're people, Jim, but I know what you mean. I also appreciate the way you handled things. I'm glad you're riding topside for the first part of this mission."

"Glad to be of help. Now go get suited up."

• • •

The meeting with Roos started on time. Tuck and Jim walked over from the hangar to the administration building and joined Roos in his small office. Lance was already there and seated in the chair most removed from the door. Roos sat on the corner of his desk dressed in black pants, black belt, and a black shirt. Thrown over the back of his office chair rested a black blazer.

On the outside, Roos gave every indication of being calm and collected. But his eyes flashed, and his words poured out in a torrent.

"The engineers have worked through the night checking everything from top to bottom," Roos said. "They told me they have every confidence that things will go as planned. *Legacy* and *Condor* are as good as we can make them, and today we put them to the real test." He stood and paced the small room. "This is what it's all been about, gentlemen. This is what I have spent millions on, this is what I have collected millions in donations for. We are on the leading edge of the future, and I want all of you to know how much I appreciate your work. Each of you has brought to the project what no one else could. I don't know how to express my gratitude."

Jim raised a hand as if he were a schoolboy. "I could use a new yacht."

Everyone but Lance laughed, and even he cracked a smile.

Roos leaned over the desk. "In a few minutes, guys, the media will come through the doors of the hangar and see for the first time what *Condor* and *Legacy* are all about. They will see the future of spaceflight. They will see the birth of a new industry in the commercialization of space, and they will have lots and lots of questions. I can think of no better men to give answers than you three. Here's how we'll play this: In precisely twenty-three minutes, I will bring in the media as a group. We have people from the major networks, radio stations, print media, and news magazines. We even have representatives from several nations here.

"I understand that you were in the hangar not long ago, and if so, then you saw the staging area where the press conference will be. Once the media has had time to shoot footage, take pictures, and jot down notes, I'll gather them in the seating area that we've provided. I'll say a few words, and then I want each of you to say a little something. Keep it short and to the point. Think sound bites. Small sentences."

"Dumb it down, you mean." It was Lance.

Roos shook his head. "Not at all. I would avoid high-end jargon; just speak as you would anywhere else. After that we'll throw it open for questions."

"What about the passengers?" Tuck wondered.

Roos smiled. "I plan to bring them in after the media has had an opportunity to ask their questions of you. I'll introduce each one and then ask if there are any more questions. Of course there will be."

Tuck asked, "How are our passengers doing? Anyone trying to back out?"

Lance answered quickly, "They are more resilient than you give them credit for, Commander. I was in charge of training them, and each one has shown a high degree of intelligence and courage. They will be nervous, but I doubt we'll have any screaming fits or panic attacks."

"That's good to hear," Jim said. "But then again it's not really my problem. I ride up alone and I ride back alone—just the way I like it."

"I didn't realize you were so antisocial, Jim," Tuck said.

"I'm not antisocial; I'm just ... well, antisocial."

Roos took charge again. "I will make sure that the press conference is over no later than eleven o'clock. After that, it'll be time to go through last-minute preparations with the passengers, then on with the flight suits. As planned, you'll enter the vehicles while they are still in the hangar and be towed to the runway. None of that is news to you since we've covered this repeatedly. I want to reiterate, however, that the tow to the runway will be slow. I want to give the media all the time they need to photograph the event. You know all the checks you need to do during that time, so use the minutes wisely. It will also give the chase planes time to get in position. As you know, cameras will tape everything, inside and out. I know I said this a thousand times, but we are making history here, and I want every moment digitally recorded."

Roos leaned back and sighed as if he had just run out of gas. He rubbed his eyes.

"When was the last time you slept?" Tuck asked.

Roos shrugged. "I don't know—a day or two or three ago. It doesn't matter; I've gone longer without sleep. Besides, after the press conference, I don't have anything important to do but watch."

The man had poured his heart, his soul, and his considerable wealth into the project. Yet Tuck sensed something different about Roos. In the halo of enthusiasm and excitement, Tuck thought he sensed doubt.

"Is everything okay?" Tuck asked.

"He's already told you that the engineer stayed up all night checking the systems out," Lance snapped.

"I'm not asking about the vehicles, Lance; I'm asking about the man himself."

Roos raised a hand and gave a dismissive wave. "Everything is fine, great, couldn't be better. I'm just a tad tired while at the same time being as excited as a kid at Christmas. I have longed for this day since I was in elementary school and now it's here. I can scarcely believe it."

"Just checking," Tuck said. "Just checking."

• • •

When the hangar doors opened and select media rushed in, Tuck heard gasps and exclamations. It reminded Tuck of something out of a film noir where the press descends upon the site of a murder like swarming flies. Camera flashes blinked in the hangar, video cameramen vied to get the best possible shot, print media reporters held digital recorders close to their lips and spoke in bursts. He couldn't blame them. Tuck had flown some of the best and most impressive-looking jets the Navy had, and piloted what may be one of humankind's greatest achievements, the Space Shuttle, but every time he saw *Condor* and *Legacy* he felt a wave of pride.

The reporters shot pictures at various angles and talked among themselves, held at arm's length from the vehicles by a thick nylon belt strung between a series of black anodized metal posts.

"Wow," Jim said, "would you look at that. I have three hunting dogs back home and that's exactly how they eat food from a bowl."

"And how did you feel the first time you got close to a fighter jet?" Tuck was feeling some of the excitement himself.

"Now that you mention it, pretty much the same."

The two stood well back of the reporters and gave them room to do all the sightseeing. Lance stood next to Roos on the other end of the hangar, still maintaining his distance.

Fifteen minutes later, Roos stepped to the microphone of the makeshift briefing area and called the reporters to their seats. He had to make the call four times. He waited patiently as media personalities took to their chairs and as cameramen set up their equipment and lights. Once certain that everyone was ready and that the tools of their trade were in place, he began the press conference.

"On behalf of SpaceVentures and all who believe that we should be a space-faring people, I thank you for being here. Today marks a new era in the history of space flight. Today we will send into space not trained astronauts, not test pilots, but everyday people."

Tuck thought the phrase "everyday people" was a stretch. Only a handful of individuals could afford the price to fly in space the way these four were about to do. Fewer still were those who can claim to be starlets, multibillionaire investors, or a high-ranking member of the government. Only the pool reporter could be considered ordinary in the sense Roos used the word.

"For the last few minutes you have been looking at my life's ambition. I've made a great deal of money in business, and with every achievement my hunger to see space travel made available to the citizens of this country, indeed of this world, has been the driving force of my life."

Roos continued his speech for an additional ten minutes, and it came across as sincere and heartfelt as any Tuck had ever heard. Roos also followed his own suggestion, breaking long sentences into short ones, each capable of being a sound bite on the evening news or the lead to some article.

Tuck jiggled his leg then caught himself, forcing the leg to be still. He was getting eager. The thrill of space flight was just minutes away. Soon he and Lance would be strapped in the *Legacy*, and behind them four people were about to experience the flight of their lives. For Tuck, the time couldn't arrive soon enough.

Tuck stole a look at his watch. He imagined that the driver with the damaged ear—what was his name again? Edwin Quain, that was it—would be leaving soon to pick up his family and drive them to the launch. He wondered how they were doing. He felt the urge to pray for them and offered a short, silent prayer.

After Roos finished his speech, he called Tuck to the lectern to say a few words. Tuck said very little, choosing just to thank his family and Ted Roos for the opportunity to fly in space in a new and innovative way, and that he hoped others would catch the same dream. Lance stepped to the podium next, where he thanked the Navy and NASA for his training and SpaceVentures for a wonderful opportunity. Jim's speech was so short as to be almost nonexistent. He clearly didn't like speaking before groups.

"We have a few minutes for questions," Roos said. "Please address your question to whomever you wish."

A reporter who didn't identify himself asked, "Will we get to meet the passengers?"

"Absolutely," Roos answered. "Being engineers of one stripe or another, we thought this approach would cause less confusion."

A man in the back raised his hand. "Are you doing this with NASA's approval?"

Roos chuckled. "This is purely a commercial venture; we don't need NASA's approval, but they are well aware of what we are doing. As you know from your briefing packets, our lead astronauts formally flew for NASA."

A man refused to yield the floor. "What can you offer that NASA can't?"

"A great many things. Those who follow the workings of NASA, and space exploration in general, know the organization is returning to an emphasis on what they call HSF—human space flight. Most of NASA's work in recent decades has been in orbital work, the Space Shuttle and International Space Station being the most obvious achievements. Now they have renewed their focus on the Moon and on Mars, and we wish them well in that endeavor. Our goal is to make suborbital flight and later orbital flight more effective, cheaper, more frequent, and available to more people. We believe that NASA will be one of our greatest clients."

A woman stood holding a digital recorder. "Jennifer Ray of the *Los Angeles Tribune*. According to my research, the commercialization of space is a highly competitive work. What separates you from the others?"

"It depends of which competitor you speak. Some in the field are not interested in manned space flight but rather the delivery of cargo and satellites into space. There are others, however, who are direct competitors. They too want to carry passengers into suborbital journeys, and I admire every one of them. In fact, we are indebted to the many that have gone before us, and whose work has opened doors for our own efforts. We made it our goal to be the first to send a group of paying passengers into near orbit. We're not the first to send a civilian into space, but we will be the first to do so on a regular basis. Other firms will follow because that is the nature of business in the United States."

A man raised a hand and Roos called upon him. "Bobby McNeil with AP. I have a question for Commander Tucker. Has the tragedy you experienced in last year's Space Shuttle mission affected what you do here today?"

Tuck rose and approached the podium and leaned toward the mike. "No." He stepped back.

The AP reporter was not satisfied. "That's all you have to say?"

Tuck again approached the microphone. "Yes."

Roos gave him an odd look and Tuck relented.

"I don't mean to be glib. I lost five friends in that tragedy and not a day goes by that I don't think of them. Space travel is inherently dangerous, but then again so is air travel. I mourn the loss of my crew … of my friends, but I can think of no better way to honor their deaths than to fly in space again. They died proving that space is a worthwhile goal, and whether we reach it because of the efforts of the government, or the efforts of fine, forward-looking men like Ted Roos, it is important to understand that the benefits are worth the risks."

The questioning continued, longer than Tuck thought it should. Finally, Roos called for the passengers.

TWENTY-SIX

Tuck had little remorse when the news conference was over. He had spoken to the press often, granted countless interviews, and been seen on television scores of times, but he had never grown accustomed to the attention. Every time some reporter held out a microphone or digital recorder, Tuck felt like an amoeba beneath a microscope lens.

As promised, the four passengers were ushered in and given a short time to speak to the press. The reporters were unleashed to do their work. Roos did a masterful job of keeping the questions on target and not letting things get out of hand. Twenty minutes later, Roos invited the media to leave, encouraging them to take their places in the media viewing area.

"Well now, wasn't that fun?" Roos seemed almost giddy. "All in all, I think the press conference went well. These things can turn into a circus."

"I'm pretty sure I saw a couple of clowns." The press conference had not removed any of Jim Tolson's wit.

"Watch it." James Donnelly used the same tone as Jim. "Remember, I represent the fourth estate."

Tuck turned to the man and saw an individual of polished good looks, dark hair, and a strong chin. His eyes looked slightly red, and Tuck guessed the man had slept no more than he had. "Jim is just having fun with you. I know for a fact that he used to want to be a reporter himself."

Jim coughed.

There was light laughter and Tuck used the time to look at the other passengers who'd gathered into a small clique. Each had been dressed in the same jumpsuit-style flight garb that he, Lance, and Jim wore. Although they stood close, it was easy to see that they were not a unit; each had erected invisible walls.

Roos directed them to another corner of the hangar where hung a tall white curtain. During the press conference, he had seen people moving in and out of the area and had a good guess as to what lay beyond the drape. Pulling back the separation, Roos led the group to tables covered with finger foods and delicacies.

"How sweet, a bon voyage party." Other than the three-minute spiel given at the press conference, these were the first words spoken by Ginny Lin.

"Nothing but the best for the first passengers of SpaceVentures." Roos moved behind the table that held the champagne and pulled a bottle from a chilled holder. "Help yourself to anything you see. These next few moments we have to ourselves. I figured we needed time to get to know one another."

"Oh, I get it," Jim said, "this is a launch-lunch."

Several people groaned.

"Will I have to hear bad jokes like that throughout the whole trip?" Burke took a chocolate-covered strawberry and popped it into his mouth. Judging by his expression, it met with his famously high standards.

"Nah, he's just the elevator," Lance laughed.

"Careful, now. You may just hurt my feelings and then where would you be?"

Donnelly circled a table scrutinizing the spread of food. He tried one of the sandwiches. "Not bad. Crab salad."

Lance said, "I don't want to be a killjoy, but remember, you're going to be flying in space very soon, so you might want to go light on the food. I imagine it'll all be here when we get back."

"I have something better planned for when you all get back," Roos said. He threw a small white towel over the neck of a champagne bottle and began to twist the stopper. A second later, a loud pop echoed through the hangar and champagne foam flowed from the opening. He poured generous amounts of the fluid into five glasses, then handed one to each of the passengers. Before taking his own glass, he opened a bottle of sparkling cider and filled three flutes, which he gave to Tuck, Lance, and Jim.

"What, no bubbly for the pilots?" Jim tried to look dejected, but failed to pull it off. He knew the pilots wouldn't take any even if Roos had offered.

"There are plenty of bubbles in this," Roos said. "No alcohol for you until you get back."

After everyone received a glass, Roos held his in the air and with obvious pride said, "To the pioneers of yesterday which made today possible; to the scientists and engineers, who gave of their time and skill; to the pilots who take us aloft; and to the passengers who make all this worthwhile."

A chorus of "hear-hear" followed.

Tuck turned his attention to the secretary of state. "I'm curious, Mr. Secretary, what did you have to do to make the president agree to this?"

"You make it sound more difficult than it was. I feel safer on this trip than most I've made over the last year."

"So you just explained it to him and he went along, is that it?"

Burke laughed. "I'd be lying if I said it was that simple. None of that matters now. I'm here and ready to rock 'n' roll."

"Rock 'n' roll?" Ginny Lin looked surprised. "I didn't think you government types talked like that."

"I grew up listening to Jimi Hendrix, Ms. Lin. I know how to rock with the best of them." He paused for effect. "I just move a lot slower when I do it now."

The comment made her smile.

Donnelly turned to her. "Ms. Lin, I know why Secretary of State Burke is here. I know why I am here, and I even know why Mr. Abe is here, but for the life of me I can't figure out why a young woman like you, who is at the pinnacle of her career, would want to be one of the first ones to fly in a commercial space vehicle."

"I've always wanted to fly in space," Ginny said simply. "Even as a child, I felt the world's greatest adventure would be to fly higher than anyone else."

Daki Abe joined the conversation. "I imagine we all have more than one reason for being here, but I also imagine we all share one motive: to do what few others have done. I for one am here for the thrill, the experience, and to see where some of my hard-earned dollars went."

"Happy so far?" Roos asked.

"I have nothing to complain about except my impatience. The closer we get to launch time, the slower the clock seems to move."

"Welcome to our world," Tuck said, and took a sip of sparkling cider.

The small launch party continued, and Tuck did his best to get to know the passengers that would be riding aloft with him. The time was enjoyable, what little food Tuck ate was good, but his mind stayed chained to the event that would begin shortly.

• • •

Less than half an hour after the toast the three crew members, four passengers, and Roos stood next to the *Condor-Legacy* joint craft. Lance Campbell walked around each passenger, inspecting the flight suits they wore. Unlike the jumpsuit-style uniforms worn for the press conference, each passenger now wore a formfitting space suit. Tuck and Lance wore the same kind of garb. It was Lance's job to make sure the passengers had donned the suits correctly and to provide last-minute instruction before they entered *Legacy*.

Lance gave a brief lecture. "Each of you has been through the training. Each of you has read and signed an agreement stating that you have read the materials about this flight. But I tend to be a little paranoid, so let's go over this one more time." He put his hands behind his back and continued. "The suits you now wear are referred to as LESs—launch and entry suits. They are similar to those worn by astronauts on the Space Shuttle. The purpose of the suit is to make you more comfortable during acceleration. Once we are on board, we will connect you to an air supply that will pressurize the suits. In the event of an emergency, you can use that same air system for breathing. The pressure in the suit helps counterbalance the stresses you'll feel when the rocket engine engages. We will be pulling close to three Gs when we begin our acceleration to space. That means you will feel as though you weigh three times as much as you do now. The suits will help you deal with that.

"Once on board, you will find a flight helmet in your assigned seat. As you know, these do not look like regular space helmets worn by astronauts during EVAs. The purpose of these helmets is to aid in communication and to prevent injury during weightlessness. Each of the helmets has your name stenciled on the front. We do this to avoid any confusion in communication. The first thing you will do once on board is find your seat and stow any gear that you brought with you. The only things allowed are digital cameras and recorders. Those of you facing a seat back may store your gear in the pouch provided in front of you. The two of you sitting in the front row will find a similar pouch next to your seat.

"Once you have stowed your belongings you will then strap yourself in. Pull the harness as tight as is comfortable and make sure the latch is secure. I will be checking everyone's harness to make sure that no one goes floating off prematurely."

The passengers smiled at the joke. Lance walked behind the four.

"Before you stand *Condor* and *Legacy*, two of the most beautiful craft I have ever seen—and I've seen many of them. As you learned in training, *Condor* is our launch platform. The two large GE jet engines you see at the rear produce more horsepower than any other engines their size. Jim Tolson will be our pilot for that portion of our journey. Once we're on board, and once the crew has done its final check, the ground crew will tow us to the runway. Once there, you will hear Jim rev the engines, shut them down, and then restart them again. This is all part of our pre-take-off checklist. Shortly after that, you will feel the craft move. You will feel something else. *Condor* flexes under strain. Rigid things break, flexible things last. As Jim starts down the runway, our speed will increase and you will feel *Legacy* begin to bounce. Don't be alarmed. It's supposed to do that.

"Our speed will increase quickly until you feel yourself pressed in your seat, much like what you feel when you fly a commercial aircraft, but slightly more. Once we reach takeoff speed, Jim will rotate ... by that I mean, he will pull back on the yoke and the two craft will take flight. At this point we're having real fun."

Lance walked in front of the four again and turned to face them. "It's much like riding in any other aircraft except you have less elbow room, and you'll fly higher than any commercial aircraft you've ever been in."

Donnelly chuckled. "Is it possible to have less elbow room than a commercial flight?"

"Point taken, Mr. Donnelly. We will fly to an altitude of fifty thousand feet, then Jim will pitch the nose up slightly. You will hear my voice in your helmet telling you to prepare for ignition. That's your cue to press your head back to the seat and put your hands on the armrests. You will hear a thud when Jim cuts us loose and *Legacy* begins its freefall. At that moment, you will feel weightless, but we haven't reached zero-G yet—it's just the effect of falling."

"Like the Vomit Comet," Daki said.

Lance gave a brief nod. "That's right, Mr. Abe, I believe you said you paid for the privilege of riding a Vomit Comet."

Ginny grimaced. "I hate feeling like a dummy, but what is the Vomit Comet and why would anyone pay to ride it? I mean ... eww."

Daki fielded the question. "It is what NASA uses to train astronauts about microgravity. It is a McDonnell Douglas C–9 that flies in a parabolic arc. When it reaches the desired altitude, it begins a fast and steep descent simulating zero gravity. There's a private company that gives paying adventurers the same experience. I believe they use a Boeing 727."

"And they call it the Vomit Comet, why?"

"Because more than one person has tossed their cookies during the experience." Donnelly seemed to take some measure of satisfaction answering that question.

"I repeat ... eww." She looked at the others then asked, "This isn't going to be *that* bad, is it? I mean, if we're all wearing helmets and one of us ... you know."

"I advise against doing that," Lance said. "You shouldn't have a problem, but if you do, we have bags for your convenience."

"They might be helpful," she said, "but upchucking in zero-G can never be called convenient."

Lance changed the subject back to the mini review and Tuck was glad for it. "As I was saying, you will feel a few moments of weightlessness once Jim cuts us loose, then a few seconds later the rockets will fire. When that happens, you will be in for the ride of your life. In a few moments, we will be traveling at twenty-five hundred miles per hour—nearly three times the speed of sound. Some movement will be difficult, but the suits you're wearing will help. There'll also be a great deal of noise, but don't let that bother you. It's just the craft doing its work.

"A short time later, the rocket will have expended its fuel and will cut off. By that time, we will be in sub-orbital space. Wait until you hear from one of us before you remove your cameras or before you undo your harness. We will let you know when it is safe to do so."

"Then comes reentry," Roos said.

"Unlike the Space Shuttle, we will be entering the atmosphere at a much slower speed, so the friction will be much less. Our angle of attack—that is, the way we fly through the atmosphere—is also different. The Space Shuttle comes in like a self-guided brick, very fast, very hard. *Legacy* uses a feathered wings system when it comes into the atmosphere. We come down like a leaf. We don't flutter down, but we do sail through the air much more slowly, and therefore do not experience the high temperatures earlier spacecraft have. The temperature in the cabin will remain unchanged."

Lance glanced at the clock on the hangar wall. "Well, lady and gentlemen, it appears it's time to mount up."

It took another ten minutes before any of the crew or passengers were able to make their way up the aluminum stairs into the *Legacy*. Photographers and videographers hired by Roos used the time to record the moment for posterity for the company and for the passengers.

Tuck was the last one on board.

TWENTY-SEVEN

Mark Ganzi had received his instructions from Anthony Verducci, and he intended to follow them to the letter. He'd been working with the man for over five months now, yet he knew very little about their ultimate mission. However, secrets were part of the private detective business. He had his secrets to keep and assumed others had theirs.

What Ganzi didn't know was why Pistacchia was so interested in Commander Benjamin Tucker. He and Verducci had been watching the family for months now, and had even broken the law by planting listening devices in their home. Ganzi's greatest fear was that Pistacchia and Verducci meant Tucker and his family harm. Ganzi had done some unsavory things in his life: he lied often, misrepresented himself, and followed adulterous spouses, never pausing for a moment in taking money for the work.

This was different.

Still, Ganzi could not assume they meant harm. After all, they had multiple opportunities to injure or even kill Tucker or any of his family had they wanted to, yet Verducci never took advantage of those opportunities. Still, here they were continuing the surveillance. His orders were to watch the family until a driver came to pick them up. After that, he was to make his way to the spaceport where an entrance pass waited for him, allowing him to join Verducci and Pistacchia in the VIP viewing area.

The black Lincoln Continental that had taken the astronaut from the hotel room to the spaceport had returned. Ganzi dutifully noted that it was the same driver—an easy man to identify.

The family came down minutes later. Since the Lincoln Continental was not a stretch limo, only three could fit in the back. Old man Tucker took the front seat. It took several moments before the car started and began to move through the hotel parking lot. Once it did, Ganzi started the van and followed. He drove at a leisurely pace, not wanting to alert the driver he had a tail.

As he drove, Ganzi moved a cell phone from the seat beside him and made a call. "They're on the move."

• • •

Verducci pocketed his cell phone. "That was Ganzi; the family has left the hotel."

The old man nodded and ran a hand through his hair. To Verducci he looked frail and ill. The trip had taken its toll, and he doubted Signor Pistacchia had slept much that night.

When they arrived at the spaceport, they received royal treatment. Guards escorted Verducci and Pistacchia to an area at the back of the hangar. The area had been cordoned off and several other dignitaries and wealthy contributors had gathered, some drinking the champagne provided by Roos and chatting excitedly. In a few minutes, they were to be escorted into the hangar, where they would be allowed to view the whole operation. Roos had promised a party.

"He's inside that building, isn't he?" These were the first words Pistacchia had uttered since arriving at the spaceport.

"Yes. He is very near."

"And soon his family will be here." The old man coughed. The last year and a half had been torture for him. Stress and grief had exacted their toll on his body, but his mind remained sharp and determined.

"I can almost feel his presence, Anthony. At long last, Anthony ... at long, long last ..."

• • •

"It looks different from down here," Gary said. "Of course it was getting dark then." He sat in the rear seat, directly behind the driver, and peered out the passenger window at the strangely formed Joshua trees, scrub oak, and tableaus of brown weeds and dirt.

Myra smiled at her son's enthusiasm.

"What do you mean from down here?" Benjamin asked.

"You remember, Grandpa. Dad brought me here last fall. Mr. Roos gave me an autographed game. He gave one to Penny too. He even hired me to review one of his new products."

"He gave each of us a game to review," Penny corrected. "You have a selective memory."

Myra suppressed a smile. Penny was in that awkward stage between child and woman. It always sounded a little strange to hear her trying to speak as an adult. "No bickering in the car, you guys. Come to think of it, no bickering anywhere."

"Anyway ..." Gary stretched the word and seasoned it with a healthy dose of sarcasm. "As I was saying, Grandpa, Dad and I flew out here on Mr. Roos's private jet. It was really cool."

Penny grunted. "You're just trying to rub it in that I didn't get to go."

"No, I'm not. You're just jealous."

"Jealous of you? No way. Nothing to be jealous about."

Myra stepped in. "All right, that's enough squabbling. I doubt Mr. Quain wants to hear you two yammering."

"Not much bothers me, ma'am. Had a brother and sister myself, and we did our fair share of quarreling."

"Do you have children of your own, Mr. Quain?" Myra decided she could keep the children from arguing if she dominated the conversation.

The driver shook his head but kept his eyes forward. "No, ma'am. Afraid I never married."

Gary turned his attention from the scrolling scenery and looked at the driver's head. "Is that because of your ear?"

"Gary!" Myra was stunned beyond embarrassment. "You know better than that."

"What a moron." Myra heard satisfaction in Penny's voice.

"Shut up!"

Myra was about to speak again when a low grumble came from the front seat. Benjamin had just cleared his throat in a very authoritative way. Both children fell silent.

"I'm sorry." Benjamin cut his eyes to where Gary sat. "Normally he's a *smart* child."

"No problem, sir. There's nothing wrong with a boy his age being honest." He turned his head slightly as if turning toward Gary. "No, I don't think my ear scared away any women ... a few crows maybe, but not women. I travel a lot. Most wives like to put roots down, and I've never been able to do that."

"What happened to your ear?" Somehow, Myra knew Gary would ask the question. She gave him an icy stare.

"Your father asked me the same question this morning."

Gary gave his mother an "I told you so" look.

"I did a little boxing while in the Navy—took too many shots to the side of the head. It's called a cauliflower ear. Boxers sometimes get it when the ear is damaged in a fight."

"Wow, I've never met a real-life boxer before." Gary sat steeped in awe. "We don't watch boxing at home. I don't think anyone in the family likes it." Gary paused. "No offense, mister."

"No problem, son. I don't watch boxing on television either. I gave up on the sport after my last bout. That was a lot of years ago."

Myra studied her boy for moment, fearful of what he might ask next. But instead of firing another question, Gary looked out the window and seemed puzzled. He turned in his seat to look behind him, then out the window on the side of the car. Myra tilted her head, then asked, "Something wrong, Gary?"

"I think we were supposed to turn back there." He jerked a hitchhiker's thumb over his shoulder. "I saw a line of cars going down one of the roads. I remember seeing that road from the air. I think."

"Things look different on the ground than they do from the air," Penny snapped.

"How would you know?"

Benjamin echoed Gary's concerns. "How about it, sir? Did we miss the turnoff?"

Myra looked at the driver and noticed he was gazing at her through the rearview mirror. He smiled.

"Yes and no. Gary is right about that being the main road in, but we're taking the alternate route. I noticed on the way out to pick you up that the road was clogged with traffic. I'm afraid that if we take the main road, we might be late for the launch. If we're not there in time for that, there will be a line of people wanting my head, not the least of which will be Commander Tucker."

Benjamin didn't seem convinced. "Won't we be traveling farther?"

The driver nodded. "Farther in distance; less in time."

Myra felt disquieted. She tried to shake it off. Everything the driver said made sense, and he gave no indication of being dangerous or untrustworthy. After all, he'd delivered Tuck to the spaceport earlier that day. Hadn't he?

Five minutes later, they turned north on a dirt road. To Myra, it seemed as though they were driving on the Moon. Gangly Joshua trees stood with their limbs lifted like the raised arms of some monster from a 1950s horror movie. Potholes marred the dirt road and washboard-like ridges ran across its width, making the car shudder as the driver pushed the big vehicle down the path. He sped up and twice the car fishtailed slightly.

"I apologize for the road," the driver said. "Fortunately we won't be on it very long."

"You could slow down some." Benjamin spoke the words aloud to overcome the noise from a vibrating car.

"Actually, driving slower makes the ride worse. The key is finding just the right speed."

No matter how hard she tried, Myra could see no buildings, no other cars, no signs indicating that they were on a road to anywhere. Her disquiet grew into fear.

A short distance ahead, an object appeared. At first Myra thought it was a house, but its rectangular structure lacked a roof, porch, a yard, or anything to identify it as a habitat. As they approached, she recognized it—a metal shipping container, the kind seen riding on the backs of freight trains, or coursing across the ocean on large container ships. She wondered what such an object would be doing in the middle of the desert. She also wondered why the dirt road led straight to it.

The vehicle slowed as the driver neared the container. It was large, white, and heavily weathered. Its protective paint coat had long ago given up its grip on the metal sides. Splotches and veins of blood-red rust replaced much of the paint.

"What are you—?" Benjamin never finished the question.

The car ground to a stop. A cloud of dust rose like a mist, and before it could settle, the driver threw open his door, reached beneath his coat pocket, and removed a handgun.

"Get out." There was no anger in the words, no ferocity, but also no room for interpretation. It was clear to Myra that he meant business, and if his tone hadn't been enough to convince her, then the gun he held in a steady hand would have done the trick.

"What do you think you're doing?" Benjamin leaned over to peer through the driver's open door. "You can't treat us this way."

"It appears that I can. I'm willing to say this one more time. Get out of the car. Now!"

No one moved.

The driver's face hardened. "To show you what a sport I am, gramps, I'll let you choose which child I shoot in the leg."

"Okay, okay, you win. Just keep your pants on." Benjamin looked over his shoulder and Myra could see the fear in his eyes. "We'd better do as he says." Benjamin slowly opened his door and exited.

"This way." Myra wanted to keep the car between the gunman and her children.

Once outside, she pushed her children behind her, interposing her body between them and the muzzle of the handgun. She knew it offered no protection, but her motherly instincts did not rely on logic. Even a one in a million chance was a chance. Her mind tumbled. What should she do? What did the man want? Was her husband safe? Between all the questions flowing like water around stones was an endless string of prayers.

"All of you to the container. Go, now, *now*."

Myra led Gary and Penny to Benjamin, and the four of them moved to the front doors of the container. Like Myra, Benjamin insisted on standing between the family and the gunman. Myra knew him when he was still on the fire department, a man unflappable then, and she could see he remained unflappable even now. She wished she had his courage.

"Open it."

Myra looked at the large container. It stood a couple of feet taller than she and was wide enough to hold a car. They stood at one end, and she could see doors— doors that reminded her of those on the back of a big rig's trailer. She took one handle and forced it up to free the latch, then did the same with the other. Fearing what she might find inside, she pulled the doors open slowly. The banshee squeal of its rusted hinges ran through Myra like electricity.

The container was empty. Almost empty. It took a moment for Myra to realize what she was seeing. Four small glass jars, spaced several feet apart and running the length of the container, hung from wires attached to the metal ceiling.

"Everyone in. Don't touch the vials."

"What are you planning?" Benjamin's words sounded more like a demand than a question.

"You watch too much television, pops. You are not going to get an explanation. Just get in."

"What do we do, Mom?" Penny's eyes were moist, but so far, she had refused to cry.

"I think we'd better do as he says, sweetheart." Myra was the first to step into the container. Gary and Penny followed, but Benjamin refused to move.

"What's the matter with you, old man?"

"I'm just trying to decide if you're the kind of man that would really kill four innocent people."

Quain shrugged. "I've done it before, and I'm willing to do it again."

"Do you mind telling me why?" Benjamin stood his ground.

"Yes, I do mind." A churning silence filled the space between them.

"Just so you know, I don't have much fear of dying. I've been ready to die for many years. The other side holds more good stuff for me than this side."

Quain shook his head as if he were dealing with a child. "I'll bet you have no desire to watch your family die. Now get in the container before I pop one of them."

Although Myra stood behind Benjamin, she could tell that a hurricane of emotion swirled within him. She doubted that there was a man alive that could intimidate her father-in-law, even at his advanced age. "Perhaps you should do as he says, Dad."

"Please, Grandpa. Please. Don't make him shoot you." The tears Penny had been holding back flowed unabated.

Myra watched as Tuck's father turned and stared at his granddaughter. For the first time, she saw tears in his eyes. He hesitated for a moment, then turned his back on the man with the gun and joined them in the container.

"Smart move." Quain went to the back of the car and popped the trunk, never taking his eyes off Myra and the others for more than a second. A few moments later, Myra saw that he held another object in his free hand. She had to gaze at it for a few long seconds before she realized what she was seeing: a small, handheld video camera. He raised the camera and Myra could see him make adjustments with one hand. "Everyone say ... 'Daddy!'"

No one said anything.

In a single blurred motion, Quain raised the gun and pulled the trigger. The sound of the shot rolled along the empty desert, the roar of it punctuated by the loud metal twang where the bullet hit the door. The children screamed. Myra tried to shield them with her body, and in turn, Benjamin tried to cover all three, wrapping them in his arms.

"I said ... everyone say, '*Daddy!*'"

Myra turned her face to the gunman and saw behind the camera the briefest of smiles.

New prayers sprung to her mind.

TWENTY-EIGHT

There was a slight jolt as the tow vehicle began a slow progression from the hangar to the runway. The combined craft of *Condor* and *Legacy* gracefully submitted to the tow. A small set of mirrors situated just above Tuck's head allowed him an unhindered view of the passengers in the rear. Lance had escorted each to their assigned seat and strapped them in with a five-point harness. Clothed as they were in their customized LES suits, they looked like an experienced, well-rehearsed crew. He knew better.

Tuck watched as Lance checked each harness one more time. The visor on every helmet rested in the up position. The passengers would not need to lower them until they reached the edge of space. Tuck could see the mixture of apprehension and enthusiasm on each face. They were frightened half to death. He couldn't blame them. Tuck and the other members of the SpaceVentures team had discussed what to do should one passenger chicken out. Of course, they could do little once they took off. *Condor* couldn't safely land with *Legacy* bolted to her belly.

By the time Lance reached the cockpit and took his seat, the tow vehicle had picked up speed. By design, the first fifty yards would be run at two miles per hour, plenty of time for the gathered crowd to take pictures. After that, the tow vehicle would increase its speed to just five mph.

"Passenger status?" Tuck already knew the answer, but he thrived on formality during flight. It was one of the few things he and Lance shared.

"All passengers are flight ready."

Tuck leaned forward and gazed out one of the many teardrop-shaped windows of the spacecraft. "A lot of people came out for the show."

"Yep, we're making history."

At the moment, Tuck wasn't interested in making history; he was interested in catching a glimpse of his family. He couldn't see them. "I assume your family made it safe and well."

"Yeah, I can see them in the stands." In an uncharacteristically soft moment, Lance touched the window as if he could feel the faces of his loved ones.

The animosity between Lance and Tuck was such that they had never discussed their families, but Tuck knew that a wife, a six-year-old boy, and a three-year-old daughter were staring back at his copilot. Tuck stared across the cockpit and through the tiny window. He was having trouble seeing. "I can't see my family."

"I can't help you there, Commander. I've never met your family."

Maybe if we stop acting like six-year-olds, we could remedy that.

"They haven't missed a liftoff yet. I'm certain they're there; I just can't make them out from here."

"Maybe they got a better offer." Lance turned to Tuck and gave a small smile.

"Trust me, pal, there ain't no better offer."

"Well, Commander, your confidence still seems intact."

What Tuck could see was a mixture of men and women of all ages standing and applauding. Some waved tiny American flags that Tuck knew Roos had provided. He also knew musical fanfare filled the air. He had heard it when the sound engineers were setting up. All Tuck could hear now was the gentle roar of fans that circulated the cabin air. The highly insulated craft kept all exterior sound out.

The craft vibrated and bumped along the tarmac as the tow vehicle drew it to its place on the runway. Tuck's heart picked up the pace. He gave up peering through the window, leaned back in his seat, and checked the indicators on his flight panel again. Everything was nominal.

Tuck keyed his mike. "Lady and gentlemen, this is your captain speaking, and on behalf of SpaceVentures, I want to thank you for flying with us. I am sorry to have to inform you that we have no stewards or stewardesses on this flight, no in-flight entertainment, no magazines or newspapers, and we certainly don't have any pretzels, but we will have an out-of-this-world view."

Nervous laughter filtered forward and through the speakers in Tuck's helmet. He continued, "The first thing on our list is to verify communications. If you're still on board, please answer when I call your name. Mr. Burke?"

"Still here and I hear you fine."

"Thank you, Mr. Secretary. Ms. Ginny Lin?"

"Present, teacher." She giggled.

"Mr. Daki Abe?"

"Ready to roll, Commander."

"Love to hear the enthusiasm. How about you, Mr. Donnelly?"

"I have to go to the bathroom."

Tuck looked at Lance. "Tell me you're kidding, Mr. Donnelly."

"Just kidding, Commander. My sense of humor goes in the tank when I'm scared."

Tuck chuckled with the others. "A sense of humor is always welcome." The tow to the runway seemed to take forever. "I assume everyone was able to hear everyone else?" A barrage of affirmative statements assaulted Tuck's ears. "By way of reminder, all your microphones are voice-activated. We as pilot and copilot can toggle off our microphones to speak to Ground Control or to one another. However, throughout the flight, you should be able to hear everything we say and everything Ground Control has to say."

"So, should one of us start screaming like a little girl ...?" It was Jim Tolson in the *Condor.*

"The whole world will know about it."

Jim said, "In that case, I'll have to put on a brave front."

The tow vehicle reached the runway and made a wide turn, centering the hybrid aircraft on the line marking the center of the long concrete ribbon. They came to a stop. A few minutes later, the tow vehicle disconnected and drove away.

Jim's voice came over the communication system again. "Ground Control, this is *Condor.* We are ready for power up."

"Condor, *you are free to power up.*"

"Roger that, beginning power-up sequence."

There was nothing for Tuck to do but sit in his seat with his hands folded in front of him. This part of the journey belonged to Jim Tolson. The passengers chatted among themselves. They discussed nothing of importance; it was just a way to handle nerves. The chatter ceased once Jim started the massive jet engines. While the *Legacy*'s well-insulated hull cut outside noise to zero, it could not prevent sound transmitted through the hard connections that held it to its parent craft *Condor.* The vibrations made Tuck's skin itch.

Tuck had never flown in the *Condor.* He admitted to a great urge to take its controls, and to fly the craft to the upper limits of the atmosphere, but Jim was the only one checked out on the craft. Since the craft had no copilot seat, only one man could be in the airplane at a time. Tuck had complained about that the first week on the job. Anytime passengers were involved, Tuck felt that a second pilot should be required. If something were to happen to Jim—a stroke, heart attack, or some other unforeseen illness that might incapacitate him—then disaster was certain.

In such a case, and if they had reached sufficient altitude, Tuck could release the stays that bound *Legacy* to *Condor* and glide the craft to safety, but there would be nothing he could do for Jim and *Condor*. Without a conscious pilot at the controls, the big plane would crash to Earth and perhaps harm those in populated areas. Roos and his team had insisted that a remote-control backup system be used, rather than another pilot. "Pilots weigh more than electronics." That had been his logic. Tuck did not agree.

None of that mattered now. Roos was the ultimate decision maker, and he had made his decision and cast it in concrete. There would be other days to argue the issue.

As the engine warmed up and reached near take-off speed, Tuck felt the craft push against the brakes, which Jim had locked. In this way, the craft was very much like a commercial airliner, which tested its engines against its brakes. It also reminded Tuck of his days taking off from an aircraft carrier.

"Ground control, *Condor* is ready for takeoff."

"You are cleared for takeoff, Condor. Godspeed, and good luck."

Tuck recognized Roos's voice. Tuck expected this. Roos had reserved the right of clearing the craft for takeoff, and since it was his money, he got his wish.

Jim's smooth Southern voice boomed in the head-phones. "Hold onto your hats and glasses, and please keep your arms and heads in the vehicle at all times."

The craft jolted forward and began its sprint down the runway.

• • •

"Mom, I can't see."

"Stay right where you are, sweetheart." Myra could hear the fear in Penny's voice. Gary was clinging to her side as if she were a life preserver in the middle of the ocean. She clung to him in the same fashion.

Small beams of light that pressed through two-inch holes near the floor broke the black of the container. It was insufficient light to navigate, but it gave enough illumination to keep the container from seeming like a tomb. It also gave her a moment of comfort knowing that the container was not airtight.

"I'm coming up behind you, Penny." Benjamin kept his voice low.

"Don't touch the things hanging down in the middle," Myra said. "I think they're dangerous."

"What are they, Mom?" Gary's voice echoed off the metal walls.

"I don't know, sweetheart."

"What are we going to do now?" Penny was on the verge of hysterics.

Benjamin answered, "First thing we're going to do is make sure we don't lose our heads. The second thing we're going to do is make sure we don't lose our faith. Are we all clear on that?" Myra and the children said yes. "Okay, give me a moment to think. When I was just a rookie at the fire department academy, one of my instructors said this, 'If you roll up to a fire and you don't know what to do, then sit down, have a cigarette, and think about it.'" He chuckled and Myra knew it was for the children's benefit. "I asked him what you are supposed to do if you don't smoke." He waited for response. Gary obliged.

"What did he say, Grandpa?"

"He told me to stop interrupting the class."

"He was telling you not to panic, is that right, Grandpa?"

"That he was, Son; that he was." He thought for a moment and took a deep breath. "First the good news: the holes near the floor will make sure we have enough air. Second, we are all still alive. And third, we may be in a pickle, but God is still on His throne."

"Amen." Myra had to force the word out. Her children repeated the word.

"Maybe there's just water in those little glass jars," Benjamin said, "but I agree that we should avoid them. I think we should move to the wall. Penny, give me your hand." There was a pause, then, "Got it. Myra, have you moved?"

"No, I'm still facing the doors, and Gary is to my left. I have my arm around him."

"Very good. That means your right shoulder should be pointed towards me. Raise your hand."

Myra did as Benjamin requested. She felt his hand touch her mid-forearm, and then work its way back to her hand. A moment later, she felt another hand, a hand she knew belonged to Penny.

"All right, Penny, let your mother pull you close to her."

"Okay."

"Got her." She never felt so good to Myra.

"Great. Now move to your left until you feel the side of the container. I mean, all three of you."

"What are you going to do?" Gary asked.

"For the moment, I'm going to stay right here."

The sound of shuffling feet filled the small area. "We're there."

"Good. Now keep your backs to the wall, or sit on the floor if you'd like. I'm trying to make sure that none of us accidentally hits one of those bottle things."

"Why ... why, what's in them?" Penny's voice carried a tremble as well as the words.

"Beats me, but I don't think he's playing with a full deck. He said they were dangerous, and that's good enough for me."

A sound came from the door.

"Tell me that's you, Ben?" Myra whispered the question.

"Yeah, it's me. I'm sure I heard that nutcase drive off. I'm going to see if I can open the door from inside."

"I think I heard him lock it," Gary said.

"Me too," Penny added.

"I think you're right." His words were calm and smooth. "But it doesn't hurt to double-check."

Myra stood with her back against the metal wall, an arm around each child, and listened as her father-in-law worked in the dark.

"Wait, I'm an idiot. Don't you have a cell phone, Myra?"

For a moment, her heart leapt with hope, but then crashed on the hard floor of reality. "Yes, but it's in my purse, which I left in the car."

"For the first time in my life, I wish I had one of those dumb things."

If she had been in any other situation but this, Myra might have laughed. Benjamin was notorious in the family for refusing to carry a cell phone. "I don't want to be that connected," he often said.

"Mine is still in the car too." Penny sounded defeated.

"I've got mine," Gary said. "I keep mine in my pocket."

"You're too young to have a cell phone," Benjamin quipped. "And just as soon as we're out of this and safe and sound, I plan on telling your father so." His voice had a forced humor to it.

"You want to use it or not, Grandpa?" Gary said. "I can let you borrow it for a real good price."

"Just like your father. I couldn't teach him any manners either. Can you get a signal?"

Myra felt Gary wiggling under her arm. A moment later, a dim light illuminated his face.

"No. No bars. I'm sorry, Grandpa."

"Nothing to be sorry about, buddy. There may not be service in this area, or the metal sides of this container may be blocking the signal. Let me see that for a moment."

The light moved from Gary to Benjamin. "Did you know that during the 9/11 attacks, the people in the Twin Towers used cell phones as flashlights to make their way down darkened stairways? I've heard of others doing the same thing during fires."

First, he held the phone near the thin crack that separated the two doors. No light came through the thin separation where the doors met because a flange on one of the doors overlapped the second. Next Benjamin used the weak light from the phone and studied the rods that ran from floor to ceiling—the rods for the locking mechanism that held the doors in place.

He took hold of the rod and tried to move it up and down, but it traveled less than a quarter of an inch. "On the outside, this thing may look like it's ready to fall apart, but it's pretty sound inside. There is no way I'm going to be able to free us this way. The guy has thought of everything."

Still using the cell phone as a flashlight, Benjamin worked his way around the base of the container and then made another circuit examining the ceiling where it met the walls. Myra watched every step. He found nothing to give them hope. Finally, Benjamin made his way over to her and the children, then sat down on the floor.

"What now, Grandpa?" Penny's question pierced Myra's soul.

"I think it's time we started praying for ideas."

They joined hands and Benjamin began to pray. Myra did her best to focus on his words, but her mind continued to run to her husband. If they were in danger, certainly he must be too.

A hot stream of tears ran down her cheeks. For the first time since being locked in the large container, she was glad for the dark.

• • •

Ganzi was confused. He had successfully followed the black Lincoln Continental along the path from the hotel to the SpaceVentures location, but just when the car should have made a right and headed north to the spaceport, it sped up and continued west. This put him in a tough spot. It was easy for one driver to follow another if one was patient and allowed sufficient space between cars, but it also required a good measure of other traffic. When he left the hotel, he had all those things, but the closer they came to the spaceport, the thinner the line of cars became. Still, there was sufficient traffic for Ganzi to keep himself somewhat hidden, but that all changed when the Lincoln shot past the only road to the spaceport. If Ganzi followed, the other driver would see him within minutes.

His training overruled his desire. He made the turn like every other driver headed to view the launching, but with one change. Five minutes later, Ganzi pulled a U-turn and resumed his pursuit of the Lincoln, hoping that enough time had passed that the driver would not become suspicious. When the Lincoln pulled down a dirt road, Ganzi's time trailing the car was over—there was no way he could follow the Lincoln without giving himself away.

He pulled the van to the side and watched at a distance. A rooster tail of dust took to the air as the Lincoln sped down the dusty path.

Not good. Not good at all.

He had no doubt that Commander Tucker's family was in trouble.

Once again, he checked his cell phone for a signal. He had none. Not willing to believe the indicator, he attempted to place a call. The phone had not lied to him—he was in a dead zone. In retrospect, he wished he had asked Verducci for a satellite phone.

In frustration, he tossed the phone on the passenger seat and lifted a powerful pair of binoculars to his eyes. At least he had those. Binoculars were standard fare for surveillance. The dust cloud left behind by the Lincoln ended about a mile down the road, too far for Ganzi to make out details. Despite the distance, however, he was able to see what looked like a small white structure, but nothing more.

Why did he go down that road? It didn't make sense. He began to run through his options, and none pleased him. One, he could drive the road itself and see with his own eyes what the driver had in mind. Of course, he would need some kind of cover story. After all, what were the odds of two cars going down the same deserted dirt road? He doubted he could fabricate any story that would pass even the least suspicious mind.

He could turn around and go back, but then he would have to explain why he had failed to follow the family as ordered. He didn't relish that idea.

The third option was the one he was doing right then—sit and wait. It had been only a few minutes, but it felt like hours, and he couldn't shake the feeling that something was very wrong. Several times he told himself that maybe this road led to a new entrance—perhaps a more secure entry point, one not known to him, but his mind refused to accept it. If the road stopped where the dust trail ended, then the car couldn't have traveled far enough to reach the southern perimeter of the spaceport. It would be several miles short.

Something moved in the distance. He refocused the binoculars and strained his eyes to see. From a place near the pale white structure came a new column of dust. This time it indicated a vehicle headed south—headed toward him. The driver was coming back. He doubted he could avoid detection. Even if he drove off now, the long, flat desert road would make him easy to spot. Ganzi needed a cover story, and he needed it quickly.

He wasted no time in pulling a U-turn and parking the van on the shoulder of the desert road. Less than two minutes later, Ganzi stood near the right rear of the vehicle, the van's jack and tire iron in clear view of the edge of the shoulder. He bent and rubbed his bare hands on the dirty tire, then marked his face with a line or two of filth. His goal was to make it appear as if he had just changed the tire. He also had taken the time to place a 9mm Beretta in his belt at the small of his back. An untucked shirt covered the weapon.

He had to wait only a few minutes before the Lincoln pulled on the macadam and turned east backtracking the way it had come. Ganzi was determined to play his part; he straightened and kept his back turned to the approaching car. He heard the car slow, its tires crunching sand between asphalt and rubber. Acting like a frustrated driver, Ganzi picked up the tire iron and tossed it into the back of the van, being careful to keep the door partly closed so as not to allow the driver of the Lincoln clear eyeshot into the surveillance vehicle. When Ganzi reached to pick up the jack, the car had come to a stop next to him.

The driver of the Lincoln lowered the passenger window. "Need some help, friend?"

The man looked to be in his late twenties, good-looking, and dressed for his part as a driver. He also had the same damaged ear that Ganzi had noted when he first came to pick up Commander Tucker.

Ganzi forced himself straight and stretched his back like a man who had just finished hard labor. He approached the car and leaned in the open window. The driver was alone—not a good sign.

"Hey, thanks for stopping. I appreciate the offer, but the deed is done. I should be back on the road in a couple minutes."

"You sure?" The driver exited the vehicle, and Ganzi's neurons began to fire all at once. "I've got a few extra minutes."

"I do appreciate you stopping, not many people do that these days. But really, I've got it taken care of. Tire is already on."

"Glad to hear it." The driver produced a gun and aimed with a steady hand at Ganzi's head.

"Whoa, what are you doing?" Ganzi took a step back, his right hand moving slowly to the weapon in his belt.

"I'm not an idiot, pal. I saw your van in the hotel parking lot and I saw you on the road behind me. You've been following me, haven't you?"

"Why would I want to follow you? I'm just here to record the launch. My day has already been bad enough. If you don't mind, I'd appreciate it if you'd lower that thing."

"You're not very good at what you do, are you? Who are you working for? You working for MedSys? You one of the dogs they sent after me?"

"I don't know what you're talking about. Just put the gun away, and we both can get back on the road."

"I don't think so."

Ganzi dove to the side of the van just as something hot and sharp pierced his left shoulder, forcing him to the ground. A cry of pain raced from his lips. Pushing himself to his knees, he reached for his gun. He was too slow. He heard the driver's footsteps on the granite; he felt the still-hot barrel pressed against the back of his neck.

"On your feet." The order came with a jerk on his shirt, and a half second later, Ganzi's face was pressed against the metal of the van, the gun digging into his flesh. The driver removed the weapon from Ganzi's belt and took a step back. "Turn around."

Ganzi did but struggled to remain erect. Blood, hot and sticky, poured from his wound. "Looks like you have the advantage." The words came out dry and not much louder than a whisper.

"I always have the advantage." He motioned to the passenger door with his gun, holding Ganzi's weapon in his free hand. "Get in."

"And if I don't?" The fire in his shoulder had spread to the rest of his body. He struggled to keep his stomach down.

The gunman aimed his weapon at Ganzi's right foot.

"Okay, okay, you win." Ganzi was doing his best to stay conscious. He made his way to the passenger door, opened it, and despite the searing pain, forced himself onto the seat. His assailant kicked the door shut and tapped the glass with the gun.

"Roll it down."

Ganzi did and the pain from the movement almost made him vomit. "All right, I'll tell you who I'm working for."

"I no longer care."

Ganzi heard nothing when the gun fired.

• • •

Two miles down the road, Quain pulled the Lincoln to the shoulder. After making sure no one observed him, he stepped from the car and threw the gun he had taken from the man into a clump of scrub oak. Seconds later, he was on the road again and headed for his next destination.

So far, the day was turning out just fine.

TWENTY-NINE

The rumbling of wheels along a rough runway stopped the moment *Condor* lifted *Legacy* into the air. Only the sound of the launch vehicle's massive GE engines permeated the cabin. Tuck watched the white concrete runway draw away from him as the craft climbed through crystalline air. With each moment, the ground below withdrew—the end of the runway passed beneath them, giving way to the brown dirt and sage of the desert terrain. Scrub brush, juniper bushes, and Joshua trees scrolled beneath them.

The whine of motors drawing landing gear into *Condor* joined the symphony of sounds. Tuck closed his eyes for a moment and offered a prayer of gratitude for the safe takeoff and for the privilege of being part of the mission. Once again, he was flying to space. He would not fly as high, he would not fly as long, he would not fly as fast—but he would fly, and at the moment that was all that mattered.

Jim Tolson's voice oozed through the headphones. "Stand by for port bank for fly by."

"Standing by for port bank for fly by." Tuck's words echoed in his helmet.

The aircraft tilted to the left as Jim conducted a wide turnabout. The flight mission called for one flyby low enough for spectators to take photos. Tuck initially opposed the idea, preferring to save fuel for any unexpected events they might experience in the flight. He had been overruled. A few minutes later, the craft leveled off and began its return trip to the spaceport. Tuck wondered if his family waved as he passed overhead.

"Film at eleven." Burke seemed to be enjoying the flight.

Donnelly added his opinion. "And at five and throughout the day. We are making history; wherever history is being made, the media will be present."

Condor tipped its wings to the left, then a moment later to the right, then leveled off again. Jim was waving to the crowd. As before, the runway passed beneath them, then gave way to the desert. From here, it would all be up, up, up.

"Off we go, folks." The electronics did not diminish the enthusiasm in Jim's voice.

The aircraft turned nose up, striking a thirty-degree angle to the plane of the ground and Tuck could hear— could feel—Jim pushing the engines to full power. There was nothing for him to do now but wait for his turn.

Ten minutes into the flight, the craft began to bounce, moving up and down, up and down. It felt as though the two craft were about to come apart and go their separate ways.

"Is ... is this normal?" It was Ginny.

Lance answered before Tucker could. "Perfectly normal. Remember we spoke about deflection. Rigid things break; flexible things don't. We're just passing through some turbulence. It should all stop when we reach higher altitudes."

"Yippie aye ay! Ride 'em, cowboy."

Tuck laughed and cut his eyes toward Lance. The comment came from Daki Abe, and hearing the old cowboy saying uttered in a Japanese accent was worth a belly laugh.

Before Tuck could respond, the craft rumbled and vibrated, the noise filling the cabin. Ginny released a little scream, Donnelly said, "Whoa," and even the unflappable Daki uttered a frightened groan. Only Burke remained silent. Tuck's eyes skipped across the instrument panel: everything was as it should be.

The plan was simple: from here Jim would fly the *Condor* in a spiral miles wide, until he reached the desired altitude twenty miles west of the spaceport. Tuck could do nothing but watch the gauges as the altimeter continued to spin: ten thousand feet, twelve thousand feet, fifteen thousand feet, twenty thousand feet and more. His fingers fidgeted. On any day and at any time, he would rather be pilot than passenger. His wife had told him on many occasions that he had serious control issues. Tuck never argued the point.

At twenty thousand feet, the craft began to shake with bone-jarring force. Tuck's stomach rose to the middle of his chest as the craft lost altitude. The rumbling and rattling left as quickly as it came, replaced by smooth, nearly silent flight.

"Man, that'll make a man toss his cookies."

"You brought cookies, Donnelly?" Tuck tried to inject a little humor into the moment.

"Maybe, but a few more bumps like that and I won't be sharing with you."

"Don't blame me. I'm just a passenger for this leg of the trip. You need to blame the pilot."

"Hey, I heard that." Jim's sense of humor was intact. "Sorry about that, folks, but we had a little more turbulence. Nothing to worry about. It happens all the time."

"I suggest you leave that part out of the brochure," Donnelly said.

The nervous chatter died as the plane continued to climb in its long leisurely circle. The altimeter continued to spin toward the higher numbers: thirty thousand feet . . . thirty-five thousand feet. They now passed the altitude that most commercial liners flew. Below, large physical objects now seemed tiny. The desert terrain revealed its wrinkles, its rills, its hills, and various hues of brown.

The higher they climbed the darker the sky became. Tuck had seen it all before but at a much more accelerated rate. Before he had been strapped into a seat on the flight deck of the Shuttle and watched blue become black as the craft was propelled into space. This was a more leisurely pace. There was nothing of rockets, no bone-vibrating roar, at least not yet.

At fifty thousand feet, the two massive engines strained to provide propulsion. The thin air at this altitude was starving the engines, and if Jim Tolson was not careful, they would quit altogether.

The time had come.

Jim's voice again. "*Legacy, Condor* approaching separation. I show all green across my board."

"*Condor, Legacy* approaching separation. We show all green here." Tuck wiggled in his seat, making himself comfortable and forcing his mind to focus on the next few events to take place. "Ground Control, *Legacy*. We show all green for separation."

"*Roger that, Legacy. Everything looks great from down here. Proceed at your discretion.*"

Tuck looked at Lance and gave a nod. Lance took the cue.

"Alrighty, folks," Lance said in a tone fitting a tourist guide. "It's time to put the pedal to the metal. Please make yourself comfortable in your seats. I trust no one has undone their harness; if so let me know right now."

No one spoke.

Lance continued. "I'll take that to mean that everyone is still strapped in nice and cozy. Please lower your visors and lay your head back on the seat. I also recommend that you take hold of the armrests and relax."

"I can't believe I ever thought this was a good idea," Ginny said.

"You haven't changed your mind, have you, Ms. Lin?" Burke's words had a fatherly tone.

"Just questioning my sanity; pay no attention to me."

Jim Tolson said, "Pitching in three, two, one."

The *Condor*'s nose rose into the air, its engines screaming.

"Stand by for release," Jim stated.

Tuck replied, "Ready for release on your mark."

Jim brought the nose up more. "In three, two, mark."

Legacy dropped like a rock and Tuck's heart and stomach took the express elevator up.

Seconds passed at glacial speeds. Finally, Tuck heard the words he had been waiting for.

"*Condor* is clear." Lance stared out the window watching as Jim Tolson steered the craft away from the plummeting *Legacy*.

As soon as Lance spoke those words came a radio transmission from Jim, "*Legacy, Condor.* I show a clear separation. The apron strings are cut. Godspeed and happy flying."

"Thanks for the lift, *Condor.* Rocket ignition in three, two, one." Tuck lifted the safety cap from over the ignition switch and pressed the button. A half second later, he was pressed into his seat. Despite *Legacy*'s sound insulation, despite the helmet with its closed visor, Tuck heard the growl of the rocket. The roar was strong, steady, and sounded exactly as it should. He wondered what the others were feeling, but he and Lance had switched off communication between cockpit and cabin, fearful that screams of joy or terror might interfere with communication.

Each new second brought greater force against Tuck's body. In a few more moments, they would be experiencing three-Gs of acceleration force. Again, Tuck was in a passive role; the computers were feathering the wings and making decisions in microseconds. It was always a blow to his ego that a computer could out-maneuver him, but he had learned long ago to accept the fact.

The altimeter spun wildly. A companion digital read-out gave the numbers in thousands of feet. Outside, an azure blue sky gave way to navy blue, which in turn gave way to cobalt, which in turn gave way to ebony.

The sound of the engine began to change, indicating the steady depletion of fuel. There was far too little air outside the craft to carry much sound, but the vibrations in a pressurized cabin did the trick on the inside. Tuck waited for what he knew would come.

Sudden silence.

Legacy continued to rise, no longer in need of the driving force of rocket engine. Its momentum in micro-gravity was enough to carry it to its planned height. Tuck let his eyes drift from the flight indicators to the window by his head—and once again fell in love with space.

"I tell you what, Lance. I don't think I'll ever get used to this."

"Roger that, Commander. Roger that, indeed."

"Would you like the honors?"

Lance toggled his mike so the passengers could hear. "Lady and gentlemen, welcome to the edge of space."

Tuck would've heard the cheer even without the intercom system.

"Ground Control, *Legacy*: *Legacy* is flying high. I repeat, *Legacy* is flying high."

• • •

Inside the hangar, Roos and the gathered VIPs let loose an ear-splitting cheer. Several large television monitors had been positioned so that visitors could see every aspect of the launch. One monitor showed only open blue sky; *Legacy* was too far up for the ground telescope to see. Another monitor showed Tuck and Lance at the controls of the craft, while still another monitor showed the cockpit of *Condor* and Jim. Of course, one other monitor provided a video feed of the cabin where four passengers made history by being the first individuals to fly in a commercial spacecraft.

Roos hugged everyone in reach, including the three people who sat at a bank of monitors and controls called Ground Control.

"Champagne," he called. "Champagne for everyone."

From outside the hangar came the applause and cheers of those in the stands.

• • •

It had taken some finagling and he had to call in more favors than necessary, but there he stood in the midst of a cheering crowd who'd witnessed one of the greatest achievements in the commercialization of space. But he wasn't here to celebrate the success of someone else.

He had other plans.

Applauding with the others, his face turned skyward, he slowly made his way to the hangar.

• • •

Quain pulled the Lincoln to the guarded barricade and waved at the guard, who immediately let him in. He drove through the gate and turned left on the back road that ran behind the spectator stands and hangar. Parking the car at the southwest corner of the hangar, he exited, moved to the trunk, and removed two dark gray backpacks. As leisurely as a man might carry a plastic bag of trash to a garbage can, Quain made his way to an area behind and just below the temporary bleachers and deposited one of the travel sacks. He carried the other small bag in his right hand.

Quain resisted the urge to whistle while he walked.

THIRTY

Amazing. No, it's beyond amazing." The words came over Tuck's headset at just above a whisper. Nonetheless, Tuck recognized the voice of Theodore Burke.

Ginny's voice was even softer. "I can't believe I'm in space."

"To boldly go ..." The words bore a Japanese accent.

Donnelly piped up, "Wait a minute, wait a minute, you're not going to quote the whole *Star Trek* prologue, are you?"

"Is there something wrong with that?" Daki asked.

"For one, it's corny; for two, it has a split infinitive."

"A split ... infinitive?"

To Tuck's surprise it was Ginny who explained. "'To boldly go where no man has gone before' should have been written 'to go boldly where no man has gone before.' It's a minor difference. Mr. Writer wants the grammar to be perfect."

"I'm impressed," Donnelly said.

"You shouldn't be. I went to school. Actress doesn't mean dumb."

Donnelly gave a nervous chuckle. "I meant no offense."

Ginny said nothing, leaving the reporter on the hook.

Lance broke up the conversation with some explanation. "Okay, folks, just a couple of last-minute things. As you look out the port side, you will see something that you know very well: Earth. I imagine you've all seen pictures of the planet from space, but I'll bet my paycheck those pictures didn't do justice to what you're seeing now. The thin, glowing blue line you see around the planet is the atmosphere. The farther in space one travels, the thinner that looks. As you can see, it is not very thick. It's always reminded me of the thin shell around an M&M candy."

"It's stunning," Burke said. "I've seen a great many things in my life, and I've traveled the world, but this beats it all."

Lance continued. "In a few moments, I'm going to clear you to release your harnesses, and you'll be free to move around the cabin. Just a couple of reminders. When you release your harness, you will experience weightlessness, but while you will feel weightless, it is important to remember that you're not massless. That means if you get moving too fast, then someone's going to get hurt. Make slow motions, and do not push off surfaces with such force you go crashing into someone else or into the bulkhead. You are free to take pictures of one another and of anything you see outside."

Lance stopped abruptly and Tuck knew why. He had heard the same thing. Someone was coughing.

Tuck spoke. "Is everyone okay?"

"That was me," Burke said. "I seem to have a tickle in my throat."

Lance started again. "If you're having your picture taken, be sure to lift your visor so everyone can see your lovely faces. Since the ship is rotating, there will be moments when the sun will pour in through the windows. Here in space we don't have an atmosphere to protect our eyes, so please lower your visors when facing bright light."

Tuck surveyed instruments on the panel before him and everything looked nominal, just as it should. "*Legacy*, Ground Control, how do you read?"

"*We have you strong and clear, Legacy.*"

"Roger that, you sound good to us too. We are unleashing the masses."

"*Understood.*"

Tuck switched his mike to "cockpit only" and turned his head to Lance. "Go have fun." He motioned to the passenger part of the cabin.

Lance released his harness and allowed himself to float free, bracing himself against the cockpit cabin ceiling. The view of the passing distant stars outside made it seem as though the universe were spinning and not *Legacy*, but seeing Lance free-floating with the cockpit slowly revolving around him brought home the truth that it was the spaceship that rotated and not space itself. Using his seat as a brace, Lance pushed himself to the passenger compartment.

Tuck heard Burke cough again; this time it sounded wet. A moment later, he heard someone else cough. It sounded like Daki Abe. Something in Tuck's stomach twisted.

Outside *Legacy*'s windows, Tuck could see stars made dim by the reflective light of Earth's atmosphere. Deeper in space the stars shone more brightly, but this close to the atmosphere Earth became a light pollutant. Nonetheless, it was still the most beautiful thing Tuck had ever seen.

He turned to face one of the onboard video cameras and gave a wave. Near the camera was a three-inch-square video monitor. On it, he could see a wide-angle view of Ground Control. One of the controllers waved back.

"Tell my wife and kids I wish they were here."

"Will do, Commander." On the tiny screen, Tuck could see the man turn in his seat and look at the crowd gathered behind him. He looked for a long time.

Over the headset came the sound of laughter, and Tuck couldn't resist the urge to look behind him. He saw exactly what he expected: four passengers and one pilot free-floating in the cabin area. Someone had brought a bag of small candies and opened it, and the contents floated around like tiny planets. Ginny had lifted her visor and was attempting to catch the candy in her mouth without the use of her hands. Daki joined in the game. Burke had his face pressed against one of the windows and was gazing into the distance. It looked to Tuck as if a magician had levitated the secretary of state. Normally an articulate man, Burke simply said, over and over, "Man, oh man, oh man."

For a moment, Tuck wished that he could join in the revelry, but his position required him to stay at the controls.

"I ... I ... don't feel so well." It was Donnelly.

"Motion sick?" Lance asked, moving toward him.

"I ... don't know. My stomach is upset. My head is starting to pound."

"I've got a bit of a headache myself," Burke said. "I think it's just a little disorientation."

Someone belched loudly. It had a feminine sound to it. "Who brought the candy?"

Daki answered, "I did. I saw a video of an astronaut doing the same thing."

"What kind of candy was it? The stuff is making me sick."

Tuck heard her belch again.

"Reese's Pieces. I bought them in California just before I came to the spaceport. It's just chocolate and peanut butter."

"Something is wrong with them. I've only eaten a few and I feel like I'm going to hurl."

"Use an airsick bag." Daki's words were sharp. "Can you imagine that stuff floating around up here? Think of the mess when we land."

Lance moved from Donnelly to Ginny. "He's right. If you think you're going to vomit use the bags we talked about. You too, Mr. Donnelly."

Donnelly groaned. "My head. It's getting worse. Something's wrong."

Lance tried to comfort the man. "It's nothing to worry about; astronauts experience it all the time. Some people get headaches."

Daki asked, "Do they also pass out? I think Mr. Burke is unconscious."

Tuck had had his attention fixed on Ginny and Donnelly, but now he could see that his most famous passenger was floating limp near the ceiling.

"Lance?"

"I'm on it, Commander." Lance moved to the unconscious man.

"Mr. Secretary? Mr. Burke? Are you with me, sir? Mr. Secretary?" Lance gently slapped the man's helmet. "He's out cold, Commander. His skin feels warm to me."

"Get him back in his seat."

Lance said, "Roger that." Then, "Give me a hand, Mr. Abe—"

Tuck heard retching and saw Ginny with her face buried in an airsick bag. A moment later, Donnelly did the same.

Headache. Nausea. Disorientation. It was all too familiar to Tuck and all too frightening. "Everyone to their seats. Now!"

Tuck turned so that he could face the video camera and activated the Ground Control switch.

• • •

Quain had walked into the staging area with a backpack in one hand and an electronic device in the other. Security guards stationed at the door gave him no thought. After all, he was one of them. Few took note of his entrance; all eyes were fixed on the monitors taking in every second of the historic event. Quain had counted on this. With the closing of the door, however, he did garner Roos's attention, who turned and gave him a quizzical look.

"Quain, where are the Tuckers?"

"No need to worry about them right now, you have other things to be concerned about, Roos." As he spoke, he set the backpack down and backed away from it. The attention of the crowd shifted to him. He held up an electronic device for all to see. "Perhaps you are all familiar with the dead man's switch, but if not let me explain. I'm holding the button. Should I stop holding the button bad things begin to happen." He motioned to the backpack.

A ripple of whispered remarks rolled through the crowd, but Quain ignored it. He made eye contact with two men dressed in suits who had fixed their eyes on him. "To our friendly Secret Service agents, let me say if you reach for your guns, I let go of the switch. If you rush me, I let go of the switch. If I see you try to communicate with anyone, I let go of the switch. If I let go, the backpack will be the death of you all. And if that is not enough motivation, then know this: an identical backpack with a receiver is situated under the crowd in the stands. Your misbehavior will not only kill you, it will kill everyone within one hundred yards." He put more distance between himself and the backpack in the middle of the crowd.

"No one moves. Everyone stays right where they are. Is that clear?"

No one responded.

"Is that clear?"

A dozen affirmative responses filled the large hangar. Quain moved to the nearest wall and put his back to it, then he ordered the guards at the doors to join the crowd. They did so without reluctance. His eyes drifted to a blonde woman of no more than thirty years. "What's your name, honey?"

She didn't respond.

Quain held out the dead man's switch and pretended to drop it. The crowd gasped. The woman shouted, "Tammy! My name is Tammy."

"It's nice to make your acquaintance, Tammy. Now you're going to do me a favor. You see the two men in suits? Those are some of the Secret Service's finest agents. It's their job to protect the secretary of state when he travels, except they couldn't go into space with him. He's up there and they're down here. You're going to walk over to each one and let them hand you their weapon. Is that clear?"

"But ..."

"I'm on a tight schedule, Tammy, and I don't have time to argue. Do it and do it now."

She shook so much as she walked that Quain feared she wouldn't be up to the job, but he let her try. Fear was a great motivator. Before surrendering their weapons, Quain ordered the agents to clear the gun and remove the clip. Each did so and Quain knew they were wondering if he was bluffing or not. Tammy walked slowly toward him, and as she did Quain caught the slight movements of the agents as they began to separate from one another, putting distance between them.

"I'd rethink that, gentlemen." Quain spoke as if he were addressing a boardroom full of executives. "A little-known fact about heroes is that they get other people killed. I promise you, I can release this button faster than you can run. Back to where you were."

Quain kept his eyes fixed on the two until they stood shoulder to shoulder at the back of the crowd and near the Ground Control console. Satisfied that he had shut down whatever stupid idea they had, he returned his attention to Tammy, who did her best to hold two guns and two bullet-filled clips. "I'll take the clips." Quain grabbed them and stuffed them in his coat pocket. He took hold of one gun at a time and threw it across the empty hangar. "All right, Tammy, I need you to do one more thing for me."

"No, please, no. I'm so frightened."

Quain smiled. "That's how I know I can trust you. Do you see that backpack I set down in the middle of the group?"

Tammy turned and looked at the object on the floor. It took her three tries to say, "Yes."

"Good. I want you to put it on."

She stepped around to face the thing again and raised both hands to her mouth, tears forming in her eyes. "No ... no ... I can't."

"Oh, yes, you can, and you will. You have ten seconds to walk over there and put that backpack on or everyone here will die."

"If you blow us up, you blow yourself up." It was one of the Secret Service agents.

"No wonder you work for a government agency; you're too stupid to work anyplace else. First, people blow themselves up all the time. Second, you make a faulty assumption."

"Then why don't you educate me." The agent was the older of the two.

"You assume I'm trying to blow this place up. I'm not. I'm far too creative to use anything as mundane as simple explosives. What you have here in your midst, folks, is a bio-bomb. That's right—you're all gathered around the most deadly pathogen that technology can create. I know this because I created it. I also created the antidote." He returned his attention to Tammy. "This is the last time I'm going to say this, woman. Put on the backpack."

"No." A man about the same age as Tammy stepped forward. He had a clean preppy look. "She's not going to do it. I'll wear the pack."

"No, Dougie. Don't." The words were awash with love.

"Let me guess," Quain said. "You're the husband, right?"

"That's right. And that's why I will wear the backpack."

Quain shook his head like an exasperated father correcting a four-year-old. "Billions of years of evolutionary history, and the human race still produces morons. Your wife is going to wear the backpack, and I have no time for a debate. If you want her to live, then take a step back and shut your mouth."

"It's all right, Dougie. I can do it. I'm just a little scared, but I can do it." She started for the pack and one minute later, it hung from her back. She started to return to Quain.

"Stay there, Tammy. I want you right in the middle of everybody. And to show you that I'm not such a bad guy, your husband may join you." He paused, then asked, "Is his name really Dougie?"

"It's Doug." The husband answered. "She calls me Dougie."

"And you allow it? Isn't that sweet."

"Just what is it you want?" Roos's voice filled the hangar.

"Several things, and they're all going to happen in quick succession. First, I assume some of those computers have USB ports. Correct?"

Roos answered, "Yes, so what?"

"Dougie the hero is going to open the back flap of the backpack and nothing more. Got that, Dougie? If you unzip the wrong thing, you're going to get a face full of death." Quain reached beneath his coat and removed the pistol he had already fired three times that day. "Or maybe I'll just shoot you. I like having options."

Dougie nodded.

"Once you've opened the first flap, you'll find a small digital video camera. I want you to remove it and take it to Mr. Roos. Next to the camera you'll find a USB cable. Take that too."

He did exactly as told, his hands shaking.

"The camera also has a media card if that will work better. There is a short bit of video footage on the camera. I want you to load it onto any computer that will allow you to send that video to your spaceship. Anything unclear about that?"

"Just motive," Roos said.

"That will come clear in time. For now, just do as you're told."

Doug removed the camera and the cable, then made his way to Roos, who took the device and handed it to one of the Ground Control technicians. "You know how to do this," he told the tech. "Get it done."

The tech hesitated, then said, "Will do."

Roos patted the man on the shoulder, then said, "Let them know what's coming."

The tech keyed his mike and looked into the video camera. "*Legacy*, Ground Control. We have a problem."

THIRTY-ONE

They're all strapped in." Lance took his seat in the copilot chair and affixed his harness. "Burke looks bad. I don't think it's motion sickness or SAS."

"But everyone is still alive, right?" Tuck's words sounded as if another man had uttered them.

"Yes, so far, but I have serious concerns about the secretary of state. We need to get him to a hospital."

"There's another problem. Ground control is sending a video." Tuck tapped the video monitor. "I don't know what's going on down there, but something has those people frightened." He waited while Lance took in the scene.

"What kind of video?"

"I don't know. Ground Control came on and said they had a problem while you were back there taking care of the passengers."

"Legacy, *Ground Control. You should be able to receive this now. Let me know if it comes through.*"

The video image of Ground Control gave way to another image that took Tuck several moments to identify, but when he did, his heart stopped beating. The video quality was poor and Tuck guessed it had been taken with an inexpensive camera. What he heard over his headset dumped a vat of acid in his stomach.

"Is that your ...?" Lance was unable to finish the question.

"It's my family. I can't make out where they are."

"One thing is for sure, they're not at the spaceport."

Tuck didn't need Lance to tell him that. The video showed his family standing in the opening of some kind of structure, but the camera shot was so tight, he couldn't identify it. Tuck keyed his mike. "Someone had better tell me what's going on and they had better tell me right now."

No answer came.

"Ground Control, *Legacy.* Do you read me?"

"*Stand by one, Tuck. We are awaiting instructions.*"

Tuck looked at Lance. "Instructions from whom, Ground Control?"

"*He wants me to ask you how everyone is doing up there.*"

Tuck was baffled. "Who wants to know?"

"*He says his name is Quain.*"

"Quain? The guy who drove me to the spaceport this morning?"

"*That's what he said.*" Even through seventy miles of atmosphere and space that separated him from the communication tech, Tuck could hear his stress.

"What's he done with my family? Where are they?" Tuck was doing his best not to yell into the microphone.

"We don't know, Commander. This is the first we've seen of it." There was a brief pause. *"He still wants to know how everyone is doing."*

Lance answered. "We've got a ship full of sick people, Ground Control. One is unconscious."

Tuck keyed off his mike and motioned for Lance to do the same. "I'm not getting the full picture here, but someone other than Roos is calling the shots. And whoever it is has done something to my family."

"How can somebody take over Ground Control? Roos hired guards, and there are two Secret Service agents in that room. Maybe it's a whole team of people."

"I don't think so, Lance. Ground Control keeps referring to 'him,' not 'they.'"

Tuck activated the mike. "Ground Control, *Legacy.* Are we to assume that you have unexpected company?"

"Roger that, Legacy. We have a party crasher."

Tuck heard Ginny's voice. "Hey, you guys? I think the reporter guy has passed out. He doesn't look so good." She began to weep. "My head hurts so much."

"I'll go back and check," Lance said.

Tuck grabbed his arm. "How are you feeling?"

Lance hesitated before answering. "Like fresh roadkill."

Tuck released him and moved to the passenger portion of the cabin. *Think, Tuck. Think.* A war raged in Tuck's mind. Competing for his attention were the sick passengers in back—each exhibiting symptoms like those that killed his crew well over a year ago—his endangered family on Earth below, and his confusion about what was happening at Ground Control. He also wondered if he had been infected too. If so, he had very little time to get his people back on the ground.

A new voice came over the headset. *"Commander Tucker. It's an honor to meet you again."*

Tuck turned in his seat and called for Lance. His copilot appeared two seconds later. "I want you to hear this."

Lance nodded but the motion came far more slowly than it should. "Donnelly is still conscious, but I don't know for how much longer." Tuck feared Lance would soon lapse into unconsciousness along with Burke.

"Cat got your tongue?"

"I'm here. You're Quain?" The civility was forced, an act on Tuck's part. He had many other words he wanted to say.

"Isn't technology amazing? I'm way down here on Earth and you're way up there in space, and we're talking as if we were in the same room together. And this wireless headset makes my life much easier. It wouldn't do for me to turn my back on some of these people. I don't think they understand me." The speaker paused, then said, *"I imagine you would like to be in the same room with me."*

You got that right. "You're the same man that drove me to the spaceport today. I thought we got along well. Why such a change in attitude?"

Laughter poured into Tuck's helmet. *"I have to say, Commander, you're one cool customer. You've just seen that your family is in danger and you're talking to me like an old pal."*

"Don't fool yourself ... pal. You have the advantage. It's in the best interest of my family to be polite."

"I think you'd be less polite in person."

"Let's cut the small talk, Quain. You must have some kind of business with me, so let's get to it."

"Polite and perceptive—now I'm rather glad you didn't die on Atlantis. *You caused me quite a bit of embarrassment, you know. You also delayed a rather lucrative payment."*

Implications of the words struck Tuck like a fist to the sternum. "Are you saying you caused that? I've heard of crazy people taking the blame for someone else's crimes, but this takes the cake."

"I assume you bought the same lie that everyone else did. I can assure you the medicinal poisoning from the dermal patches was no accident."

"Like I said, crazy people take the blame for others."

Quain's tone chilled. *"I'd go easy on the crazy-people talk if I were you. I have over fifty hostages in the hangar and several hundred more outside. Oh, and I almost forgot, four others hidden away—others you care a great deal about. So from now on when you speak to me, you will speak to me with respect, or you will be returning home to an empty house—if you get to return home at all."*

"All right, Quain, I believe you. Tell me what you want."

"Let me bring you up to speed. In the midst of these VIPs is a backpack filled with a bio-bomb. It contains the same genetically engineered germ that killed your crew on Atlantis *and was supposed to kill you, except it doesn't contain the delaying agent. Unlike your* Atlantis *crew and your current passengers, these people will die quickly. Badly, painfully, but quickly. I've placed another such bio-bomb under the bleachers of the crowd waiting for your return. In my hand is a dead man's switch. If I release the switch, both bombs will go off and my personal brand of*

biowarfare will be released into the air. You have a sample of my work with your passengers. Tell me, Commander, how many are sick now?"

"I think you know the answer to that. All of them."

"Everyone except you."

"How do you know I'm not sick?"

"Because I didn't contaminate your flight suit."

"Is my family still alive?" It was the hardest question Tuck ever had to ask.

"For now. I have them locked away safe and sound."

Why would he do this? Why poison an entire space crew? Why kill dozens of people he didn't know? Tuck had no idea.

"What is it you want, Quain? You must have some kind of goal. I can tell you're no dummy, so I know you aren't doing this for kicks. What do you hope to gain?"

"You're right about that, Commander. I'm no dummy. People are motivated by only a few things: love, money, and power. I don't care about love, but the last two weigh heavy in my decision making. I'm in this for one thing and one thing only: wealth. If you have wealth, you have power; if you have wealth and power, you can buy love."

Lance moved his hands to his stomach and leaned his helmeted head back against his seat. "Well, I can see why he doesn't teach philosophy." He coughed.

The same feeling of helplessness that had washed over Tuck during those horrible hours during the *Atlantis* crisis inundated him once again. His family needed him, and although only seventy miles separated him from the surface of the Earth, he was several hundred miles of flight path away.

"So you're holding everyone down there hostage, is that it?"

"Bingo. But not in the way you think. I will be out of here in a few minutes. It's surprising, Commander, you haven't asked the really important question yet."

"You mean, why did you poison everyone but me?"

"Exactly. It's not that I like you, but for the moment I need you and that really galls me. You should've died those many months ago, but you had to wear the wrong patch. Had you worn the patch designed for a man your size and weight you would be taking a dirt nap now. I hadn't planned on your choosing a patch designed for women."

"Yeah, well, I'm a twenty-first-century kind of guy."

Lance whispered to Tuck, "Don't antagonize him. He may be smart ... but I don't think he's stable."

Tuck switched off his mike. "I'm trying to keep him occupied and hoping someone down there can do something." He was grasping at straws, but straws were all he had.

"I know your glibness is an act, Commander, and that's all right with me. Every second you waste is another second closer to death for your passengers and your family. So don't let me hinder you; you waste all the time you want."

"I'm listening."

"The rest of my plan I think I'll keep to myself. Here's all you need to know: you are to stay in space until everyone on board is dead. Then and only then may you make reentry. The reason you are alive is that I'm afraid Mr. Roos here has some auto-control system installed on Legacy. I'll have to admit I never thought NASA could land the Shuttle without a crewman at the controls. If you break my little rule, your family will die. How's that for being stuck between the devil and the deep blue sea?"

"I think you have more than money in mind. There's someone on board you want dead."

"Very astute, Commander. Very astute, indeed. I also want you to suffer, and watching your passengers die is one way to do it."

• • •

"That went well," Quain said.

Roos grunted. "If you say so." He avoided eye contact.

"I do. Now it's time for you to get to work. I assume this building has wireless connectivity."

"Of course."

"It's time for a little online banking, and you're going to do it."

It took Roos a few moments to catch the man's drift. "You're . . . robbing me?"

"I prefer to think of it as a free-will offering—my will and your offering. You're going to transfer money from your bank accounts to my offshore account."

"US banks—"

"Don't trifle with me, Roos. You have six offshore accounts. Don't ask how I know. Money and fear will buy all types of information. You're going to skip all the US laws and transfer funds from your Cayman accounts to mine. Get a laptop and get online. I don't want to spend any more time here than I have to."

THIRTY-TWO

Tuck's mind spun like a windmill in a tornado. Nothing in his experience, not even the tragedy on *Atlantis*, had prepared him for such a moment. He tried to control his mind and his emotions, but images of

Myra, Penny, Gary, and his father flashed on his brain with strobe-light intensity.

"Your family ... you must save your family." Tuck could sense the effort required for Lance to utter those words.

"You stay with me, pal. You got that? You think we've had tension in our relationship before; if you die, I promise it will get worse."

Lance chuckled. "If I die, I'm going to haunt you."

Hearing Lance suggest that Tuck sacrifice him and the others for his family pulled the rubber band of tension within him to the breaking point. Tears burned his eyes and the ache that began in his stomach now ran from head to sole. "I'm serious, Commander. You are not to die on me. That is an order."

Lance's head moved from side to side and at first Tuck assumed he was shaking his head, then realized the man was now too weak to hold his head up. Tuck activated the inner ship communication. "This is Tucker. I need to know who is still with me. Ginny?"

"I'm ... I'm still here. My head hurts so much." She whimpered. "I'm ... getting sleepy."

"Stay awake, Ginny. Do whatever you have to, but stay awake. Mr. Abe?"

Tuck waited for a response but none came.

"Mr. Abe? Can you hear me, Mr. Abe?"

"I think he's out." The weak voice came from Donnelly. "Same with the secretary."

"How about you, Donnelly? How are you doing?"

"Not good. I've never felt this bad. Hard to stay awake ... nausea ... head pounding ... feels like something's going to break." He coughed, then groaned. "What's wrong, Commander? Why are we all sick?"

Tuck thought about feeding him a lie. What good would it do to tell the truth? But the man was dying and deserved the truth of the matter. In his situation, Tuck would want the facts. "Someone has put a biological agent in everyone's flight suit. He's holding Ground Control hostage—he is also holding my family."

"You don't sound sick. Why aren't you sick?" Ginny's voice sounded a shade weaker than a moment before.

"He didn't poison my suit. He wants me to keep everyone up here until you are all dead."

Tuck heard Ginny weeping. "I don't want to die. I don't want to die in space. You have to do something ... it's your job. We trusted you. We trusted you."

"I know," Tuck whispered. "I know."

"Family first. No one will blame you. Do the right thing." Lance's words were thin.

The right thing? Exactly what was the right thing? He had one more name to call before finishing his survey. "Mr. Secretary? Mr. Secretary, this is Commander Tucker." No answer came, nor did Tuck expect one. Burke had been the first to go unconscious.

Tuck closed his eyes, laid his head back, and struggled for words to say to the One who created the space in which he flew. To his surprise, he didn't plead for help, nor did he ask for miracles. Instead, the prayer came in simple words: "God of heaven and earth, grant me wisdom and give me courage. Bless that which I'm about to do. All things rest in Your hands."

Tuck blinked back tears and took a deep breath. Once again, he looked at the distant stars; once again, he took in the bright, beautiful blue of Earth.

Then he reached to the console before him and flipped the switch that turned off all communications.

He began punching commands into the onboard flight computer.

Lance muttered, "No."

"Lance ... shut up and relax. That's an order, pal."

"You ... you can't."

"Try and stop me."

• • •

Verducci's mind chewed through options like an adding machine chewed through numbers and it kept coming up empty. If he were facing a man with a knife or gun, then his options would be clear. If properly done, a trained man could disarm an armed assailant. The dead man's switch was the surest way to ward off such an attack. Even if Verducci could get a clear shot at the man or land a skull-crushing blow, he would be unable to prevent Quain from releasing the button and infecting everyone with whatever biological agent he had created.

He wished Ganzi were present, but the man had not shown and that did not bode well. Over the months, the private investigator had demonstrated endurance and loyalty. Verducci could think of only one reason to explain Ganzi's absence, and he hoped he was wrong.

Glancing around the crowd, Verducci saw that there was little help available. There were the two Secret Service agents who were undoubtedly thinking the same thing as he. But like him, their hands were tied as long as the dead man's switch remained operable. It had crossed Verducci's mind that the dead man's switch was nothing more than a prop and for a few seconds had considered challenging Quain, but common sense reined him in. If he was wrong, then fifty or more people in the hangar would die, and possibly several hundred enthusiasts outside.

For what must have been the one hundredth time, Verducci looked at his boss. Since the arrival of Quain, the old man had not taken his eyes off the intruder, and Verducci knew why.

Pistacchia took a step toward Quain, who remained huddled close to Roos as Roos worked the wireless computer. Verducci took his arm and gave it a gentle squeeze. Pistacchia stopped but gave no indication that he was aware of a hand on his elbow.

"I've been waiting for you." The old man's voice carried farther than Verducci thought it could.

Quain looked up, stared at the old man, then returned his attention to Roos and his activity.

"All these days ... all these months ..."

"Signor—this is not wise," Verducci whispered.

With surprising strength, Pistacchia pulled his arm free of Verducci's grip.

Quain turned his eyes on the old man. "If you know what's good for you, gramps, you'll shut your mouth."

Pistacchia stopped and took a deep breath, thrusting out his chest. "I am Vincent Pistacchia."

"Well, good for you, old man. Now shut up."

The fire that burned in Verducci turned white hot. In any other circumstance, in any other situation, such an insult would be punished. If Pistacchia took the comment as an insult, he didn't show it. Verducci knew his employer well enough to see that his mind was fixed on only one thing: confronting his son's killer.

Pistacchia repeated his words, "I am Vincent *Pistacchia.*"

Quain stood fully erect and his eyes blazed. He raised his gun and said, "I told you to shut—" Quain

tilted his head to the side. "Pistacchia? Vincent Pistacchia ... Where have I heard that name before?"

"You killed my son. It took me a long time and a
great deal of money to find out how and who, but now I
know it was you."

Verducci could almost see Quain's mind working
like gears in an old clock. He took a step forward and
put an arm on his employer's shoulder.

"Vincent Pistacchia? Vinny Pistacchia? The astronaut? Vinny Pistacchia was your son?"

"He was, he is, he will be forever. You took his life,
but you can't take his memory."

"What are the odds?" Quain laughed.

"No odds, Quain. I've spent close to three million
American dollars to track you down."

Quain's laugh reduced to a smile. "I'm honored.
That's a lot of money."

"I will spend ten times that to see you dead."

"I would've thought you would have been tracking
Commander Tucker."

"Oh, I did. At first, I blamed him. At first, I hated
him, but the more I came to know, the more I came to
believe someone else must be behind my son's murder.
My investigators learned of MedSys; my investigators
learned of you."

"So what, old man? You are in a group that doesn't
give two cents for your sorrow or pain. All they want is
for me to let them go. What are you going to do? You
going to attack me, pops? You going to make a move?
Are you going to be responsible for the death of all those
around you and all those people outside?"

"Before I am in my grave, I will see you moldering in
the ground. Then you will be God's problem."

A subtle movement caught Verducci's eye. One of
the Secret Service agents had been slowly working his

way closer and closer to Quain. He had no idea what the man intended, but he knew that his boss's outburst was distracting Quain, and perhaps some good could come of that.

"You Italians are so poetic; you even make death sound important. Old man, you will be worm food long before I will. I'm not afraid of death, pops. It happens every day. Thirty thousand children die of starvation daily. What have you done about that? I'll tell you what you've done. You've done absolutely nothing. As we speak thousands are dying of cancer, heart disease, and thousands more in civil war."

"You care nothing about those people." Pistacchia's words were sharp as nails.

Quain nodded in agreement. "You're right, of course I don't care. That's my point. No one gets out of this life alive; not you, not me, and I don't care. I plan to live as long and as well as I can, and if people die in the process, that's just part of the price. It's not as if they weren't going to die anyway. All I've done is change the date."

"You make a profit from it," the old man spat.

Quain shrugged. "Well, there is that."

Quain spun on a heel, facing the Secret Service agent slowly moving closer. "I told you to stay put." Without another word, Quain raised the gun.

THIRTY-THREE

Jim Tolson felt the landing gear lock in place one hundred feet above the runway. Moments later, the *Condor* touched down and continued its taxi. As the plane slowed, he had time to look out the cockpit window and see the crowd in the bleachers standing, applauding, and pumping their fists in the air. He gave a polite wave.

He let the craft slow to just a few miles per hour, then turned it and taxied back to the hangar. The plan was for him to exit, spend a few moments waving at the gathered enthusiasts, and then walk to the back of the building to enter a private door to join the VIPs and others at Ground Control.

When he finally brought the plane to a standstill, he exchanged the cockpit for the concrete tarmac and moved toward the hangar. Jim found a guard and a stranger waiting for him. The guard he recognized as being part of the "rent-a-cops" that Roos retained for flight day, but he had never seen the other man before. He was tall, trim, and wore a grim expression.

"Something up?" Jim asked the guard.

"This man thinks so."

Before Jim could speak again the stranger said, "My name is Alderman, Garrett Alderman." He retrieved his wallet, and opened it, showing identification. "I own a private investigation business in Chicago. We do business only with large companies."

Jim frowned. "Sorry, buddy, I don't make those kinds of decisions here. Besides, this is rather an inappropriate time to be drumming up business."

Alderman didn't move. "I'm not here to drum up business. I need your help and I need it now."

Jim looked at the guard, who offered only a shrug. "It's all right; I'll talk to the man."

"Very good, sir," the guard said, then left to return to his post.

Jim studied the man for a few moments. "This had better be good."

"I wish it were good, but your security has been breached. I believe a man—a very dangerous man—is inside the main hangar. I further believe that everyone inside may be in great danger."

"I don't see how that's possible. We have guards everywhere. The place is crawling with them."

The stranger held his ground. "With all due respect, you have a host of undertrained, part-time mall security guards. None of them is armed and I doubt any of them has received training beyond the basics. Besides, those guards are on the outside of the hangar, not the inside."

Jim walked slowly around the building toward the back. The man named Alderman followed. "If there's a problem, I'm not aware of it."

"Have you spoken to Ground Control or whoever you talk to in there?"

That had been a bit of a puzzler. "Of course."

"Was it everything you expected?"

Jim hesitated, reluctant to admit that he had detected a note of stress and detachment in the Ground Control tech's voice, but beyond that, there was nothing indicating a problem. The pilot told Alderman so.

"What about communication with your spacecraft. Have you been able to maintain contact with them?"

Jim told him no. "Once the craft separate I lose contact with *Legacy*. Part of that is by design—too many people trying to speak to the spacecraft at one time muddles communication. Even in Ground Control, only one person can speak to the pilot at a time."

"You don't know if everyone is safe?"

"If they weren't, I would know about it." Jim started to turn.

"Then tell me why the monitors are blank."

Jim redirected his gaze to the monitors spaced out before the crowd—the monitors that allowed some of the guests a view of the video feed from *Legacy*. "It's possible we've lost the video feed for a short time. Such things happen."

"It happened during test flights?" Alderman was becoming edgy.

Jim was beginning to lose patience with the man. "Just what kind of bad guy do you think is in there?"

Alderman looked around, lowered his voice, and said, "I've been tracking Edwin Quain for well over a year. He's smart, he always has a plan, he never makes a mistake, and he has a loose gear up here." He tapped his head. "He also has a thing against Commander Tucker."

"What do you mean 'a thing'?"

"Quain was in the Navy but not for very long. He never finished his enlistment. Our background research shows that he was bounced out of the service for several things, including a complaint filed by then Lieutenant Tucker."

"What kind of complaint?"

"Quain was a pharmacist mate on the same aircraft carrier as Tucker. His name then was Edward Yates. Since then, he's had several identities. Someone told Tucker that Quain had been stealing medications— drugs—and selling them to other members of the crew. Tuck confronted him and with the help of Quain's supervisors was able to find Quain's stash."

"That would get a man booted pretty quick," Jim agreed. The pilot looked Alderman over again as if in doing so he would somehow be able to read the man's thoughts. "All right, let's assume for moment I believe you. What do you think your man is doing in there?"

"He has a sophisticated MO. His weapon of choice is a biological agent he created while working for my client's firm. Actually, I think he's created several bio-agents. Some work faster than others. Maybe he has a way of slowing the effects or speeding them up. I don't know for sure. Some have died quickly, while others die hours later."

"What firm?"

"I'm not going to tell you that. Truth is they're not really my client anymore."

Jim crossed his arms. "Did you get canned?"

A shadow of emotion passed over Alderman's face. "No, I would be fine with that. Quain killed the people who hired me. He used a biological agent spread on a letter that appeared to be from the IRS. I'm afraid he's planning on using the same agent inside the hangar."

"Look, pal, if this guy is such a bad man, why haven't you called the police? If what you say is true, there should be cops all over the place."

"We don't have time to argue about this. I've told you, Quain always has a plan. I'm the best there is in this business, and he's been evading me for well over a year. If cops show up, then I'm sure he will turn this into a hostage situation. I don't want that and neither do you. I can guarantee that several, maybe scores of people would die."

Jim placed his hands behind his back and began a slow stroll away from the hangar to the area behind the bleachers. He could hear the crowd talking eagerly, and a few complaining about the blacked-out monitors. Alderman walked by his side.

"There's something else you should know." The words came from Alderman with difficulty. "Quain is responsible for the *Atlantis* tragedy."

Jim stopped and stared Alderman in the eyes. "Investigators deemed that the accident was caused by a faulty dermal patch ..." Jim let his words trail off as the comment percolated to the forefront of his mind. Alderman was telling him who his client was without actually revealing the name. A mistake? No, Jim reasoned. "The company that made the dermal patch was investigated thoroughly and found guilty of producing a faulty product. As I recall, it was all due to the malfunction of a machine."

"You remember correctly."

"You're telling me somebody inside a company purposely poisoned the dermal patches that killed the *Atlantis* crew?"

"I have said no such thing."

Jim narrowed his eyes. "You're not denying it either."

"I don't think we have much time."

"Hey, mister?"

Jim looked down and saw a blond-haired boy no older than eight. He held a pen and piece of paper. Jim knew where this was headed. "Yes."

"You're the guy who flew the plane, right. The one that took the spaceship up?"

"That's me."

"Can I have your autograph?"

"Um, sure. Why not?" Jim took the pad and pen and began to write. A moment later, he handed it back to the child and as he did, he caught sight of something beneath the bleachers. "Is that your backpack, son?"

"No, sir. It belongs to the man who drove that car."
He pointed at a black Lincoln Continental. "He left it
there. I think it's his lunch or something. He was kind
of strange."

"Strange how?"

The voice shrugged. "I don't know. Maybe it was his
ear. He had a funny-looking ear. Anyway, thanks for
the autograph, mister."

Jim said the boy was welcome and looked at Alderman. The blood had drained from his face.

THIRTY-FOUR

Mayday, Mayday, Mayday. This is Benjamin Tucker,
commander of the commercial spacecraft *Legacy*.
I'm declaring a medical emergency. Repeat, I'm declaring a medical emergency. Request instructions for
landing."

The return to Earth had been painfully slow for
Tuck. Had the situation been otherwise, he would have
enjoyed what amounted to a leisurely fall. With family
and friends in danger, the cabin full of dying people,
he longed for the rapid descent of the old Space Shuttle. The computer provided the proper guidance and
brought *Legacy* into the thickening atmosphere in long
lingering loops. It had taken an eternity to reach this
point.

Tuck keyed the mike again and tried to raise the
control tower at Edwards Air Force Base fifty miles
away from where he had taken off that morning. He
had changed the radio frequency to match that used
by military aircraft. "Mayday, Mayday, Mayday. This is

Benjamin Tucker, commander of the commercial space-craft *Legacy*. I have a medical emergency. Repeat, I'm declaring a medical emergency. Request instructions for landing."

"*Stand by*, Legacy." Even over the headset, Tuck could tell the air traffic controller was confused. In his mind, he could see the man speaking to his superior and wondering if this were some kind of drill or joke. "*Um*, Legacy, *this is restricted airspace. You do not have clearance to land.*"

"Edwards, I repeat this is a medical emergency. I need ambulances standing by." Tuck wasn't going to take no for an answer. In point of fact, he couldn't take no for an answer.

"*Legacy, you are hereby ordered off approach. We rec-ommend SCLA.*"

Southern California Logistics Airport was too far and much too public. Not that it mattered now; Tuck had committed himself to Edwards Air Force Base the moment he entered information into the onboard com-puter. "Negative, Edwards. I am without power and in direct line with you. It's you or nothing."

"*Stand by*, Legacy."

"You're going to make some general very unhappy." Lance's words were soft but clear and the sound of them gave Tuck a moment of hope. His mind stumbled back to Jess and her fractured speech as the effects of the stroke that took her life manifested.

"Not a problem, buddy. I plan to blame you."

"Somehow ... I figured that."

Tuck reached to his copilot and gave him a pat on the shoulder. "Your job is to live to give me a bad time about it later."

"Count on it."

A new voice came over the headset. "Legacy, *this is Colonel Riggins. Did we hear you right? You said your name was Benjamin Tucker?*"

"Roger that, Edwards. Commander Benjamin Tucker, United States Navy, retired."

"My intel says you're supposed to be on the other side of the desert."

"Affirmative, Colonel Riggins. I hate to be a party crasher, but I need to sit down on your runway and I need to do it soon."

"Legacy, you're cleared to land on runway two-two. Please be advised that we have gusty winds at one thousand feet. Winds diminish below that. Copy that you have a medical emergency. How many souls on board?" The voice came from the traffic controller.

"Six souls. Two are crew. Five need immediate medical attention. Please be advised that we have a high-ranking member of government on board."

"High ranking? Understood, Legacy."

"Runway two-two, Edwards, and ... thanks."

"You may thank me in person, Commander Tucker— and you had better be Commander Tucker. Have I made myself clear?" Riggins had come online again.

"Colonel, there are days when I wish I wasn't."

As they descended toward the long wide runway of Edwards Air Force Base, Tuck hit the switch that lowered the landing gear. He heard them rumble and lock into place. The airspeed of *Legacy* immediately dropped.

Approaching from the east, Tuck could see the brown desert turn pale beige as he passed over the dry lakebed on approach to the runway. It was the long runway and the land-capable lakebed that made Edwards Air Force Base the alternate landing site for all Space

Shuttle missions. More than one crew had set down here; now *Legacy* was about to do the same.

As they dropped to a thousand feet of altitude, strong gusts of wind pushed the craft to the side and caused it to bounce in unsettling ways. The computer compensated beautifully and a few minutes later, it was clear flying. Tuck took hold of the controls and finished the landing manually. The *Legacy* rolled along the hard runway, and the sound of rubber tires on concrete reverberated through the spaceship. To Tuck, it sounded like music. A few minutes later, Tuck brought the craft to a halt.

Tuck released his harness and made his way to the door, where he released its locks, opened it, and extended the airstairs. Several military vehicles pulled alongside, as did the military police. Colonel Riggins was easy to identify both by bearing and in the way the men looked to him for leadership. Tuck didn't need to see the icon of rank.

Four medics started for the stairs, and Tuck extended a hand to stop them where they were. They looked confused. "Masks and gloves. There's something in their flight suits that made them sick. This is the same thing that happened on *Atlantis*. Watch their blood pressure." No sooner had the last syllable flown from Tuck's lips than he was down the stairs. The colonel was there to meet him.

"I hoped to meet you, Commander, but I never expected it would be like this. Let me get a medic to look at you."

"No need, Colonel, I'm fine, but I do need your help, and I need it fast."

• • •

Jim entered the code into the keypad lock on the rear door to the hangar and pushed it open, making certain it closed behind him. He entered like a man victorious from a successful flight, took several steps, and then stopped in his tracks. He stood frozen in place, taking in the scene. He already imagined what it would be like, but it was important for him to play his part. "Well, I feel like I'm interrupting something."

"That's because you are. Who are you?" The man asking the questions did so with a confident air about him. Jim took in every detail of his appearance and couldn't help noticing a banged-up ear on the side of the man's head.

"Maybe I should be asking you that."

"I'm your new host and I brought party games." He held up the gun and an electronic device that Jim couldn't quite make out. "Now once again, who are you?"

Jim didn't answer. He was afraid that if he appeared too cool he might tip his hand.

Roos spoke up. "His name is Jim Tolson, and he's the pilot for *Condor*. He's supposed to be here." Roos addressed Jim. "This man is holding us hostage. The woman with the backpack—well, the backpack has some kind of bio-bomb. The device the man is holding is a dead man's switch."

"Man, did I pick a lousy day to be punctual."

"That you did, Jimmy boy. That you did." Quain motioned with his gun. "I would feel a lot more comfortable if you joined the party."

Jim said nothing as he blended in with the others in the huddled crowd.

• • •

Myra's back hurt and the cold seeping in through the metal side of the container made the pain worse. Still she didn't move. Tucked under each arm and pulled tightly to her body were her children. Under her left arm, Penny quivered more from fear, Myra was certain, than from the cold. Beneath the other arm, Gary rested. He had not succumbed to tears, but she could feel the tension in his body. Myra wished she could do more, but embracing her children was the best she could offer. She decided that if she were to die, and her children along with her, then they would die in one another's arms. Although no ideas for saving themselves had come to her, she had not given up on the process. Her mind alternated between heartfelt prayer and cold logical reasoning, but despite her best efforts, no ideas came.

Benjamin had yet to sit down. Perhaps it was the old firefighter in him; perhaps it was because he was the only male adult available; but he had resisted the temptation to settle in one of the dark corners. He tested the doors a dozen times and used the meager light from Gary's cell phone to examine and reexamine the small pendulums of death that hung from the ceiling. Myra had no idea if what their abductor had said was true, but she didn't want to test the validity of his statements. Perhaps the glass vials contained nothing more dangerous than water. Then again, they might hold a horrible, torturous death.

"Any ideas, Grandpa?" It was the first words Gary had uttered in the last hour. Myra assumed it had been an hour. There was insufficient light for her to look at her watch and she saw no benefit in doing so.

"No, Son. Not yet. I feel like I'm overlooking something."

Myra could feel Penny raise her head. "Dad sometimes tells me I overthink things. He says that I'm always looking for the complex answer when the obvious would do the trick."

"He would know," Benjamin said. "I can't tell you how many times I told him that very thing when he was your age."

"I didn't know that." Penny's words were soft. "I wish I could hear him say it one more time."

"You will, kiddo." Benjamin's words carried a note of confidence.

"I'm scared, Grandpa. I feel all broken inside." The last few words came from Penny with tears.

"How can you be so calm, Grandpa?" Gary's voice was shaky. "Aren't you scared?"

"I'd be lying if I said I wasn't." Myra could hear Benjamin's footsteps as he continued to walk around the perimeter of the container. In her mind, she could see him taking one slow step after another, being certain he avoided the dangling vials. "I'm plenty scared."

"You don't show it," Gary said.

The footsteps stopped. "Many years ago, years before your father was born, I was assigned to my first fire station. I was wet behind the ears and eager to do my job. Just putting on my uniform made me feel brave. I thought I was really something.

"Then my first call came. It was a big house fire—we called them boomers. I was on the pumper. We rolled up and my feet had no more than hit the ground when the captain told me someone was inside and trapped in the flames. The captain looked at me, pointed, and said, 'Tucker, get in there.'" Benjamin paused, then said, "The smoke was thick and black and I could feel the heat from the flames all the way to the curb. It rolled out of broken windows. I had never seen flames licking at the eaves. I donned my tank and mask and then turned to face the house again."

"What did you do, Grandpa?" Penny asked.

"I was shaking in my boots, but then I noticed something: none of the other firefighters seemed afraid. They just went about their business. They did their jobs. They did what was required of them. So I pretended not to be afraid, and I went into the house."

Gary straightened. "Did you save the man trapped inside?"

Benjamin gave an actor's laugh. "Turns out, there wasn't anyone trapped inside after all. Nonetheless, it did me a world of good to stare fear in the eye and still do my job. Later, a guy on my rig took me aside."

"What did he say, Grandpa?" Penny's voice had strengthened.

"He asked if I had been afraid and I admitted to it. 'Good,' he said. 'Because the day you stop being afraid is the day you retire.' He said at such a blaze, every firefighter was frightened and that I shouldn't trust anyone who wasn't. It was a good lesson—and he taught me something even more important. He's the one that led me to faith in Christ. He said that there were many courageous men in the world, but a courageous man with faith was unstoppable. I never forgot that, and I don't want you to forget it either. Got that?"

Gary and Penny said they did.

"Tell you something else; everyone experiences death. Our faith enables us to face it with courage."

Myra heard the old man approach and judging by the source of his voice knew he had squatted down next to them. He spoke softly. "We're not giving up. Everyone dies, but that doesn't mean today is our day.

We need to use the faith, the courage, and the brains God gave us."

Myra heard him stand again. "Thanks, Dad. That helped."

Benjamin didn't respond. Instead, he resumed his pacing, and once again, Myra could hear his footfalls on the metal floor.

"Have you figured out what those things are, Grandpa?" Gary sat straight, pulling away from Myra. She resisted the urge to pull him back in place.

"I don't know, Gary. I've been giving it a lot of thought. The driver told us not to touch them and implied that doing so would be deadly. That means that these glass vials hold some kind of chemical or poison. I've been afraid to touch them because someone who's gone through this much trouble must have assumed that we would try just that. My concern is if I touch one the others will fall."

Benjamin paced a little more, then stopped. "Why would he go through such an elaborate scheme? If he just wanted to kill us, he could have driven us to this isolated spot, shot us, and been done with it, but he didn't. He found this container here or maybe he had it put here, but why imprison us? Why set up these vials?"

Myra had not thought about these things and Benjamin's questions bored into her mind. "It's Tuck, isn't it? It's the only thing that makes sense. It must have something to do with today's space flight."

"So we're hostages." Benjamin's words were a statement, not a question. "That means he plans to keep us alive until he doesn't need us any longer. That's why these things haven't dropped yet."

"So he's going to release this after he gets what he wants?"

"No, Penny, I wish it were true." Benjamin's words hung heavy in the air. "I don't think these vials are just for us. I think he intends to kill us—and whoever tries to rescue us."

Myra listened to the conversation and her mind flew to her husband, who she knew must be miles away in space.

"Why keep us alive?" Myra asked. "Why not just kill us and store our bodies in here? If he's after Tuck, then he could tell him that we were still alive even though we weren't."

"He's not sane, Myra. No one does this kind of thing, goes to these lengths without being at least a little batty." Benjamin's voice faded, then, "Maybe he gets some kind of thrill out of all this, like those serial killers who leave clues for the police or send them letters. It's a way to make people suffer longer." He sighed. "The reason doesn't matter now. Escaping does."

Myra agreed. She started a new prayer.

Her prayer was interrupted.

"Did you hear that?" Benjamin asked. He stopped his pacing.

Myra strained her ears to catch a sense of whatever Benjamin had heard.

"I hear it." Gary's words echoed in the container. "What is it?"

Before Benjamin could answer, Myra heard a distant thumping. At first, she thought she heard thunder, but then noticed the sound came in rhythmic pulses. "Helicopters?"

"Yes," Benjamin said. "From the sound of them they're big—maybe military helicopters."

"When Dad and I came out here to visit Mr. Roos, he told me that he had been stationed at Edwards Air Force Base. He said it wasn't far from where Mr. Roos did his work." There was excitement in Gary's voice.

"He's right, Edwards is close by."

Penny asked, "Is it Dad? Is he coming to save us?"

Myra could hear Benjamin take a deep breath. "I pray so, but it could just be a routine flight. There's no way for us to tell, no way for us to signal them."

The *thumpa-thumpa* of the sound grew louder, and Myra could feel vibration through the metal skin of the container.

"Oh no," Benjamin whispered.

Myra returned her gaze to the direction of his voice and saw her father-in-law activate the cell phone again. He raised the dim light to one of the vials. What she saw made her courage drain from her.

"This is not good," Benjamin said with a calm that belied the situation.

Myra's eyes fixed on the same thing as Benjamin's. The vials that dangled like pendulums on a string were vibrating in resonance with the sound made by the powerful rotors of approaching helicopters.

Benjamin moved the light to another vial and Myra saw the same terrifying sight: a delicate glass container dancing to the music of heavy motors.

If the helicopters get any closer ... Myra couldn't finish the thought.

• • •

Colonel Riggins's voice stabbed Tuck's ear as the officer shouted into the onboard communication system. "Could that be it?"

"Where?" Tuck tried to keep his wishful thinking in check.

"Two o'clock off our heading—on the ground—a structure."

Raising binoculars to his eyes, Tuck looked in the direction that Riggins had indicated. It took a moment, but he soon locked his sights on a worse-for-wear metal box. Its peeling white paint stood in contrast to the taupe ground. Through the powerful lenses of the binoculars, Tuck studied every inch that he could see from a low-flying CH–53E Super Stallion helicopter. The aircraft belonged to the Marine Heavy Helicopter Squadron–769 stationed at Edwards. At the controls sat a man who looked too young to be manhandling such a large craft. At the moment, that didn't matter to Tuck; he felt grateful that Riggins had been able to call in favors with the squadron commander.

"It looks like a storage container," Tucker said. "I can see tire marks leading to the door."

The pilot chimed in. "I just got word that our second chopper has found a van on the roadside. They could see a body in the passenger seat from the air. They've landed and investigated: one male, dead."

Tuck felt sick with worry. "Can they describe the man?" Tuck's thoughts ran to his father.

"Stand by one, Commander." A moment later, "Male Caucasian, midforties, short, and thick build." Another moment ticked by before the pilot asked, "I hate to ask, but does that sound like one of yours, Commander?"

A wave of relief rushed over Tuck, followed by another wave of guilt. The description did not fit any member of his family, but nonetheless, a man lay dead in the desert. "No." Tuck tried to picture the image he'd seen over the video monitor. He could see his family and could tell that they were in some kind of artificial surroundings, but the camera angle was too tight for him to see anything more than darkness behind them. Could they have been confined in the container below? Tuck knew only one way to find out. "Let's take her down, Colonel."

The helicopter began a slow descent fifty yards away from the large metal box. The rotor blast kicked up dust and sand, and Tuck could feel the vibration of the powerful engine run through his body. If his family were indeed trapped inside that container, they would feel and hear his arrival.

THIRTY-FIVE

I asked a straightforward question!" Quain's temper flared. A few feet away from where he stood lay the bleeding bodies of the two Secret Service men. Quain had not wanted to use the gun. There was always the risk of a gunshot being heard, but when he caught sight of the Secret Service agent slowly and foolishly making his way toward him, Quain did the only thing he could. The percussion of the 9mm blast rolled through the empty space of the hangar. The first Secret Service agent staggered back, clutched at his chest, then dropped to the concrete floor. Quain gave no thought to his next action: he turned and squeezed off another round, striking a second agent in the left shoulder. The man spun, cried in pain, and dropped to his knees.

At the first shot, nearly everyone in the hangar hit the ground. Several screamed, women wept, as did several men. Quain gazed over the frightened masses. Some covered their heads as if the bomb had gone off; others huddled on their knees as if in prayer. Only

Tammy remained standing, shivering as if she stood on an Antarctic plateau with nothing more than a T-shirt and shorts to protect against the icy wind. Most amusing to Quain was the way old man Pistacchia stared at him. The man with him—a chauffeur, his guard, his personal assistant, whatever he was—had done his best to cover the old man's body with his own.

It was then that Quain had noticed the video feed from *Legacy* had gone black. He had been standing over Roos's shoulder watching every keystroke as he transferred money from one offshore account to Quain's. He turned to the three people seated at the control panel and asked, "What happened to the video?" No one answered.

Quain moved closer, put his face close to the communication tech's ear, and shouted at the top of his lungs, *"What happened to the video feed?"*

The man shivered in fear. "I don't know. It just went blank."

Quain stood erect. "When did it go blank?"

This time, he didn't have to ask twice. "Maybe five minutes ago."

Quain nodded as if mulling over the statement. "Listen up, people. This man is lying to me, and it's about to get you killed." He held up the dead-man's switch so that everyone in the room could witness his next act.

He released the switch.

The moment he did a piercing beep emanated from the backpack hanging from the frightened woman's shoulders. Her limbs shook as if suddenly struck by palsy.

"No, no, no, no. Please, please. Don't kill me. No, no, no."

• • •

Before the helicopter had fully touched down, Tuck was out the door and sprinting toward the battered container. "Myra! Dad? Kids?" he shouted the words while still ten yards from his destination. His heart no longer just beat, it pounded against his chest with rib-cracking intensity. He stopped just two feet away from the container and looked down. Footprints. Shoe prints of various sizes. Tuck didn't consider himself an expert in tracking, but he knew enough to know that four or more people had been standing here not long before.

"Myra? *Myra!*"

A muted voice: "Tuck! We're in here."

"Are you all right?" Tuck put his face close to the doors.

"Unharmed. Scared. It's wonderful to hear your voice. The kids are here. Dad is here."

Tuck looked down at the doors and saw that the two handles that opened the container were bound with a large Yale lock. "Hang tight, I'll be right back."

"Tuck ... wait ..."

Tuck didn't wait for the rest of it. He sprinted to the helicopter. Riggins met him halfway. "They're in the container. There's a lock on the doors. Is there anything on the chopper I can use to break the lock?"

Riggins said, "I don't know, but I know how to find out." He and Tuck ran through the soft dirt toward the chopper. What they found was a disappointment.

"We have a toolkit and a hacksaw; what you really need are bolt cutters." The pilot and the copilot moved to the back of the craft and opened a toolkit. "The hacksaw might do the job, but it's going to take some time. Wait, I have a better idea. We just got a report from our other helicopter. The police and fire department have arrived at the hangar. I know the fire department carries bolt cutters on their trucks."

"How long?" Tuck asked.

The pilot smiled. "A lot less time than it will take you to saw through a lock."

Riggins looked at the man. "Make it happen."

"Will do."

• • •

The piercing beeps stopped five seconds later as Quain once again pressed his thumb upon the dead man's switch. Verducci had watched it all with a kind of detachment like a theatergoer watches a play.

Five seconds. He let it run five seconds before pushing the button again. There's a delay.

Verducci stood, and then carefully helped his employer rise to his feet. Pistacchia showed no signs of fear. The old man was as unshakable as concrete.

"Next time, folks, I won't stop the little countdown. Is that clear?"

Several people said, "Clear."

Once again, Quain stepped to the young man at the control panel. "How long have the monitors been blank?"

"I don't know. They went dark not long after you spoke to Commander Tucker."

Quain released a hot stream of obscenities. He turned to Roos, who still hovered over the laptop. "If you're not done by now, I will assume you're stalling."

"It's done," Roos said almost too softly to hear. "It takes time to transfer all six accounts. Offshore banking requires a lot of hoop jumping. But then again, I assume you already know that."

"I know everything I need to know." He moved to the laptop computer that Roos had been using and examined the screen. It appeared to Verducci that the man was satisfied. "Turn it off. I don't want you using the Internet to call for help." As soon as Roos had powered down the laptop, Quain addressed the group. "All right, who are the jet jockeys that fly the business jet?"

"There you may have a problem." The newest man in the group, the pilot of *Condor*, stepped forward. "They're not here."

"Explain."

"This is a VIP gathering," Jim Tolson said. "In my book every pilot is a VIP, but unfortunately these guys weren't invited to the party. However, they are outside with the others. You want me to go get them?"

Verducci had never seen a man frown as much as Quain did at that moment.

Tolson spoke up. "If not, then I'm your man."

"You're qualified to fly the business jet?" Quain looked doubtful.

"Listen, buddy, I'm clear to fly everything. In case you've forgotten, I just flew *Condor* to near-record altitudes. I think I can handle a business jet."

"Then that's the way it's going to be. Don't mess with me. Remember, I still have a way of killing everyone here."

"You'll get no trouble from me. I know how to take orders."

• • •

It took only ten minutes for the second helicopter to arrive and for one of the crewmen to emerge with bolt cutters in one hand and a sledgehammer in the other. Tuck allowed himself a few moments of hope.

The crewman reported to Colonel Riggins and Tuck, "The fire department is on its way, just in case these don't do the trick. There was nothing for them to do there. California Highway Patrol will stay with the van and the body until the medical examiner and homicide arrives."

It appeared that the man was going to give a longer report, but Tuck was in no mood to listen. He seized the bolt cutters and jogged to the container. By the time he had the powerful jaws of the scissorslike device clamped around the hardened steel of the lock, Riggins and his crewmen had joined him. It took Tuck two tries, but the lock gave way. Handing the bolt cutters to Riggins, Tuck quickly removed the lock, slipped open the latch, and swung the two doors wide. What he saw inside made his breath catch.

Tuck's family stood in line, each facing the same wall of the container, each standing with his or her hands extended. He took a step closer and examined what they cupped in their palms. Each held a small glass bottle.

Myra was the first in line, and she squinted through nearly closed eyes as the bright light of the desert sun poured into the makeshift prison.

"What—?"

Tuck quieted the Colonel with a raised hand. "Um, hi, sweetheart."

"Hi yourself, good lookin'." Her words sounded sweet to his ears, but he knew something was wrong. He turned to Riggins. "You better let me handle this."

With deliberate steps, Tuck walked into the container and stood before his wife. "Is that a present for me?" He studied the tiny glass bottle carefully, but could make no sense of it. It had a screw-top lid and a wire hanging from it. He looked up and could see where the distal end of the wire had connected to the ceiling.

"He told us these vials contain something that would kill us." Her hands began to shake.

Tuck leaned forward and kissed her on the forehead. "If you don't mind, I think I'll take that."

"Be careful."

"You know me, I'm always careful." As far as Tuck was concerned, the glass objects contained nitroglycerin. He doubted it would explode in his hands, but he treated it as if it would. As if in slow motion, he lifted the object from her palms and took it in his own hands. "Walk outside, and don't stop until you're at least halfway between us and the helicopter. Understand?"

"I'm not leaving without the children."

"You're going to do exactly as I say." The order came in the softest tone. "The kids will be right behind you. Now go."

Myra hesitated only a moment before stepping from the shadowed container into the bright sun. Tuck turned, moved to the wall behind him, and gently set the vial on the metal floor. He moved to Penny. Tears flowed down her cheeks and dripped to her blouse; her lower lip trembled faster than Tuck thought possible.

"Hi ... hi, Dad." Had he not feared for her life and the life of the others he might've taken a moment to feel proud of her courage.

"Hi, baby. How are you?" As with Myra, he studied the object in his daughter's hand. It appeared to be the same as the one Myra had held.

"Scared. Real scared."

"Yeah, you've had a rough day. You saw what Mom and I did?"

"Yes."

"Okay, we're going to do the same thing. I'm going to take this thing from you, and then you're going to slowly and gently walk outside. Go to your mother."

"But what about you?"

"I'll be out soon to collect hugs from everybody. Got a hug for your old man?"

"I've got a thousand of them." She began to cry harder, and her hands shook. Tuck didn't waste another second; he reached forward and removed the object. As soon as he turned, he heard Penny leave. Sweat was forming on his brow and dripping into his eyes, stinging and blurring his vision.

He rose again and turned to Gary. His son stood like a statue, but Tuck could tell the boy was terrified. "I can't leave you alone for a minute," Tuck said with a slight laugh. "I can't even leave the planet without you getting into trouble."

"I'm starved for attention." Gary's words were almost too quiet to hear.

"You know the drill, right?"

Gary looked into his dad's eyes, and for a moment, Tuck thought his knees would give way. "Yeah, I know. You take it and I leave."

"Just make your steps soft and light, like a cat."

Gary nodded. "Like a ninja." Tuck knew the boy was doing his best to stay brave.

With the same gentle caution as before, Tucker removed the small bottle from his son's hand, turned, and set it on the floor with the others. By the time he stood from his crouch, Gary was gone and he could see him running toward his mother. Tuck moved to his father.

"I've been praying for you, Son. Praying real hard."

"It just so happens I've been praying for you too. I take it these things were spaced out along the ceiling."

Benjamin said they were. "I knew I couldn't catch them all, and when we heard the helicopters and felt the container begin to shake, I knew we were in for real trouble. Having everyone lined up to catch these things was the only thing I could think of."

"You always could think on your feet. Okay, we're going to do the same thing."

"No. I think I can set this one down myself. If something goes wrong, then better that it should happen to me than to you. Children need their father."

Tuck studied his father for a moment then said, "Which is precisely why I'm willing to take that from you. I still need you and don't think about arguing—I brought the Air Force and the Marines with me."

"Still rebellious at your age." Benjamin lifted his hands and Tuck took the vial. As before, he set it on the uneven metal floor once his dad was clear. He began a slow egress. The moment his trailing foot passed the threshold, Riggins and a crewman closed the doors and latched them. Tuck took a couple of steps, stopped, bent forward, and placed his hands on his knees. He drew several long breaths.

Riggins barked an order to the nearest Marine. "I want this thing secured, and I want a guard on it until we know what's in there. No one is to approach it. Is that clear?"

"Crystal clear, sir."

Tuck straightened, then jogged to his family, who met him with tears and warm embraces.

The feel of his family in his arms struck a chord deep in Tuck's soul—and from that soul came a heartfelt prayer of thanksgiving.

Tuck began to weep.

THIRTY-SIX

Everyone on the floor. Everyone but you, Tammy. You get in the middle of everyone." Quain marched around the Ground Control console, the dead man's switch in his right hand and the 9mm pistol in the other. He jerked the pistol from side to side and up and down, pointing at a different head every few seconds. He was becoming more animated and tense.

Verducci helped Pistacchia to the floor, and he could see from the old man's eyes that it was the last thing he wanted to do. Since he first set eyes on Quain, Pistacchia had fixed his gaze like a hawk circling its prey on the ground. Had Pistacchia been younger, stronger, faster, he almost certainly would have charged Quain.

Verducci took his time helping the old man to the floor in hopes that Quain would approach in an effort to intimidate him. Then he would make his move. Quain might be smart, he might be devious, he was certainly insane, but Verducci was certain he was much faster than Quain was.

Quain didn't take the bait. "I can shoot the old man from here, and if that isn't enough motivation I can shoot someone else. Now get on the floor."

Pistacchia complied, but Verducci was sure he could feel the heat of the old man's anger radiate from his skin. Verducci lay on the floor next to his employer. His head raised slightly, just enough to keep an eye on Quain.

"All right, ladies and gentlemen. One quick reminder. This little device that I hold has quite a range. If I see anyone leave this building before that jet is in the air, I'll release the button, and then you can all kiss your lives good-bye."

Roos spoke up, "How do we know you won't do it anyway?"

Quain smiled. "You don't." He took one last look around the room, then said, "You, pilot man, let's go."

Verducci watched the man named Jim Tolson rise to his knees and then to his feet. "I assume you want to use the back door."

"No, Einstein. We are going to use the one closest to the jet and that's at the front of the building right next to where it's parked. Move out."

Tammy was on the verge of a nervous breakdown. "What about me? Can I take this off? Please, I can't take it anymore."

"It stays right where it is."

Jim Tolson and Quain disappeared through the door. The moment the door hit the jamb, Verducci was on his feet. He approached Tammy. "Give me that backpack."

Gratefully, she let it slip from her shoulders and he took it.

"What are you doing?" someone said. "He might come back."

"We have to get this thing out of here," Verducci snapped.

From outside came the sound of jet engines winding to a start. At that moment, the sound of loud beeping cut through the air.

Tammy screamed, and the crowd backed away. Verducci took the bag and ran. *Five seconds. Five seconds.* He seized the first opportunity he saw: a door with the words *Rest Room* on it.

He fell into the room, landed hard, and had just enough time to kick the door closed.

Something erupted in his face.

He rolled his body to back against the door—a human doorstop. He lifted his arms, saw them covered in an oily powder.

He was finding it hard to breathe.

• • •

The Cessna Citation rolled along the tarmac, its powerful dual jet engines warming up for flight. Jim sat at the controls and hoped that his plan would work. He had to trust a man he had never met before, and that made him uncomfortable.

"Let's you and me get something straight, partner." Quain's words dripped with threat. He placed the barrel of the 9mm behind Jim's ear. Jim could smell the acrid odor of spent gunpowder. "You start to play any games with me, and I'll give you a copper-clad memento to remember me by."

"Oh, I think you're quite memorable enough."

"Don't use the radio; just take off."

"You're the boss. I need to move to the end of the runway. This baby needs a little longer runway than most."

He caught Quain looking at him like a biologist who has found some new form of life. "I would think a modern plane like this would need *less* runway."

Jim shrugged. "I'll give it a try if you want, but there's a good chance we will run off the pavement and into the sand. That won't be good for anyone." As he spoke, he turned to face his abductor and noticed that the dead man's switch was no longer in his hand. He said nothing but Quain caught his gaze.

"I let go of that thing the moment you started the engines. You have no reason to be a hero now. That batch was particularly toxic; those who aren't already dead will be in the next few minutes."

Jim thought of the backpack under the bleachers—the backpack he and Alderman had carefully locked in the empty Lincoln Continental before Jim entered the hangar. "Why should I bother taking off?"

"Because you have no more desire to die than I do."

Jim caught the movement out of the corner of his eye and immediately turned to look out the windscreen. "I have no desire to let a mass murderer go free either. And let's face it, you're not going to let me live when we get to wherever we're going."

"You might be right about that, but then again, I have my moments of reason."

"Had any recently?"

The thud was followed by a sting as Quain's gun hit Jim on the side of the face, opening a gash that released a warm thick fluid. "I find pain a great motivator, don't you?"

"I know I do." The voice came from behind Quain, who spun toward the unexpected passenger. The blow landed square on Quain's nose. Instinctively, Quain raised a hand to his face, and the next punch landed hard and deep in his stomach.

Moving as fast as his hands would allow, Jim unbuckled his safety harness, pressed on the pedals to bring the business jet to a stop, and switched off the engines. He started to turn when something hot hit him in the right shoulder. He felt the bullet leave his stomach. Instinctively his hands reached for his abdomen and a moment later, he saw them covered in blood.

Jim slipped back into his seat and watched as a bright high desert day narrowed to a tunnel of darkness, then black.

• • •

Alderman's hand ached from the first punch. He wasted no time thinking about it, but he knew something was broken. Fire raced from his knuckles up his arm, but that didn't prevent him from throwing a punch to the midsection of the man he had tracked for so long. Quain backstepped into the cockpit and tried to raise the gun. Alderman seized Quain's gun hand and pushed the muzzle of the weapon away.

"My name is Alderman ... and I have been looking for you—" He jabbed a knee to Quain's inner thigh and heard him cry in pain, but didn't release the weapon. If Alderman weakened for just a moment, Quain would put a bullet in his head. Alderman pushed Quain back to the cockpit door, hoping Tolson could help.

The gun went off.

Tolson screamed in pain.

"Tolson? Tolson!"

The sudden discharge and the realization the accidental firing had hit Tolson made Alderman pause for a second—a second too long. Quain roared in anger and forced his way forward. First Alderman felt a knee strike him at the belt, then another caught him in the groin. Despite the pain, Alderman tried to yank the gun from Quain's hand. His side flared with pain as his opponent's fist plunged into his side. White sparkles filled his eyes. He couldn't breathe. He tried to straighten but his body wouldn't cooperate. He felt a hand on the back of his head, then caught sight of Quain's knee just before it landed hard on his face.

Blood ran from his mouth and nose; his vision flashed with pain. Alderman had to get himself together if he were to survive. He stood motionless for a moment and waited for what he knew Quain would do, what any man with a gun would do. Quain lifted the weapon and pulled the trigger, but Alderman had anticipated the move, and despite the protestations of his body, he turned to the side as he saw the trigger finger tighten. The bullet missed him by less than an inch, but a miss was a miss.

Alderman shot out his right hand and seized the weapon, twisting it up and back. The next second, he brought his left hand to the gun. He lifted until the barrel pointed to the ceiling. It went off, but Alderman refused to surrender his grip.

"I'm going to kill you—" Quain snarled.

Alderman brought a knee hard to his thigh, then again to the man's knee. The weapon discharged again as Alderman struggled to wrestle it away.

Quain proved stronger than Alderman had imagined. He decided on a dangerous move. Releasing the gun with his right hand, Alderman drove his elbow into Quain's already broken nose. The scream rolled through the cabin, but Quain refused to loosen his grip. Alderman groped Quain's face with his free hand until he found his mark. He pressed his thumb into the man's eye. With a scream of pain, Quain released the weapon and Alderman pulled it away. Quain took a step back to free himself from Alderman's thumb, then swung a right cross that caught him hard on the cheekbone. Alderman's head snapped to the side.

"I don't need a gun to finish you." Quain took another step forward and landed a punishing body shot. Alderman dropped to a knee and struggled to draw even a short breath.

He felt the next punch, then the next. Alderman lost consciousness a second after his head bounced on the thinly carpeted deck.

• • •

Tuck had had to peel his family from him. "I have one more thing to do." They resisted and he longed for nothing more than to ride with them back to Edwards, but other lives were at stake.

The vision of them staring at him as the helicopter took flight haunted him. He had broken their hearts again, and the guilt of it ate at him like a piranha. As they crossed the short air distance from the container to the SpaceVentures complex, something drew his attention to the present.

"Someone has moved the Citation." Tuck was so close to hanging out the open door of the Super Stallion that Riggins had taken hold of his arm.

"Hey, Commander?" It was the pilot. "I'm getting word from Edwards that someone has been trying to reach you over your aircraft ... spacecraft radio."

"Is there a message?" Tuck turned his attention to the pilot who flew the large helicopter just a few hundred feet above the ground. "Roger. Someone named Roos is hailing you."

"Ask your man to get a sit rep."

"Will do, Commander."

Tuck again leaned out the open door. He could feel the powerful downdraft of the rotors. If it weren't for the communications in the helmet he wore, Tuck wouldn't be able to hear a word.

"Commander, a man named Roos says everyone in the hangar is fine. Someone named Quain and Jim Tolson have taken off in the business jet. He said Quain is armed."

"You know those names?" Riggins asked.

"Tolson is one of the good guys. Quain is the man we want. I'm guessing that he took Jim hostage to fly the jet."

"Then why isn't it moving?"

"You don't know Jim." Before Tuck could start another sentence, the Citation's door opened and the automatic airstairs descended. A second later, a man appeared—the man who had driven him to the launch and who had abducted his family. He looked dazed, and even at a distance Tuck could see he was bloodied. He staggered down two steps, then took note of the helicopter.

"Watch it, he's got a gun!" Tuck ducked his head inside just in time. A round bounced off the skin of the copter in a glancing blow. Tuck moved to another window as the chopper banked away.

"Should have brought a gunner, Colonel."

Riggins swore. "I would have had I known we were going to be shot at."

"Wait," Tuck shouted. "He's down." Just before the craft banked, Tuck saw another man appear at the door, pause, and then leap toward Quain just as he pulled the trigger. He had just enough time to see both men tumble down the steps and onto the runway. "Down, put us down."

"Colonel?" The pilot looked to Riggins for confirmation.

"Put her down, Marine, and make it quick."

The helicopter was still two feet off the runway when Tuck sprang from it and charged the two men. Twenty feet away, he recognized Jim Tolson and could see he was injured. Quain punched him several times, punches that landed without the slightest defense from Jim. Quain struggled to his feet, raised the handgun, and aimed at Jim's head.

To Tuck, it felt as if he had tackled a barrel of concrete, but he put all he had into it. He and Quain hit the ground hard, Quain landing face first, and Tuck rolling over him. Pain ricocheted through his body, but he forced himself to rise and charge again. Quain still had the gun and tried to raise it. Tuck launched his body at the assailant again. This time, he managed to hold onto the man. Tuck's head hit the concrete and the edges of his vision darkened. He shook his head to drive the pending unconsciousness away. Still rattled, it took a moment for him to notice that someone else had joined him. He looked up to see Colonel Riggins with a well-placed boot on Quain's wrist.

"Can you hold him?"

"Oh, yeah. No problem. He's not going anywhere."

Tuck moved to Jim, who lay gazing up into the darkening blue sky. Blood slowly pooled beneath his right shoulder and oozed from the exit wound in his stomach.

"Did ... did you get 'im, Tuck?"

"We got him, Jim. You did great."

"I wish I ... could fly one more time ..."

"Stay with me, Jim. You stay with me. Do you hear?" Tuck slapped his friend's face.

"Where never lark ... nor even eagle flew ... And, while with silent lifting mind I've trod ..." He coughed blood.

Tears ran hot down Tuck's cheeks. He tried to finish the poem that had meant so much to him and any pilot: "The high, untrespassed sanctity of space, Put out my hand and ...

"... and touched the face of God." Jim raised a hand to the sky. It dropped to the ground.

"No. No." Tuck lowered his head. "Not again." He pulled Jim's head back, opened his mouth, placed his own mouth over his friend's, and blew. He started chest compression. "One ... two ... three ..." Every compression reminded him of the same act he performed on Jess on the flight deck of *Atlantis*. Now as then, he prayed between every compression and every breath. *Please, God.*

EPILOGUE

SIX MONTHS LATER

The feast of finger foods were once again served by Ted Roos. This time the gathering was small and the only people present were there by special invitation.

"Nice spread, Mr. Roos," Riggins said.

"Eat up. I owe you and Commander Tucker a great deal."

"Careful who you tell to eat up. Those Marines over there will lick the plates clean."

Roos laughed. "Let them. They all played a part in saving lives and my business."

"They're good men—just don't let them know an Air Force colonel said so." Riggins popped a deviled egg in his mouth. "So no crowds this time?"

Roos shook his head. "No, this is my way of saying thanks."

"I can think of another way. I'm still a little confused. What was Quain's motive?"

"Money and revenge. His skills in synthetic biology allowed him to create a bioagent that he could use to kill an individual or thousands at a time. That made it valuable to many people around the world. Of course, he couldn't sell it here, since biological warfare is governed in the US by strict treaty—at least technically."

"Technically."

"Anyway, he had several buyers including North Korea, a couple of Middle Eastern players, and others. However, the money he was asking demanded proof of usability. So, driven by that ego of his, he set up an impossible assassination: killing astronauts two hundred miles in space. He did it by contaminating dermal patches manufactured by MedSys. Since he worked there, it was an easy thing for him to do. Dermal patches release their meds slowly, so Tuck and the others wouldn't feel the effects of the bioagent until well into the mission."

"Except Commander Tucker lived."

"The feds are guessing that that was a sore spot. While he did manage to kill most of his targets, he failed with the key player. I doubt his buyers knew this, but he had borne a grudge against Tuck for years. Tuck tells me he had long forgotten about it. He said the ear should have been a clue, but he never made the connection."

"So to get top dollar, he decided to prove his product by killing all the members of your first official flight?"

"Except he wanted Tuck alive. Quain was a sick man. He decided that making Tuck suffer was more fun than killing him, and he could still prove his point by killing only those he wanted to."

"So he tried to take out the secretary of state?" Riggins took a sip from a water bottle and declined the temptation of champagne.

"Burke was just one target. The feds think Quain was paid for that as well as for Daki Abe. Certain Chinese interests had a problem with the Japanese businessman's tactics. They wanted him out of the way."

"It's all nuts. The world is nuts. This guy takes money from US enemies, creates a weapon of death, and still has time to try and bleed you dry."

"And he almost did it. I transferred every dollar I had to his offshore accounts."

"He certainly covered his bases. The man had to be insane."

"Fortunately, there are still some good people in the world." Roos looked at his watch. "Come on, it's almost time."

"It's hard to believe you're up and running again in just six months." Riggins strolled to the large monitors in the hangar.

"The vehicles were fine ... well, my jet took a bit of a beating, but repairs were made. The hard part was clearing my name. Once that was done, sponsors began to come forward, and we're back in business."

"What about your first passengers? I read about the lawsuit."

"Only Ginny Lin sued, and we settled out of court. Burke wants to fly again, as do Donnelly and Abe. In fact, Abe has contributed a substantial amount of money to keep things going. Your medics and the doctors did a great job keeping them alive. It's fortunate that Tuck reentered when he did. Had he waited as Quain demanded, the passengers would have all died in space."

"Just like on *Atlantis*."

Roos agreed. "I think that was one of Quain's points. He wanted Tuck to relive the whole tragedy. We owe Tuck a lot, and Jim. And of course, we owe Verducci our very lives. Not many men will sacrifice themselves for strangers."

Colonel Riggins reached for another deviled egg. "Don't forget Alderman, another of Quain's victims."

"He died from the beating Quain gave him. Sad really. He saved a lot of lives."

Riggins pursed his lips. "You've done an amazing thing here. I don't think I'll ever get used to the idea of space tourism. I hate flying airliners."

Roos laughed. "Everyone hates flying airliners."

• • •

"All right, folks. Here we go. The next few minutes will be the most exciting ride of your life." Lance switched the mike so he could talk to Tuck without others hearing.

"I have an odd sense of déjà vu."

"Considering all you've been through, it's a good feeling to have. You were one sick puppy for a while."

"Thanks to you, it wasn't permanent."

"Don't get mushy on me now. It'll ruin your reputation."

"Let it. For once in my life, I don't mind riding second seat." Lance reached across the console and gave Tuck a friendly slug on the shoulder.

"Pitching now. Stand by for release."

Jim Tolson's voice sounded good to Tuck. It had taken two surgeries, a week in the hospital, and three months of physical rehab, but Jim was back at the controls of *Condor*. The bullet that had entered his shoulder had pierced his lung and large intestine but had missed the descending aorta—by an inch.

"Oh, and Tuck, this time try and land at the right airfield."

"Will do, Jim. Will do."

A few moments later, *Legacy* dropped from beneath *Condor* and did a ten-second freefall to the excited squeals of the passengers.

The rockets engaged, propelling *Legacy* to space. Once the fuel had depleted and they were in low-Earth orbit, Lance began his spiel. Ten minutes later, he freed the passengers to release their harnesses and enjoy zero-G. One passenger floated to the cockpit and raised her visor.

"I think I understand now, Dad. I think I finally get it. It is so beautiful." Penny's smile matched her father's.

"Hey, you're not letting her drive, are you?" Gary said.

"Shut up, squirt." Penny pushed back to the cabin.

"Do they always bicker like that?" Lance asked.

"Yeah. Doesn't it sound wonderful?" Tuck looked over the indicators and gauges. "Say, Lance—"

"Of course, I will. Go back there and enjoy your family for a while."

Tuck was out of the harness in seconds. "No speeding, okay."

"No promises, Tuck. No promises."

Finder's Fee

Alton Gansky,
Bestselling Suspense Author

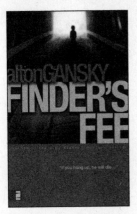

"If you do not do exactly as I instruct, he will die."

A terrifying phone call sweeps rich and powerful businesswoman Judith Find into a desperate search for a kidnapped boy. If she involves the authorities, the child will die ... and "The Puppeteer" will reveal Judith's darkest secret to the world.

Judith is teamed with a mysterious stranger with a carefully guarded secret of his own. But is Luke Becker an unwilling ally or an agent of the kidnapper? As Judith and Luke's mutual distrust wars against a growing attraction, the life of a small boy hangs in the balance. A boy unlike any other Judith has ever met.

Eight-year-old Abel Palek will help Judith discover a faith and a life she has never imagined. But freeing him could cost her everything.

Her career.
Her reputation.
And very possibly her life.

Softcover: 0-310-27210-6

Pick up a copy today at your favorite bookstore!

Before Another Dies

Alton Gansky

Running for congress is hard work for Madison Glenn.

But she never expected it to be murder.

Running the coastal city of Santa Rita. Campaigning for a congressional seat. Staying one step ahead of a high-powered corporate broker's demands. Life couldn't get more difficult for Mayor Maddy Glenn—or so she thinks.

Enter three murders in three days. Rumors fly of a serial killer at large, and the press has a field day with Santa Rita's embattled mayor. Especially when a strange pattern emerges: the victims were all fans of a radio talk show whose enigmatic host specializes in the weird and unusual. Coincidence or clue?

For Maddy, the search for answers is about to become personal. Refusing to play it safe, Maddy is caught in a lethal game in which seconds count. But even her renowned grit and tenacity—and her emerging faith—may not be enough to prevent more brutal deaths.

Including her own.

Softcover: 0-310-25935-5

Pick up a copy today at your favorite bookstore!

Director's Cut

Alton Gansky,
Author of The Incumbent

Mayor Madison Glenn has worked hard
to get where she is. Standing on the brink
of a brilliant congressional career, the last
thing the colorful mayor of Santa Rita,
California, needs is trouble.

Enter Maddy's cousin, Catherine Anderson, a beautiful young
actress newly returned to her hometown, Santa Rita, to take pos-
session of her lavish new home and star in a local dinner theater
production. And find the body of her chauffeur floating in the
swimming pool.

As Maddy is determined to protect Catherine from danger, a
revised script arrives at Catherine's door with a disturbing new
dialog that suggests someone is watching Catherine's every move
… and waiting to make her part in the script turn deadly.

Softcover: 0-310-25936-3

Pick up a copy today at your favorite bookstore!

The Prodigy

Alton Gansky

Patients in a hospital ward are instantly healed.

A killer tornado is stopped in its tracks.

A dying businessman is cured of cancer.

Undeniable miracles are following a rusty station wagon on its journey west. But the person behind them is no charismatic religious figure. He's the six-year-old son of a poor single mother and the possessor of a gift he can't explain. To multitudes, however, Toby Matthews is about to become a New Age messiah—and to unscrupulous opportunists, a ticket to undreamed-of wealth.

But one person besides his young mother will see Toby for who he really is. Thomas York, a gifted but searching divinity student, finds in Toby a kindred spirit—brilliant, intuitive, hungry for truth. And as an evil beyond their comprehension unfolds, Truth will become their only weapon against a terrifying enemy unseen by all except Toby.

A taut supernatural thriller, *The Prodigy* probes the influence of the invisible realm on the world around us and the indomitable power of the Light that shines in the darkness.

Softcover: 0-310-23556-1

Pick up a copy today at your favorite bookstore!

Out of Time

Alton Gansky

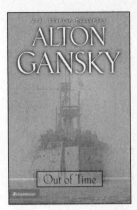

The fog released more of the ship. As he watched the bow slowly emerge, Stanton saw something that made his gut twist. "This can't be." Stanton stared at the gray-white battleship. "It's a dreadnought."

But that kind of ship ceased sailing three-quarters of a century ago.

It starts as a trip to help five troubled teens, courtesy of a new Navy youth program. With retired submarine commander J. D. Stanton serving as captain and two young naval officers heading the expedition, the state-of-the-art catamaran leaves port. It's a routine voyage ... until a mysterious storm pulls Stanton and his crew into an eerie world of swirling mist and silence.

There is no sun, no moon or stars, no way to take a bearing. Electrical appliances fail. The diesel engine is sullen and unresponsive. And then, out of the mist, a ship slowly appears — H.M.S. Archer, a pre-WW1 dreadnought.

A ship missing since 1913.

The antique vessel holds disturbing surprises: a ghostly crew ... evidence of a mass murder ... and a thousand questions. Now J. D. Stanton and his untried team must discover the answers — before this ship out of time leads them to their destruction.

Softcover: 0-310-24959-7

Pick up a copy today at your favorite bookstore!

ZONDERVAN®
.com

Three ways to keep up on your favorite Zondervan books and authors

Sign up for our *Fiction E-Newsletter*. Every month you'll receive sample excerpts from our books, sneak peeks at upcoming books, and chances to win free books autographed by the author.

You can also sign up for our *Breakfast Club*. Every morning in your email, you'll receive a five-minute snippet from a fiction or nonfiction book. A new book will be featured each week, and by the end of the week you will have sampled two to three chapters of the book.

Zondervan *Author Tracker* is the best way to be notified whenever your favorite Zondervan authors write new books, go on tour, or want to tell you about what's happening in their lives.

Visit *www.zondervan.com* and sign up today!